CROWN ME

THE ROYALS SAGA

Alexander & Clara

Command Me

Conquer Me

Crown Me

Smith & Belle

Crave Me

Covet Me

Capture Me

A Holiday Novella

Complete Me

Alexander & Clara

Cross Me

Claim Me

Consume Me

Smith & Belle

Breathe Me

Break Me

Anders & Lola

Handle Me

X: Command Me Retold

MORE BY GENEVA LEE

CONTEMPORARY ROMANCE

THE RIVALS SAGA

Blacklist

Backlash

Bombshell

THE DYNASTIES SAGA

London Dynasty

Cruel Dynasty

Secret Dynasty

FANTASY & PARANORMAL ROMANCE

FILTHY RICH VAMPIRES

Filthy Rich Vampire

Second Rite

Three Queens

CROWN ME

GENEVA LEE

ESTATE

CROWN ME

Estate Publishing + Entertainment

www.GenevaLee.com

First published, 2015

Cover design © The Book Bar.

Image © SergValen/Adobe Stock.

To the ladies of the Royal Court,
  we'll use that term loosely.

CHAPTER ONE

The sun peeked cheerily through the kitchen window. Purple hues painted the sky, casting the quiet Notting Hill neighborhood in a rosy glow that was unusually vivid for February. But despite the beauty of the peaceful London morning unfolding outside, I only had eyes for the man lounging against the counter. Black silk pajama pants hung low off his hips, displaying his carved abs and the deeply hewn V that I loved to run my fingers over. His black hair was still tangled from this morning's lovemaking session. It hadn't even been an hour since his crystal blue eyes had been locked on mine while he coaxed my body to two toe-curling orgasms.

But as gorgeous as his body was, it had nothing on his heart. My chest tightened as I considered that he was mine. It seemed impossible that this brutally beautiful man belonged to me.

Alexander's sinful mouth curved into a knowing smirk as I drank him in. He held out a mug. "For you, Poppet."

I took a cautious sip from it and nodded approvingly.

"Am I finally getting the hang out of it?" he asked.

"Not bad," I confirmed, taking another drink.

"The least I can do is to caffeinate you after last night, even if it means making coffee."

"If you're going to keep me up half the night, I have to agree," I teased lightly, trying to ignore the way my lower belly tensed at the memories of how he'd kept me up. Being late to work was becoming a bad habit, and I didn't need to tempt myself any further.

Alexander and I had fallen into a comfortable routine during the last few months despite our ongoing argument regarding coffee versus tea. We'd survived the holiday season and both our families along with it. That was no small feat, given that his father would prefer I vanished into thin air and that my own parents' marriage was hanging by a thread. Still, our relationship was more solid than ever. The lies and secrets that had once created a wall between us had been replaced by trust and understanding. Now it was time to start focusing on the changes this year would bring. It wasn't that I didn't want to marry Alexander. I couldn't wait to be his wife. It was that it meant spending time with people I'd rather avoid, as well as facing just how much my life was about to change.

His hand cupped my chin and drew my attention back to him. Back to this moment and away from the future. "You've got that I'm overthinking things look on your face."

I forced a smile and shook my head. "There's a lot on my plate."

"One less thing on your plate soon." His tone was casual as he spoke, but it didn't stop me from sucking in a defensive breath.

Here we go again. This was exactly the conversation I wished to avoid with my overprotective lover.

"I'm going to miss my job. They need me there," I reminded him. It might not seem like a dream job to others, but the work I did with Peters & Clarkwell was important. At least to me. Despite being new to the company, I'd already worked on several environmental and social campaigns that had received global attention. The best part was that the work I did writing press releases and creating social media campaigns actually did something to bring positive change to the world. I would never have gotten rich doing it, but that hardly mattered given the balance of my trust fund. However, joining the Royal family meant taking on new responsibilities that prohibited me from continuing with my job. It had been a bitter pill to swallow—in fact, it still was.

Alexander's blue eyes flamed to life, and he crooked a curious eyebrow at me. "I need you, and you don't need to work."

"I want to work. Being independently wealthy isn't an excuse to spend all day shopping and going to the spa."

"You're not going to become your mother," Alexander assured me, bypassing subtlety in favor of directness. Of course, he knew what this was about. At least I thought so until he added, "And believe me you'll have plenty of responsibilities besides shopping and mud wraps soon."

I set down my coffee mug and faced him, my hand slipping down to finger the drawstring of his pants. "Like?"

His arm hooked around my waist, pulling me against him violently. His cock thickened between us until it was a rock hard reminder of exactly what he expected from me. But despite the desire awakening in my blood, this wasn't a subject I would let slide. "Can we start with spending all day in bed?"

"As much as I love the idea of you naked every waking moment, I meant your other responsibilities. There will be expectations when you become my wife, Poppet." His tone had softened even if his grip on me was still firm and unrelenting.

"Oh." Of course there would be. I knew that. At least I thought I did. Months ago, I'd given notice to my boss that I'd be leaving in February, so why couldn't I process that it was actually happening? Probably because it meant turning my back on everything I'd worked to accomplish at university in favor of navigating the choppy waters of the Royals. To most of them I was simply an American pretender who had no place marrying the heir to the throne. My education, my upbringing—none of that mattered to them, which made giving up my career sting even more.

Alexander's lips cruised along my jaw. "It's not a death sentence."

"That would mean more if you didn't act like it was," I shot back, unable to quash my own defensiveness.

"Clara, you'll still work with charities, but when we're married, you'll have all my resources and connections at your disposal. You'll be meeting with world leaders to affect change instead of doing online campaigns."

I had a feeling he was making those opportunities sound far more glamorous and empowering than they'd actually prove to be. The trouble was that I knew there was a difference between activism and politics. Alexander understood that as well. But regardless of how I felt, I also knew that choosing him meant giving up my previous life, and I'd made my choice. I'd expected a bit longer to acclimate myself to the idea. Of course, nothing involving Alexander was gradual. Everything between us happened too quickly—meeting him at my graduation party, falling into bed and unexpectedly falling in love. Our early relationship had been rocky, but once we'd recommitted to each other last fall, things had moved swiftly. Now the wedding was less than two months away. My head had been spinning for months, trying to keep up with my own life.

"I'd rather stay in bed with you than sit through meetings with politicians," I admitted with a sigh. At least, if I had to give up my career, I had a lifetime of Alexander to soften the blow. No matter how much changed, he was the constant. My center. My core. As long as I had him, I could handle all the chaos.

His hands slid from my hips to cup my ass. "We could stay in bed today."

"No way, X." I shoved at him playfully. "I promised Tori lunch, and I swore I wouldn't be late."

"Tell your boss that there were pressing matters of state." He swiveled his hips to show me exactly what pressing matters we were discussing.

I bit back a moan, but the momentary loss of concentration was all the time Alexander needed to shove my skirt into a bunch around my waist. A low growl vibrated through him as he touched my delicate lace garter and thong set. A finger pushed aside the scrap of lace, exposing my sex, and anticipation rolled through me.

"I can't let you leave without a proper send-off," he murmured silkily.

"You gave me two proper send-offs this morning." But it

was already a lost cause. My body responded to his gentle strokes with hunger and I rocked my hips against his hand.

"Oh God, I love you," he said as my fingers slipped past his waistband and closed greedily over his cock.

Work could definitely wait.

Half an hour later, I was definitely late to work. Maybe it was a good thing that my last day was near. If this kept up, I was likely to be sacked anyway. Slamming the red door of our house shut behind me, I shouldered my bag and waved to the Rolls-Royce parked at the curb. I couldn't see Norris, Alexander's personal security guard, who was now mine as well, but I knew he was there waiting to take me to the office. I stepped forward and my heel crushed something soft under foot. Stumbling back, I found a smashed rose. I crouched down and picked it up with trembling fingers. Immediately I scanned the small garden that provided privacy to our residence. At least, it was supposed to offer privacy. My stomach plummeted as I dropped the remains of the flower.

Someone had been here.

Norris appeared before me, and although his kind, weathered face remained impassive, I could tell by the tension in his posture that we were wondering the same thing: was the rose a token of admiration or a threat?

"Did you see anyone here?" I asked. It was a silly question. If Norris had found someone this close to our home, they'd already be on their way to the nearest police station.

He picked up the flower and inspected it. Without thinking, I plucked one of the petals and mashed it between my fingers. It was cold, nearly frozen. It could have been here all night, which meant that whoever had left it had managed to get in past the security that maintained a constant, if distant, presence outside at all hours.

"Miss Bishop," Norris said in a measured voice as he guided me back toward the door, "please wait inside while I speak to Alexander."

That wasn't going to work. My life was already upside down and I couldn't let every perceived threat frighten me. Staying behind locked doors wasn't an option. "I'm already late for work."

"It will only take a moment," he reassured me.

I sucked in a frustrated breath, squared my shoulders, and allowed him to see me back inside. I didn't have much of a choice. As much as I wanted to pretend nothing had happened, Norris was my ride to work, so I either waited outside—alone—or I followed suit. But it wasn't fear that made me choose retreat, it was the possibility that I might overhear something important. Security had been tight since I'd been attacked by my crazy ex-boyfriend, Daniel, on the night of our housewarming party. He was in jail, charged with attempted murder amongst a number of other lesser charges. Alexander and Norris were careful to keep discussions regarding my personal safety to a minimum—at least in front of me. After the proposal, I'd been more than happy to turn a blind eye in favor of romantic bliss. But this changed things. If something more was going on, I needed to know.

Alexander appeared in the hallway as soon as the door opened. His face was unreadable, a skill he'd perfected after years of constant media scrutiny, but there was no denying from his rigid stance that he was on alert. I was torn between running to him and staying close to the door, uncertain if my touch would calm him or upset him further. He feared for my life, having already lost both his mother and sister, and Daniel's attack had only made his anxiety on that front worse. No security measure seemed to soothe him.

Norris passed the rose to him. Neither spoke, but the look they shared said enough.

"What's going on?" I demanded.

"Could you wait outside?" Alexander asked his trusted bodyguard.

So much for getting any information.

As soon as Norris was out the door, I rounded on my fiancé. "Tell me this is just the token of a very stealthy admirer."

"Perhaps." It was all he said, but the words he didn't say spoke louder.

"Daniel is in jail awaiting trial," I reminded him.

"Clara." His tone was rich with warning, but I ignored him.

"Don't Clara me," I snapped. "You've had this place watched like it's a nuclear test site for months. If something else is going on, I need to know."

We were under twenty-four-hour surveillance in our own home. Most of the time, I could ignore that. The men Alexander had hired to protect me were ex-military and very good at their jobs. They kept out of sight, but I still felt their presence at home. At work, I couldn't even go out to lunch without an armed escort parked nearby. It was beyond controlling, especially if the biggest threat to my safety was locked up. Unless...

Realization crashed through me, and my hand shot to the wall to steady myself. "Oh my God."

Alexander's arms were around me before I could voice the fear tripping on the end of my tongue. "You're safe."

But I wasn't. Not if...

"How long?" My words were hollow. I wouldn't allow myself to feel the fear building in my belly, which meant I couldn't allow myself to feel anything at all.

"There's no danger. Not with Norris and the team—"

I held up a hand to stop him and repeated myself, "How long?"

"Since Switzerland," he said in an unusually quiet voice.

"Switzerland?" I squeaked. We'd been there months ago, before Pepper had gone to the press with accusations that Alexander had drugged her and before he'd changed the course of my life with a simple question. "You've known this whole time? You knew when you proposed!"

"I did," he confirmed.

I pushed him away, suddenly needing space to catch my breath. The hallway spun and I fought to regain control over the emotions warring inside me. Fear tore down the barriers I'd erected, liberating itself with a surge of panic that flooded through me. I couldn't ignore it anymore.

"I didn't want you to be scared. If you had known, it wouldn't have changed anything."

"Like hell it wouldn't have!" But it was a lie. Knowing Daniel was back on the streets wouldn't have made me feel safer. In this instance, knowledge wasn't power. The last thing I felt in this moment was empowered. That didn't change the fact that I knew now. "How?"

"An overzealous attorney." Alexander's lips twisted into a

rueful smile. "By the time I was informed, he was long gone."

"Gone?" I repeated. Disbelief added itself to the chaotic mix of feelings churning in the pit of my stomach. How could he be gone? Even if he'd been released temporarily, I hadn't dropped the charges against him.

"For someone with no military background, he knows how to hide."

This time when Alexander reached for me, I let him wrap his arms around me. I melted into the safety of his embrace, willing myself to believe he could protect me. But if Norris couldn't find Daniel—if all the men Alexander employed behind my back hadn't even seen him leave that rose—what hope was there? The thought chilled my blood and settled deep in my bones.

I pulled away from him and reached for the door. "I need to go."

"Clara, if I—"

"I don't want to hear it," I stopped him. I'd spent the last few months believing Alexander was too overprotective—because I'd thought the source of his paranoia was behind bars. "I don't know what's worse—that Daniel was released or finding out you've been hiding it from me. You lied to me. I need to think."

"Clara." His voice was sharp, but I ignored him.

"I thought we were past this shit. Later, X." I left before he could offer me more excuses. He'd been protecting me, I knew that, but it didn't make it any easier to swallow the betrayal or the fact that my fragile happiness had been shattered. Right now all I wanted was space to consider what I'd just learned:

No one could protect me.

CHAPTER TWO

A familiar redhead popped into view at the entrance to my cubicle. Tori shot me a tired grin and I waved her inside. Plopping into my spare chair, she rubbed the small bump that was just making its presence known and sighed heavily. The weight of it mirrored my own current frustration. Apparently Monday wasn't going smoothly for anyone. I could only hope that whatever was on her mind had nothing to do with crazy stalkers or possessive boyfriends. Of course, she was dating one of the kindest men I knew, so it probably didn't.

"That bad?" I asked sympathetically. Leaning back in my chair, I folded my arms and waited patiently. I couldn't help but notice that she looked absolutely exhausted. Tori's fair skin was pale against the dark circles ringing her eyes and the red hair she usually wore in glamorous waves or funky up-dos sagged into a limp ponytail.

"I'm behind with the PostAid campaign. I thought I'd get caught up this weekend, but I'm so tired. Things were supposed to get easier in the second trimester."

"You should talk to your boss," I said dryly. I added a wink for good measure.

"I think he's more tired than I am. The twins had the flu. Apparently, we're all falling apart." Her gaze traveled down. "I swear my poor back is already a mess. I can't believe I have five more months to go! I looked into getting one of those chairs. But I saw the price tag and it's going to have to be a knockoff for me."

"My workaholic father's idea of a Christmas present. I have to admit it's pretty nice though," I said, tapping my fingers on the arms of my new Aeron Chair. I didn't mention that the extravagant gift was yet another attempt to smooth things over with me. The gesture was ridiculous, given that I had been neither avoiding nor punishing my dad after catching him with another woman. My mother and sister had received similarly lavish presents. But we all knew that no gift was going to erase what he had done. "You know, I don't really need this anymore."

I stood and pushed the chair to her. At least something good could come of my father's emotional bribery.

"Really?" Her eyes lit up, but then her face immediately fell, tears sparkling in her eyes. "I keep forgetting this is your last week."

"I keep forgetting that everything makes you cry right now," I teased. "Look on the bright side, you get my chair."

She managed a tight smile. "This is making me feel even worse. The doctor called and I need to pop over to the clinic. Can we reschedule lunch?"

"Absolutely." I hoped my response didn't seem too forced. I was more than a little sad to miss out on one of my last lunch dates with her, even though I was thrilled about the baby.

It was going to be hard to maintain my professionalism when I packed up my desk. I'd see Bennett and Tori again—they were on my personal guest list for the wedding and the engagement party. Sadly, Tori was going to have to sit out of the raucous hen party Belle had planned. And of course, I was dying to hold the baby in a few months. They'd be around, but it wouldn't be the same. I'd become attached to them as a couple, even though I suspected part of that stemmed from being more than a little jealous of how normal their relationship seemed. Date nights. Movies at home. No paparazzi tailing them or tabloid speculation. Gathering my notebook and a pencil, I braced myself and headed to my boss's office, knowing our morning strategy sessions were numbered. I paused at the door as Bennett finished a phone call, but he beckoned for me to come in.

"Understood." Bennett swiveled to face his office window. His view was blocked by the reflective glass of the neighboring Gherkin building, but he stared, unblinking, into the glaring sunlight bouncing back at him.

My heart churned, full of conflicting emotions, but I managed to keep it together. My mother had helpfully passed along a magazine article that talked about the top twenty-five stressful life events last week. I stopped counting the number that currently applied to me when I hit ten. No doubt the actual number was much higher. All the tension and change had made me nearly as weepy as Tori, but I refused to cry when Bennett spun around and asked me how my day was. I wouldn't cry. Not until my final day in the office, at least.

Instead I launched into the strategies I'd managed to

write up over the weekend. The only perk of Alexander's increasing familial responsibilities was that I had a bit more time to devote to projects outside of work. An hour later, I'd managed to get Bennett's half-hearted approval on everything I'd pitched to him.

"What am I going to do without you?" he asked when I'd finished rattling off the latest specs for a public health campaign we were putting together with the BBC.

I wagged a finger at him. "Don't start!"

"You don't really want to marry that guy, do you?" Bennett said.

"Speaking of marriage," I said pointedly, "when are you making an honest woman out of Tori?"

"Hey, I've asked." He threw up his hands defensively, laugh lines crinkling around his warm brown eyes. "She said the first night she gets a full eight hours of sleep, she's dragging me to the nearest church."

"In my defense," Tori interrupted from the doorway, "I look like a zombie. All I want is one decent, quick photo of my wedding day where I don't look like I'm ready to eat someone's brains."

I laughed along with them, excusing myself so that I could get back to work. The number of projects I needed to wrap up before I left was staggering. An hour later, I'd sorted through the files I'd kept at my desk and dropped them off to the project managers that would be taking over the various campaigns. I'd just seen the last stack safely delivered when my mobile rang. Lola's face blinked on the screen, and I dashed back to the safety of my cubicle before accepting the call. Enough of my day-to-day life was aired across tabloid covers, the last thing I wanted was for my parents' marital difficulties to be thrown into the mix. It was silly that anyone cared about what I bought at Tesco when I grabbed groceries, but it was unthinkable to invite people to speculate on the affairs of my family.

"Hey Lola," I greeted her breathlessly.

"Were you running?" she asked. The hint of confusion coloring her tone quickly shifted to annoyance. "And why are you whispering?"

"I'm at work," I reminded her, keeping my voice soft. I loved my kid sister, but her unapologetic bluntness meant she wasn't always terribly perceptive.

"I thought you worked in an office, not a library."

I shook my head, marveling at the strange mix of British and American that comprised my sister. She'd been young enough when we'd moved to the U.K. that she'd picked up a subtle accent, but her forwardness was all-American. I, on the other hand, spoke like an American and chose my words carefully like a Brit—most of the time.

"I figured it would be nice to keep a little of my personal life private." My eyes rolled involuntarily, glad that she couldn't see me through the phone. "I'd like to keep our family issues out of the tabloids."

I had no reason to suspect anyone at Peters & Clarkwell had sold me out, but the paparazzi's interest in me had grown into a frenzy since my engagement to Alexander. The press had run stories on everything from analyzing my apparent preference for free-range eggs to interviews with people who'd attended classes with me at university.

"Mom loves being in tabloids," Lola said.

Normally I'd say she had a point, but my mother's stubborn refusal to admit Dad was cheating suggested this was a line in the sand. A juicy story like my father's affair would be worth a pretty penny—and it might destroy my mother. Of course, Lola didn't admit that she was enjoying the cover time she'd been receiving herself. Our shared genetics meant that she looked like a younger, slimmer version of me—that dressed better. Much better. As such, she'd quickly become a fashion trendsetter, even starting a craze for American handbag designer Kate Spade across the pond. The gossip rags had begun a Lola watch, breaking down her wardrobe choices and linking her to a dozen of the world's most eligible bachelors. As far as I was concerned, it was too much, but I'd rather she distract them from what was happening behind closed doors. Plus, Lola didn't seem to mind.

"Regardless," she continued, "she's asked me to go dress and hat shopping for a certain blessed event. Please tell me your last day at that job is coming up. She's insisting we go together."

"No date yet. Soon," I lied. "Take her to buy a hat for the engagement party. That's next weekend."

"She's had that hat picked out for months," Lola said emphatically. "Word to the wise, she's going to ask you at our family meeting next week."

"Of course, she is." I sighed and checked the clock. "I better run."

"You probably should run if you keep Mom waiting any longer," Lola warned and quickly hung up.

I pushed thoughts of dates and hat shopping into the back of my mind. Yet another reason I would miss my job was that it provided distraction from the topic of my wedding. With everything so complicated at the moment, the last thing I needed to add to my plate was more wedding preparation.

Not while Alexander was still keeping secrets from me. Not while his father refused to give his blessing. And certainly not with Daniel out there. A thick lump formed in my throat, and I swallowed against the sudden swell of fear. Right now burying myself in my work meant not having to face that fact. A few spreadsheets and a PowerPoint later, I was surprised to glance up and realize it was nearly my lunch hour. My stomach growled, accustomed to the carefully timed schedule I kept regarding meals. But I had no appetite. Without Tori around to distract me from the security detail that would follow me as soon as I left the office, I didn't feel like grabbing lunch. My phone buzzed insistently, and I grabbed it to silence my reminder-to-eat alarm, surprised to discover it was actually a call from Edward.

"Clara Bishop's desk," I said with mock formality.

"Is the tart in?" Edward asked in a voice dripping with British dryness.

My mouth twisted bemusedly at his saucy pet name as I typed out a final note and closed my file. Edward, Alexander's younger brother, was the only living member of the Royal family I could stand. "I'm afraid she's busy."

"Too bad. I was calling to inform her that her presence is demanded at a mandatory girls' night this weekend."

I couldn't stop myself from snorting at this. Since he'd officially come out of the closet, he'd fully embraced his sexuality. It only made me love him more. "Girls' night, huh?"

"Don't bother telling me I don't have the necessary equipment, I have the necessary attitude," he said, adding, "and the emergency to boot."

"Please tell me there's not trouble in paradise for you, too."

"Absolutely not. I've been reformed," he assured me cheekily. "I just want some time with my two favorite brides-to-be. Belle's already in, and if Alexander cannot bear to be parted from you or your vagina for the evening, we can do it at your place."

"You're shameless."

"You love me."

I couldn't disagree with him there. "I'll have to..."

The words fell off my tongue as Alexander seized the chair next to mine. He lounged back, smirking wickedly, as I struggled to regain my composure.

"Sorry...I'm distracted. I'll have to call you back," I finally managed.

"Tell him I said hello," Edward said knowingly.

I took a steadying breath as I hung up and shoved the phone into my purse.

"What? You couldn't just send a note?" I bit out, allowing the turmoil I'd felt all morning to spill over.

"We need to talk." His voice was low, but firm. Domineering. Powerful. A dizzying sensation washed over me as I fought against the effect he had on me.

I knew that domineering tone. I was being commanded, and while I couldn't deny I'd come to crave that in his bed, I wasn't about to put up with it now. "Now you want to talk? Did something happen that you couldn't coordinate behind my back?"

"Poppet."

"I need to get to lunch."

And I needed to avoid a screaming match in the office.

"That's why I'm here." Alexander moved closer, brushing a finger along my arm. My reaction was instantaneous. A ripple of longing shivered from the point of contact and up my neck. My body curved, lured toward him with the same instinctual magnetism that had drawn us together since the moment we'd first met.

But I refused to roll over that easily. "I had a lunch date, remember?"

"And it was cancelled," he said, shrugging his broad shoulders in a far too innocent gesture.

"Un-fucking-believable." Snatching my purse up, I beelined for the lift, but before I could reach it, he was at my side. His arm slipped through mine, claiming me, as we waited for the lift.

"Do you have this whole place bugged?" I hissed, unable to contain myself and hoping none of my co-workers would hear.

Alexander was more patient, exhibiting an almost super-natural control that drove me crazy. When the lift doors slid open, he released his hold and gestured for me to enter. My simmering annoyance had reached full-blown fuming as he calmly pressed the down button. "I am made aware if your schedule changes."

"Do you even hear how crazy that sounds?" I exploded.

"It's a safety precaution. Your life might be in danger." The evenness of his voice only made me angrier.

"Might? It might be? You also *might* be driving me crazy!" I'd gone along with the initial security precautions following Daniel's attack, because I was as desperate to feel safe as he was to protect me. Maybe I was approaching this the wrong way though. Alexander could be reasonable. I just needed to be logical. "You weren't honest with me. I accepted the security so that you would feel better. I thought we'd both be able to relax soon, but instead I find out that there's actually been a real threat the whole time. How would you feel if every moment of your life was watched, recorded, and reported on without you even knowing why?"

But he only cocked an eyebrow. "Every moment of my life has been exactly that."

"Right." I sank against the cool metal wall of the lift for support. Of course it had been. It still was. This was entirely normal to him, which meant the expectation was that it would be normal for me as well. I didn't move when we reached the ground floor.

Alexander's hand closed gently over my upper arm, urging me into the lobby. This time he didn't try to loop arms, instead he guided me in silence until we were on the sidewalk. The bustle of London foot traffic afforded more privacy than the quiet office building, but even with the anonymity, I couldn't find words.

"I should have been more honest with you," he admitted. "We can discuss that over lunch, but right now I need to see you eat something."

My purse strap slipped and I shouldered it with determination before pointing to a bistro a few buildings down. I'd been there before and knew it was frequented by businessmen too preoccupied with their own deals and conversations to care about us. Alexander caught my hand as we crossed the street, purposefully placing himself on the side of oncoming traffic. But the street was relatively quiet and a few moments later, he held open the brass door to the restaurant. The low hum of a dozen conversations filled the room accompanied by soft music. The bistro itself sat in the shadow of several of the larger financial buildings, dimming the room considerably for the lunch hour.

"Two," Alexander informed the hostess, who was in the process of stacking menus. She glanced up and her mouth fell open.

"Of course," she chirped, her fingers trembling as she checked the seating chart.

Alexander dipped down until he was eye level with her. "Somewhere...private."

My legs buckled, causing me to sway slightly in my heels. His grip on my hand tightened, pressing my sizable ruby engagement ring into my flesh. The brief smarting pain mixed with the frustration I felt, sending a jolt of unexpected arousal traveling through me.

Hardly anyone noticed as we followed the girl toward the back of the restaurant to a fairly private table tucked into a recessed nook, but awareness prickled through me. Were we being watched right now? Followed by a special security team? Were any of our private moments private at all?

"Will this do?" The young hostess wrung her hands nervously as Alexander pulled out a chair for me.

"This will be fine," he said in a gracious tone, tilting his head slightly. Her eyes darted from me to him and then she did a small curtsy and scampered away.

Possessiveness flared inside of me, I hadn't mistaken the lust in her eyes. I couldn't exactly blame her for that. Not only was he the Prince of England, but he exuded a raw sensuality that most women couldn't ignore. But the reaction had been uncontrollable and unexpected. Jealousy wasn't really my thing, except when it came to the toxic Pepper Lockwood. Gripping the sides of my chair, I willed my pulse to calm. I was being paranoid. Alexander had been lying to me again, and my body had responded possessively to a perceived threat. That was all.

But that didn't make it okay.

"You're quiet." There was no accusation in his voice, but there was an undercurrent of something else hidden amongst his words. Pain.

I lifted my gaze slowly to meet his, preparing myself for the momentary electricity I always felt when I saw him. It rocked through me, but this time I focused that scorching desire into fuel for my anger. Betrayal and desire were a volatile combination, and it took what little self-control I had to keep my voice low enough that only he could hear me. "I feel like I've been living a lie."

"I should have told you about Daniel," he repeated. "But there was never a good time. I expected to have a lead on him much more quickly."

"That's no reason to keep the truth from me!"

"I assumed it would be resolved weeks ago. Months ago. The longer it took, the harder it became to bring up."

I shook my head, dismissing the lame excuse. "That probably should have been a clue that what you were doing was wrong."

"Poppet." He brought my hand to his lips and kissed each knuckle, stopping at my ring finger as though to gently remind me that I'd promised myself to him.

"Don't think that if you are all sexy and sweet, I'll forget what you did."

"You think I'm sexy?" The cocky grin that suited him so well twisted over his lips, making it impossible not to want to kiss him.

"Once again, you're missing the point, X."

"We came here to talk, and we will, but I also came to tell you I have to go out of town." His blue eyes stayed trained on me as he dropped the bit of news.

I swallowed and nodded. "For how long?"

"My father has asked me to attend a jubilee dinner. I'd like you to come with me."

"I can't." The refusal was out of my mouth before I could think about it. A time was coming when my presence would be expected, but for now, I wanted to relish the last bit of freedom I had left.

Alexander stiffened, surprised by my refusal.

"I have plans," I continued in a rush. "And this is my last week at work."

"So this has nothing to do with our fight earlier?"

"No." I paused. "And yes. Maybe some time apart will give us some perspective."

"I don't like time apart," he growled.

"I can't go," I repeated, but this time the refusal came out weakly.

"Fine, but I want to make one thing perfectly clear." Alexander grabbed the arm of my chair and jerked it closer to him. The scrape of its feet on the wooden floor vibrated through my body, dialing up my shredded nerves and making me all the more aware of him. Heat radiated from him, drawing me in even as I tried to stay away. He might have lied to me, but the safety I always found in his arms was a surer truth than any I'd ever known. It was his own screwed up way of loving me. That made it even harder to maintain the space between us, especially when it was his solace I longed for.

His shoulders slanted and he inclined his head until the warmth of his breath skimmed across my neck. I breathed in his scent—spice and heat, earth and fire—my eyes shutting as his hand closed over my knee and snaked under my skirt. His fingers drifted up teasingly as he traced a path across the sensitive flesh of my thigh.

"What I do is for your protection, Poppet. Not only from anyone who might wish to harm you, but also from yourself." With his free hand, he tucked a strand of hair behind my ear and then tipped my chin up. My eyelids fluttered open expectantly, knowing exactly what he wanted from me— what he demanded. Our faces were a fraction of an inch apart, close enough to kiss. "Fear is your enemy. It controls you when you let it, and then you try too hard to take control back."

So he controlled fear for me. He protected me from myself. Or, at least, he controlled what I knew. Sometimes I suspected he still wanted me to fear him. He'd tried hard to sabotage our relationship early on. I swallowed and held his gaze unwaveringly even as the tips of his fingers brushed across the lace of my panties. I was soaked through, wildly turned on despite my confusion, and his eyelids hooded as he felt my wetness.

"Are you ready to order?"

My own dreamy eyes popped open when I realized we'd been joined by the waiter, but Alexander's face remained impassive as he looked over the menu, his hand staying, decidedly, in place between my legs.

"I'd like the lamb shank and the fennel salad," he answered smoothly as he pushed the lace to the side and thrust a finger past my folds. I bit the inside of my cheek, trying to keep a moan of pleasure from spilling out as he continued with his order. No one would guess from his casual demeanor that he was expertly fucking me with his hand under the table.

"And for mademoiselle?" The waiter shifted his attention to me.

I felt heat rise to my cheeks. I didn't dare look up. I didn't dare move. If I opened my mouth now, I wouldn't be able to keep up the pretense of normalcy. I clung to my last thread of self-restraint, hanging in an ecstatic limbo. The thought of being caught—the mere idea that the stranger in front of me might suspect what was happening—held me in check while heightening every brush. Every caress.

"She'll have the same," Alexander said, coming to my rescue, his thumb massaging a teasing circle over my aching clit. He held out the menu, and as the waiter accepted, Alexander slipped two fingers inside me. I forced a polite, if strained, smile onto my face as the waiter took his leave. As soon as he was gone, I pressed my face into Alexander's broad shoulder, biting into the bone and muscle in an attempt to control my pleasure.

"This is how it will be with us," he spoke huskily, his voice rich with restrained lust. "Whatever I ask of you, whatever I assume is best for you, you will comply. I live for two things, Clara, to give you pleasure and to protect you. I won't restrain myself in either regard. Do you understand that? Nod, Poppet."

His fingers curled inside me, massaging my g-spot. It was impossible to find my voice, but I could nod.

And I did.

My body belonged to him.

I belonged to him.

"And now you will come for me," he commanded in a whisper. "I want to feel your teeth in my skin as you try not to scream. Leave your mark on me as I claim you right here in front of all of these people."

My mouth clamped down to stifle the rapturous sob his dominance provoked within me. I couldn't deny Alexander's hold over me any more than I could deny myself air. He infuriated me, but that anger only stirred my desire for him more. He knew that. He knew that he owned me.

CHAPTER THREE

"Why is Hugh Grant always so charmingly stupid in movies?" Edward asked as he rounded the corner with a bowl of popcorn. He sank onto the guest bed next to me and turned his attention back to the television.

I scooped a handful from the bowl and popped a few kernels in my mouth. "It's for all the dreadful Americans."

"Does that work on you?" he asked with a chuckle. His bright eyes danced with laughter. "I'll have to keep that in mind."

Belle's head swiveled around to stare him down, eyebrow already crooked. "You're taken," she reminded him. "Don't make me text David."

"Where is he anyway?" I asked.

"Now, now. Need I remind you that as Prince of England I have to deal with all sorts of dreadful Americans?" Edward held a hand up in surrender, and then pointed to me. "Especially this one. I'll take whatever help I can get."

"You're avoiding the question," Belle accused, a knowing smile stealing across her full lips.

"I resent that." Edward shook his head. For a moment he looked just like a younger version of Alexander—handsome and defensive. His eyes darted downward, displaying the curly black mop that he kept stylishly coiffed. Suddenly the popcorn was much more interesting than the cute British guy on the television. Something was definitely up.

Belle sat up, completely obstructing the view, and turned to face us. "Spill, Your Highness. You're jumpier than a prostitute in church."

"You're blocking the best scene," he said, craning to see past her. "I like the idea of the Prime Minister dancing through Downing Street."

"Well, I hate to ruin it for you but the Prime Minister isn't nearly as cute as Hugh Grant. Now stop avoiding the question. You called us for a girls' night," I reminded him. "So out with it."

Truthfully his timing couldn't have been better. With Alexander out of town, I'd made up an excuse to crash at my parents' the night before. It hadn't been my proudest moment as an adult, but I wasn't prepared to sleep here alone even with Norris keeping watch. Alexander would be back tomorrow, and a girls' night seemed like exactly what I needed to clear my head.

"As if I'm the only one keeping secrets." Edward pushed his horn-rim glasses to the of his nose and stared me down. "You're in your own world."

"I'm getting married in a few weeks!"

"Am I the only one without trouble in paradise?" Belle asked, not buying my excuse either.

"Trouble?" Both Edward and I repeated at the same time.

"Clearly, I'm misreading you both," Belle said, sarcasm

dripping from her voice. She twisted a string of honey blonde hair around her finger and narrowed her eyes. With her high cheekbones and elegant bearing, she looked graceful even in her pajamas. "Don't make me turn this television off."

Sighing, I slumped back against the upholstered head-board. If Alexander believed it wasn't worth it to make me worry about Daniel, it definitely wasn't worth making Belle and Edward worry about him. Still I didn't particularly like the idea of lying to my best friends, especially since it seemed to prove Alexander had a point when he'd chosen to keep this information from me. Of course, that wasn't the only thing on my mind. "Alexander is going to be traveling more and more. My mom is on me about wedding stuff every waking minute. And I'm officially unemployed as of this morning."

"You'll have plenty to keep you busy soon," Edward said in a soft voice.

"Exactly." I grabbed a nearby pillow and hugged it to my chest. "It's not like Alexander makes becoming a Royal sound appealing."

"It's not like he has any other choice," Belle jumped in. "And neither do you if you want to marry him."

Edward and I shared a look. Apparently I wasn't the only one thinking about this.

"What was that?" Belle demanded.

I hesitated, unable to voice the possibility, so Edward told her for me, "He could renounce the throne."

"Would he really consider doing that?" she asked. "I can't imagine he would now if he hasn't already."

"I don't know," I lied. I was positive Alexander wanted nothing more than to dismantle the monarchy piece by piece, but his position afforded him access to private security and the funds to pay them. He was doing it for me. "I'm not sure I know anything anymore. If I think everything's fine, I find out it's all a lie. Everyone thinks I'm living a fairy tale!"

Edward wrapped an arm around my shoulder. He flashed a look at Belle. "I told you we should have gotten more wine."

"It doesn't go with popcorn anyway," I mumbled, rubbing my belly. The whole situation was making me sick. I'd had a perpetual stomachache since I'd found that rose Monday morning. "I think he's also worried that if he renounces, he can't protect me. He's been a little manic since Daniel's attack."

"That's just stupid. He renounces and you two could move wherever you wanted, shag like rabbits, and make lots of beautiful babies."

The air was knocked from my lungs and I gasped. Recovering, I shoved some popcorn in my mouth. Apparently girls' night was going to be full of conversational land mines.

Both Belle and Edward fell silent, obviously sensing that they'd hit on a touchy topic.

"We're not going to have babies," I blurted out past the raw ache in my throat. "I don't even want to have babies, so it's not a big deal."

"Who would?" Edward said conspiratorially, trying to make me laugh. "Stinking nappies and getting woken up in the middle of the night."

"Stretch marks," Belle added.

I forced a small but grateful smile out and rubbed the back of my eyes with my sleeve. "I have no clue where that came from. I really never thought about having children, and suddenly, it's off the table and bam! Instant blubbery mess."

"Did you find out..." Belle searched for the right words, thought better of it and gave me a meaningful look instead. She'd been there over a year ago when I'd thought I might be pregnant. I'd been suffering from malnourishment, but she knew that I'd purposely avoided getting answers from my doctor.

"Nah." I shook my head and took a deep breath. "Alexander doesn't want kids."

"Father's going to love that," Edward said in a flat voice.

"I suppose it's up to you to carry on the monarchy."

He laughed hollowly. "Then the monarchy might be doomed."

"Look at us." I leaned into him. "Sitting here, slowly destroying a thousand years of tradition."

"Just another Saturday night."

"I feel like I'm not doing my part," Belle said with a fake pout.

"We might need backup," I said purposefully.

"I'm good for that," she promised. She lifted a slender finger and pointed at Edward. "Now, how are you destroying the monarchy?"

"You mean other than being gay as a picnic basket?" He hesitated, his eyes darting from Belle over to me. "I'm thinking of asking David to marry me."

"You wanker!" Belle's still pointed finger stabbed the air violently. "You've been sitting here keeping that to yourself the whole night!"

Genuine laughter bubbled through me and spilled over. "Wanker?"

"Well, if you think it was hard for the lovely, demure

Clara to win over my father, imagine poor David." There was a bitter edge to his laughter. "A black, gay commoner!"

My joy curdled at the mention of Edward's father. It seemed the only duty he felt to his children was to ruin their lives. It was hard to imagine a parent could be so intentionally cruel, but he hadn't minced words regarding my relationship with Alexander. His behavior had been somewhat more reserved in the past few months, but there was no doubting how he truly felt about his sons' partners. He shared the same blue eyes with both of his sons, but his always glinted of disappointment. "Who cares?"

"Oh, are we all renouncing the throne?" Edward asked. "It's going to be a brilliant year for jolly old England."

"Who cares if your father supports your marriage?" I continued, ignoring him. "What matters is the commitment you two make to each other. You don't need anyone's approval to decide to love someone, and you certainly don't need it to choose to spend the rest of your life with them."

The room fell silent and I felt a little silly for letting my passion get the better of me, but then Belle lunged, squeezing between us.

"You do realize that this means we're all getting married this year!"

Edward snorted at this point of fact. "Do you honestly think I can plan a wedding in less than a year?"

But he couldn't keep a sheepish smile off his face.

In no time, we'd completely abandoned watching the movie in favor of discussing proposal ideas. We talked so late that Belle curled into a ball and fell asleep between us.

"It will be hard to top Alexander's," Edward whispered, trying not to wake her.

"Alexander's proposal was a challenge," I said, remembering the over-the-top event he had staged at the London Eye. It had been thrilling and overwhelming, and although I'd said yes, his private proposal later that same evening was the moment I'd truly said yes.

Edward shook his head. "It was a message that he chose you. I want David to feel that. I want him to know that I've chosen him the moment I ask him."

"He will," I promised him softly.

He sucked in a long breath. "Want to shop for rings tomorrow?"

"I thought you'd never ask," I said, smiling widely.

"Clara." Edward paused, the boyish exuberance slipping from his face as he reached over and took my hand. "I know things are uncertain right now, but I want you to know that I'm glad you're going to be my sister."

I squeezed his hand. "Me too."

Between us, Belle rolled over and began to snore.

"We should take a video of this," Edward suggested.

"We should," I agreed, "but we won't because we're her best friends. We'll just tease her mercilessly about it in the morning."

Edward shot me a bittersweet smile.

"What's that about?" I asked.

"I'm just happy that I'm getting a sister."

"And I'm getting a brother."

"Hardly seems like a fair exchange."

"I'll be the judge of that." I stuck my tongue out at him for good measure. There were a lot of things that scared me about marrying Alexander, but gaining Edward as family was definitely on the pro list. "I love Belle, but I can't sleep with this racket."

Edward scooted down in the bed, laughing. "David says I could sleep through a hurricane."

"Night." I bent down and pecked him on the cheek. "Tomorrow we go ring shopping."

He grinned sleepily. "What would you dreadful Americans say? 'Hell yes?'"

"Hell yes!" I giggled. It really was going to be like having a kid brother.

I crossed to my empty bedroom and was halfway inside when I realized the lights were on in the kitchen. Yawning, I ambled down the stairs, tugging at the pair of boxers I'd stolen from Alexander's drawer, hoping whoever was on duty out front wouldn't look in and see me.

The click of a cabinet stopped me dead in my tracks. I was torn between running upstairs to Belle and Edward, heading for the front door, or grabbing an umbrella from the stand by the door. I thought of being followed, of the constant security, of the lies that kept stacking up between Alexander and me. I was tired of running. My fingers closed over the umbrella handle and I pulled it slowly from the rack.

I took a deep breath and rounded the corner.

"Expecting rain?" Alexander's mouth pressed into a thin line as he tried to hide his amusement.

"What are you doing home?" I dropped the umbrella and ran to him. His arms folded around me, and I drew back to drink him in.

"Did you miss me?" he asked, his voice taking on a husky tone that sent a flutter of expectation throbbing through me.

I fiddled with the tie that hung loose at his neck and shook my head playfully. "It's only been one night."

"Are you sure, Poppet? You're wearing my pants." He ran his index finger along the band of elastic that hung loosely on my hips. "Turn around and let me see. Slowly."

I pivoted obediently. His watchful gaze burned through me, igniting a flame deep within my belly. I had missed him, and my starved body reacted with throbbing pangs of hunger. My legs clamped shut as I tried to control my arousal. Alexander slid a hand between my thighs and urged them back apart, brushing across my sex as he did. Even the light touch, mostly obstructed by the now-soaked cotton that covered me, drew a gasp from me.

He hooked a finger in my waistband and drew me roughly against him. Sliding a hand under my tank top, his fingers circled my nipples, tugging and pinching them until they were almost painfully hard and I was panting. I pressed my ass back until his erection prodded against my soft backside—a silent signal of what I needed.

His lips moved against my ear, teeth catching and nipping its shell. "Now, did you miss me?"

CHAPTER FOUR

M y pulse quickened, my breathing shifting to shallow puffs. I'd expected our time apart to provide some perspective away from his influence, but I'd spent it craving him instead. With everything changing, with my whole life in limbo, the only thing I could be certain of was him.

"Answer," he prompted, squeezing my swollen breasts and drawing my thoughts away from the outside world. "Tell me that you missed me."

I moaned a yes, barely able to find the word in my fervent state. I wanted to turn around—to kiss him—but I recognized the tone of his voice. Tonight he was in control, and my body knew that. It was what I wanted. I still refused to believe that I needed submission. It was a conscious choice to place myself completely in his hands. It was the only way it could be healthy for either of us. Still, knowing I would be at his mercy soon sent the sweetest pang echoing through me.

"If you will not speak, then you must show me," he commanded. He released his hold on me and pressed his hands gently to my shoulders. There was no need for him to be rough—not yet.

I knelt, the cool hardness of the kitchen floor providing a jolt to my already frayed senses. Iciness traveled through my blood, spreading so rapidly that instead of shivering, I grew feverish.

Alexander circled me thoughtfully, pausing in front of me so that I could see the proof of his own arousal straining against his trousers. "We have guests?"

I nodded.

"Is that why you're being quiet?" A smirk played at his shapely lips, and I thought about running my tongue across them. I imagined them pressed between my legs. "Then we'll make a game of it. If Clara wants to be quiet, she will be. But I won't make that easy for you."

It wasn't so much that I wanted to be quiet or that I was worried about waking the others, it was that something about Alexander demanded it this evening. His dominant side had overtaken him just as the submissive side he'd uncovered in me longed to surrender. Part of me fought against it, still wounded from the information he'd kept from me.

"A gentleman would take you upstairs and close the door. He would make love to you slowly so that your screams wouldn't wake your friends." He bent and tipped my chin up with his index finger. His gaze smoldered through me, melting the last of my inhibitions. "I'm not a gentleman."

His words ignited me. Desire sought out each nerve ending until my skin sung with near-electric desire. Need sizzled and crackled across my flesh as if warning that even the slightest touch might spark an inferno.

His thumb glided over my lips and paused expectantly for them to part before plunging inside my mouth.

"Perfect lips," he murmured appreciatively. "Do you like to have your mouth filled?"

I started to nod and changed my mind, unprepared to give in entirely even as I shifted on my knees, desperate to ignore the longing growing rapidly in my core. But my squirming was met with firm disapproval. Alexander drew back and shook his head. "Naughty Poppet."

He crooked his finger, beckoning me up, and I scrambled onto my feet.

"Strip," he ordered.

I was powerless to resist the request, because in the end I couldn't deny him. I didn't want to resist him. I shimmied out of the boxer shorts and kicked them away, aware that I was now stark naked in my kitchen.

"Does it make you uncomfortable to know that your friends are upstairs? That any moment a guard could walk by to check the perimeter and see you like this?" His palm trailed across my bare abdomen, leaving a path of fire in its wake. "You may speak."

"No," I murmured.

"If you aren't afraid, why are you whispering?" he asked, pausing to pluck a silk scarf from the collar of the coat I'd left strewn on the kitchen table.

"No," I repeated in a clear, steady voice even as my knees nearly buckled. I considered what he was going to do.

Alexander wrapped the scarf around his hands and pulled it until the silk was as taut and stretched as my own desire. An ache grew into a painful pulse that thumped between my legs. I dipped under the weight of his darkening eyes, returning to my knees instinctively. Conscious thought fled, replaced only by the sensations crowding in my body, each begging to be freed.

"That's better." He took a few steps until he stood behind me and then the silk slipped over my eyes. The filmy fabric obscured my vision, transforming the room around me into a collection of hazy shapes.

"Show me your beautiful cunt." His words were sharp, his voice more commanding with the scarf's impediment.

I bent forward with caution, my movement controlled as Alexander gradually slackened his grip on the makeshift blindfold. The scarf drifted, passing over my mouth and gliding down until it loosely collared my neck as my palms met the cold floor. I shivered both from the added chill on my bare skin and from the agonizing promise of the moment.

"You're cold." Concern colored his voice, but he didn't urge me up from the floor. "I'll light a fire."

You already have. The lone thought broke through my clouded head, but I didn't speak. I was high on him, drunk on my own submission. Without thinking, I crawled forward, tugging gently against the scarf. Alexander sucked in a breath behind me, but he didn't move, forcing me to a halt as my neck strained against the fabric. I waited as he stepped to my side before resuming my progress toward the hearth in the living room. I'd never felt so blatantly sexual, even with Alexander. I was his to control—to consume. Each movement forward—each press of a palm to the floor, each slide of my knee—fueled my wantonness. I'd submitted to him before but he had always taken the reins. Tonight I'd literally handed them over to him.

"Stop here," he said as we crossed onto the plush Oriental

rug situated in front of the hearth. He dropped the scarf entirely. It fluttered to the floor beneath me, but I didn't move even as he lit a match and stoked a small flame into a roaring fire. Its warmth licked across my face, searing down my shoulders, and enveloping my body physically in the heat already in my blood. I remained on all fours, sensing Alexander's enjoyment of the pose.

"Do you feel the fire?" he asked, his fingers closing over his belt buckle. "It's turning your skin such a lovely rosy color. It makes me think of other things that turn your skin pink."

I tensed with delirious expectation as he drew his belt free of his trousers. It clattered to the floor, followed by his tie. My eyes were glued to him as he unfastened each button of his shirt with slow precision until it hung open, revealing the dips and ridges of his abdomen. I wanted him to take it off so I could see every chiseled groove of his upper body and the scars that I'd grown to love, but I didn't dare speak. In the firelight, his blue eyes were as dark as the inky black hair that he ran his fingers through as he studied me. His hand shifted to rub the slight stubble that peppered his jaw after the long day. I pressed my thighs tightly together as I imagined how it would feel against them, but with my ass in the air it did nothing to allay the resulting twinge of want.

"You've been so patient," he told me with approbation. The praise in his voice reached inside me and soothed an anguish I didn't know I carried. "That will be rewarded, but first I want to see how much you can endure. Can you handle that, Poppet? The pleasure without the release? I want you to contain it—to hold on. To beg. But to not let go until I say."

I whimpered, knowing he could take me to the brink and

hold me over the edge without letting me fall. He'd done it before but never to this extent. Usually he wanted me to succumb to the clawing, relentless orgasms he unleashed from me. This was new.

And it was exactly what I wanted—to relinquish my body while remaining in control.

He wet his lip with his tongue as he undid his fly and moved out of view. I stared into the flickering blaze, my eyes clenching shut as he softly kicked my bare feet open and stepped between them. His body grazed against my swollen sex as he sank to his knees, his hands gripping my hips then traveling to the soft roundness of my bottom before the hot suction of his mouth closed over me. I swallowed back a groan, my teeth sinking into my lower lip as I concentrated on staying in one piece. His tongue flicked and swirled, dipping into my hole and then settling over the bundle of nerves twitching at my core, making abstinence feel like an impossible feat. The sharp nip of teeth on my engorged clit broke my focus and I cried, dangerously close to coming.

He drew back, smacking my ass with disapproval.

I sucked at the air, my chest heaving as I struggled to center myself.

"Feel it," he urged. "Feel how close you are to satisfaction. Enjoy it. But don't let go."

"Please." It was out of my mouth before I could stop myself.

"No, Poppet," he refused, rubbing my back in soothing circles. "You can hold out longer. I won't be happy until you're begging like it's your very life at stake. In fact, perhaps you need a moment to collect yourself. Turn around."

I did as he demanded, turning my trembling sex toward

the hearth and its heat. My head tilted, gazing up at him hopefully, as I moved closer and pressed a soft kiss through his trousers to the rigid outline of his cock. He smiled, reaching down to free it from the confines of his pants and I wasted no time. I wanted him to feel half as turned on as I did. I wanted to torture him—just a little. My mouth closed over his crown and I relaxed, taking in his shaft until it bumped the back of my throat. A guttural sound rumbled from him as I stroked his length with my tongue.

"You are so fucking beautiful with my cock in your mouth—eyes wide and innocent. It makes me want to do all sorts of depraved things to you."

My moan vibrated across the velvet marble of his dick, and he responded to the sensation by grabbing a handful of my hair and driving into my mouth with furious abandon.

"Do you want me to come?" he growled. I hollowed my cheeks in response and his head fell back as my lips plunged swiftly over him, sucking him as hard as I physically could. Alexander's body froze for a split second and I relaxed my throat in anticipation of his climax. But instead he pulled abruptly out of my mouth, his fist jerking his shaft roughly as he released in hot spurts across my bare breasts.

He'd never marked me like this, and I sat back, astonished, on my heels, staring at the milky cum dribbling over my nipples.

"Up. Now," he commanded through gritted teeth. His erection wagged, undiminished, as he gripped my elbow and hauled me to my feet. He practically dragged me to the corner of the room, turning me at the hips and shoving my knees onto the bench of the grand piano that had sat here untouched since we'd moved in. I narrowly caught myself, my fingers splaying across the keys and sending a jarring cacophony of notes into the air. Somewhere it registered that we were no longer being quiet, but I couldn't care less. There was only him. Only his touch. Only his skin and his palm as he lightly spanked me.

"That wasn't very patient of you." His accusation was followed by a playful smack. He massaged away the sting before another landed on the opposite cheek. "I wanted to come with you, Poppet. Now I'll have to make you come twice."

Yes, please.

He read my mind. His forearm hooked around my waist, drawing my hips lower, so that my ass hung over the edge of the bench. Alexander lowered to one knee behind me and positioned his wide crest at my entrance, and then he waited.

"Please," I whimpered.

But he didn't move.

"I need to feel you. I need you to fuck me, X."

He remained motionless and I wiggled my hips, trying to lower myself onto him. His arm tightened, restricting my movement.

I gasped, gulping for air that I couldn't catch as frustration and arousal warred inside me. Want had taken me past rationality, and I struggled against him, bucking and howling as tears spilled down my cheeks. A litany of pleas streamed from me, coupled with sobs that rolled violently through my limbs. Alexander's lips lowered to the curve of my neck as he restrained my writhing figure, and he kissed the spot softly. The simple act electrified me, and I screamed.

But he didn't try to silence me—instead he slammed into me, burying himself as deeply as possible with one swift thrust. I was impaled on his cock and his hands shot out, seizing my wrists and pinning them behind my back. My head fell forward, meeting with the cool ivory as he pounded against my cervix, turning my sobs into cries and shrieks that exploded from the very center of my being. My orgasm ripped through me. My muscles splintered and the ball of tension in my core burst as I shattered over him. He'd wrecked me—destroyed me—and I dissolved into his embrace, folding into him as he rocked me slowly to a gentle encore.

By the time he gathered me in his arms, covering me with his shirt, and carried me upstairs, my eyes were heavy and my body exhausted. His scent clung to the stiff cotton and I breathed it in, allowing it to lull me closer to my dreams. He nudged open the bedroom door and was two steps inside when a worried voice called my name.

"Clara! Are you okay?" Edward's sleepy voice called in our direction.

Alexander paused and stuck his head into the hallway, while keeping my spent, languid body safely out of sight.

"Never mind," Edward said with amusement. "Hurricane Alexander is home."

"Good night." Alexander kicked the door closed behind us and took me to bed.

CHAPTER FIVE

E dward tapped on the spotless glass case. "What do you think of this?"

"Too ostentatious," I said decidedly. The thick yellow gold ring featured large square diamonds circling the band. Whoever wore that ring would be hard to miss—not exactly what seemed important to someone like Edward's boyfriend. "I can't imagine David wearing that."

"Neither can I." Edward released a long sigh and shook his head. "Remind me that this isn't the most important decision of my life."

I inclined my head thoughtfully, my fingers twisting my own ruby engagement ring. "Asking him to marry you certainly is."

"But not the ring," Edward clarified.

"You could probably give him a rubber band and he would be thrilled," I agreed. "He wants to be asked."

"God, I hope you're right." Edward pointed to another band, which the saleswoman swiftly retrieved for his inspection.

"Hey, no cold feet." I bumped his shoulder with my own, trying to cheer him up. "Don't get angsty unless he says no."

"And if he says yes?" Edward asked, turning the ring over in his palm before slipping it onto his own finger.

"That's a whole different matter."

"How are your feet?" he asked.

"Toasty warm," I assured him, before adding, "most of the time."

"And the rest of the time?"

"I wear thick socks."

His lips pressed into a thin line before he turned his attention back to the task at hand. "Thanks for coming along with me on this. The tabloids would have a field day if someone snapped a photo of me here alone."

Here was Hammond's—London's premier private jeweler, located in posh Belgravia. I'd never heard of the shop until today. I'd assumed Edward was actually referring to Harrods, the famous department store nearby. Instead I'd found myself in a tiny shop tucked back in an unassuming line of stores. As it catered to a very exclusive clientele, the Royal family included, the only thing on the sign was the store's name and the year of its establishment: 1875. The well-appointed interior full of luxurious leather chairs and plush imported rugs made it a surprisingly welcoming space —that was until I saw a price tag.

No wonder the shop was the Royal family's jeweler. Each piece cost a king's ransom.

"I am the perfect alibi." I leaned closer to the glass, my breath fogging the pristine surface. "I need to buy a wedding band myself."

"I don't think you can give Alexander a rubber band." Edward smirked as he teased me.

"Probably not." At least not with the whole world dissecting every decision we'd made about the wedding. I sighed, struggling to convince myself that public expectations didn't matter. The fact was that they did. The closer I grew to Edward, the more I longed to see the rest of the family stop merely tolerating one another and actually love each other. I wasn't about to admit that to Alexander though.

"This one," Edward said triumphantly, pushing his glasses on top of his head so he could inspect it more closely.

My purse vibrated and I nodded encouragingly while I dug my phone out.

"Very nice choice," the girl behind the counter opined. "That's brushed 14-Karat white gold and of course these"— she pointed to two thin yellow gold rings on both edges—"are also 14 Karat."

The number on the screen was unfamiliar but I recognized the area code. Oxford. I silenced the call with trembling fingers and dropped my phone back into my bag.

"Are you okay?" Edward asked.

"Yeah," I lied, pretending to look at the jewelry case. I stepped away as they discussed price and tried to turn off the sudden onslaught of fears the phone call had provoked. Running my fingers along the glass, I paused as a simple band caught my eye.

"May I show you something?" A man in an expensive tailored suit stepped from the shadow of the back room. He was striking—classically handsome, save for a nose that looked as if it had been broken a few times. And judging from the salt and pepper in his hair, he was close to my father's age. I nodded and gestured to the ring that I had just spotted.

"I don't believe we've been introduced. It's a pleasure to have you in my shop, Miss Bishop."

I started, caught off guard by the fact that he knew me. Then I remembered that I was no longer an anonymous woman. He reached out and grasped my hand, drawing it to his lips. Charming, handsome, and he owned a jewelry store —he was a triple threat. I couldn't help but wonder if Belle's Aunt Jane was seeing anyone yet.

"Mr. Hammond, I presume."

"Please call me Jack." Despite the warmth of his greeting, there was a coldness behind his flinty eyes that sent a chill running down my spine.

"Then you must call me Clara." I started to pull my hand away but his grip on it tightened.

"Such a lovely ring. My father made it for Albert."

I raised an eyebrow. Alexander's father wasn't the type to be on a first name basis with his jeweler. I smiled politely. "I'm very attached to it."

"I was certain you would be. No doubt owing in no small part to the man who gave it to you." He studied me for a moment, and I squirmed under his gaze, my discomfort growing with each passing second. "Tell me, how is Alexander? I've expected him to pay me a visit since I heard of your engagement."

"I plan to wear his mother's ring as my wedding band," I explained to him.

Jack released my hand and smiled wanly. "Still, a man should keep his jeweler close if he wants a happy marriage."

I laughed politely. Jack Hammond bent to reach into the

case and I shot daggers at Edward, who merely returned my glare with a puzzled shrug.

"This would suit your fiancé," he said as he handed me the ring. It was a simple platinum band but the inside was coated in rose gold. It reminded me of the night he'd proposed to me with dozens of red roses.

"Could you engrave it?" I asked, handing it back to him.

"Certainly." He placed it on a small, velvet square. "And I'd be happy to deliver it to your house."

I had the oddest instinct to say no. "Can you send it with Edward's order? I don't want him to see it before the wedding."

Jack inclined his head in agreement, and relief washed over me. I immediately felt silly. There was no reason to be so paranoid.

The store's doorbell—another measure of its exclusivity—chimed, distracting him and saving me from any further consideration on the matter. It had been months since Daniel's assault, and I was still seeing wolves behind every friendly face.

We arranged for payment and delivery, and I tried not to think about the extravagant price tag. If Alexander was going to wear this ring for the rest of his life—and he was if I had anything to say about it—it was worth the cost.

As Edward finished signing his check, I glanced up, noticing the shop's newest customer for the first time. And the fact that she was studying me. Her gaze didn't waver even when I caught her staring. I flushed, turning away, but not before I'd gotten a good look at her. She was about my age, but that was where our similarities ended. Dressed in tight jeans and leather boots, she didn't look like the type of client I expected to find here. Except that she was gorgeous. Thick, black hair hung loose past her shoulders. Full lips that pouted without trying. I couldn't remember the last time I'd seen a woman as stunning as this bold stranger.

"Miss Bishop," Jack called. "Allow me to introduce one of my partners. This is Ms. Kincaid."

Ms. She looked like the type that would insist on Ms. Maybe it was her boots or the fuck-off look plastered on her face.

She sashayed a few steps closer and stuck out her hand. "Georgia."

"Clara." I stumbled over my own name, feeling slightly confused.

"Ms. Kincaid is a...matchmaker," Jack explained, tacking on, "of sorts."

"Unfortunately, we've met too late then," I joked.

Georgia laughed, but her amusement didn't reach her eyes. I couldn't help but get the sense that she was taking my measure.

"Are you ready?" Edward asked, completely oblivious to the introduction occurring behind him. When he turned, he froze, just as quickly composing himself. "Thank you again, Jack."

Edward hooked an arm through mine and led me quickly from the shop.

"That was a little rude," I told him. "But thank you. They just kept staring at me."

"Well, you are going to be the next Queen of England." There was an edge to his words.

"Who was she?" I demanded. "You knew her, and she was sizing me up the whole time."

"No one," Edward said too quickly.

"I don't buy that," I said as we reached the Rolls.

Edward slid into the back without answering, and I followed him in, more determined than ever to uncover Georgia Kincaid's mystery.

I crossed my arms and stared him down.

"You aren't going to let this slide, are you?"

I shook my head.

"Someone from the past."

"Alexander's past?" I guessed. My stomach plummeted, but I shook off my unease. "No wonder she was staring at me."

"You can't blame her for being curious." He lounged against the leather seat.

Curiosity, but not exactly jealousy, got the better of me. "Was it serious?"

"I don't think so. Honestly, I was young. I never really met any of Alexander's girls."

"Until me?" I teased.

"Exactly," he said. "So who cares about that girl? Not Alexander."

I hoped he was right.

I WAVED goodbye to Edward from the front stoop. Shooting an awkward smile at the guard stationed near the gate, I stepped inside and closed the door softly. I waited for a moment, listening for Alexander, before I ducked into the study off the front hall.

My fingers shook as I found the missed call and hit return.

"Oxfordshire Clinic," a perky voice chirped.

"I, uh, missed a call earlier." I stumbled over the simple statement. My heart began to pound so hard that I could feel my chest moving.

"Name?"

"Clara Bishop," I whispered, questioning if this was a good idea. Hospitals had privacy policies, but I was no longer just some university girl. Privacy without anonymity didn't feel all that private anymore.

"Bishop," she repeated, pausing for a moment. "Oh yes! We received your request for your medical records."

I wet my lips, nodding. "Yes."

"My apologies for the delay in responding. Unfortunately, we were unable to locate any record of treatment for you."

"What?" I pressed a sweaty hand to the back of my neck, rubbing out the knot of tension that had suddenly formed. "I was hospitalized a little over a year ago."

"I'm sorry," she said. "We've been updating our computer system, it's possible it just got lost."

"Is there anyone I can speak to?" I fumbled for a solution, but I knew it wasn't there. It was no coincidence that they had no record of my hospitalization.

"I can put in a request for you to speak with a patient liaison, but I assure you that I've done a thorough search."

I didn't miss the annoyance in her voice.

"Thanks anyway." I ended the call and stared at the phone.

I'd expected answers. I'd dreaded them as soon as I'd seen

the caller ID. Instead I'd only been left with more questions. Daniel had claimed I was responsible for the death of our unborn child. Was he right? Had I actually been pregnant? Now I would never know. Alexander claimed he didn't care. I believed him. So why had I requested those records? I hadn't been sure then.

But now I knew it was because I did care.

I also knew those records hadn't just disappeared.

Taking a deep breath, I redialed the number and clutched the phone to my ear.

"Oxfordshire Clinic."

"Hello. I just called. I thought of one quick question. Do you have a Clara Bishop listed in your system at all?"

She paused. "No. I am sorry. Are you certain you have the right hospital?"

"Quite." I hung up the phone, stunned. Part of me wished that I had the wrong hospital because the alternative was worse. Much worse.

I'd been scared for the last few weeks that I'd lose myself in all the changes. I had never considered that I might be being changed.

"Poppet?"

I jumped, startled as Alexander leaned against the doorframe.

His blue eyes swept over me. "Is everything all right?"

I didn't answer. I just walked into his arms. He folded them around me without any more questions. I told myself it wasn't a lie. I told myself I had nothing to lie to him about. I told myself he wasn't lying to me.

I suspected I was actually lying to myself.

CHAPTER SIX

ALEXANDER

C larence House was stuffed full of diplomats and
distant relatives. The few friendly faces in the crowd
were courtesy of Clara's guest list and Edward's good sense.
Still, I had to hand it to my younger brother, he'd managed to
make the whole event somehow feel festive—a rare feat for
any Royal gathering. The crowd had been trickling in for the
past hour, swelling until the party spilled throughout most of
the main floor. Despite the party's liveliness, the fact that I'd
been separated from Clara for the third time in the space of
that hour was unacceptable.

Spotting her, I sidestepped a Russian diplomat with a
terse nod and headed in her direction. She was huddled with
Belle, no doubt avoiding her parents, whispering. My breath
rasped at the sight of her. I wondered if she'd been advised to
play up the blushing bride bit for today. If she had been, I
wished I could thank whoever had suggested it. Her dark hair
was gathered loosely, cascading in waves over her shoulder
and providing contrast to her porcelain skin. But it was her
dress that made my cock twitch. The ivory lace skimmed over

her curves in a tempting mix of innocence and sensuality. Drawing up behind her, I pressed my palm to the small of her back. Under my hand, her skin heated through the thin fabric.

It took considerable effort to remind myself that now was neither the time nor place. It took even more effort to convince my dick.

"I thought we were celebrating our engagement," I said in a low voice, "but I can't seem to keep track of my fiancée."

Belle grinned, shaking her head. "Should I leave you two alone? Word to the wise, this place has like fifty rooms, but please find one that locks."

"Get your mind out of the gutter." Clara smacked her best friend lightly on the arm.

"Speaking of dirty minds," Belle said, "I see Philip. Maybe I'll go find one of those locking rooms."

Clara sighed, leaning against my shoulder. I wrapped my arm around her, enjoying what was certain to be a brief moment of privacy. "I wish I was half as comfortable at these things as she was."

I narrowed my eyes thoughtfully, watching Belle navigate the room with a beaming smile. Clara's best friend was pretty and charming, but nothing compared to the woman I loved. "I rather like when you get flustered at these events."

"You do, huh?" She folded against me, pressing more of her sinful body against me—and doing nothing to alleviate the ache in my balls. "Why is that, X?"

I leaned in, brushing my lips over her ear. "Because it gives me an excuse to take you away to collect yourself."

A shudder rolled through her body. My hand dropped, catching hers and heading toward the hall before she could stop me. I needed her alone. Now. A strong hand clapped onto my shoulder, startling me from my mission. I turned to discover a familiar face.

"Brex!" I dragged him into a tight hug. Next to me Clara shifted, nudging me expectantly.

I drew back, my arm thrown over his shoulder. "Clara, allow me to introduce you to Brexton Miles. The man who is largely responsible for keeping my sorry arse alive before we met."

"Then it is a pleasure," she said, reaching out her hand. Brexton caught it and brought it to his lips.

"She's taken," I reminded him, shoving him away.

Clara's cheeks flushed, her arm hooking around mine. I glanced to my old friend and saw him through her eyes—hair clipped short in traditional military fashion, broad shoulders, warm smile, and a pressed uniform. I closed my hand over hers, my smile tightening a little.

"Don't look so offended, poor boy," he said, tucking his hat under his arm. "I'd never go after another man's girl. Now if you cock it up—and I know you will—then all's fair."

I smiled in spite of myself. He had no idea how likely it was that I would fuck this up. Not that I'd ever let him—or any other man, for that matter—get that close to her. Regardless of me being in the picture or not.

"Poor boy?" Clara repeated with a laugh, looking at me with curiosity.

"Some wanker gave him that call sign," Brexton explained. He managed to look innocent except for a mischievous twinkle in his green eyes.

"Some wanker, huh?" I said, pointedly. "This guy walks

into training, takes one look at me, and then yells 'who's getting stuck babysitting poor boy?'"

"The nickname stuck." Brex shrugged. "And that poor wanker got stuck on babysitting duty."

Clara bit her lip as if she was trying to hold back more laughter. "So you two served together."

"I'm not certain you could call it that," Brex said with mock solemnity.

I rarely discussed my time in Afghanistan with Clara. Unlike many who had returned from the warfront, I hadn't brought home any ghosts. But only because I'd left them all locked away there in the first place.

"Excuse me," Brex said, his eyes trained on something over my shoulder. "I think I just found my soul mate."

"Soul mate?"

"At least for tonight." He winked at Clara and her blush deepened.

"What poor woman have you got in..." I turned to see who had caught Brex's eye this time and stopped mid-sentence.

That was the thing about locking your past into closets— ghosts could walk through doors.

"Georgia Kincaid," Clara said, putting a name to the face I wished I could forget.

I glanced at her, hardly able to suppress my discomfort at hearing her speak that name.

"Then you know her." Brex stepped to Clara's side and took her free arm. "Introduce me."

"I don't know her as well as Alexander."

How the fuck did she know that? How the fuck did she even know Georgia's name?

"You know all those times I saved your life?" Brex said, as he nodded toward Georgia.

But before I could come up with a good excuse to keep him away from her, Clara started toward her.

Georgia had worn a slinky black dress to my engagement party, which pretty fucking well summed up where her and I stood. I had no doubt she was here at the request of her employer. Something I would be certain to speak to Hammond about.

"The happy couple!" She lifted her glass and smiled as though we were all old friends.

"It's nice to see you again," Clara said in a clipped but polite tone.

"I had no idea you two had met." I couldn't quite keep an edge of accusation from my tone, but I wasn't certain if my displeasure was directed at Georgia for being here or at Clara for not telling me they'd met.

Because it was pretty goddamn clear that Clara had some idea about my past with her.

"I'm certain Clara didn't want to ruin the surprise, and now I've ruined it." Georgia looked anything but sorry.

Clara shrugged the thin shoulders that I wanted to shake. "No secret. Alexander knows we're getting married. My purchasing a wedding band shouldn't surprise him."

Despite her nonchalant attitude, her body had gone rigid as soon as she saw Georgia and still hadn't relaxed. I drew Clara's hand up to my lips and kissed it softly. How she'd met Georgia didn't matter, the fact that she was clearly upset at the woman's presence did matter. She obviously knew that we'd been involved, but I couldn't imagine that she understood the true nature of our relationship.

I suspected we'd be discussing that very soon.

"I, however, am not getting married." Brex shifted forward and extended a hand.

The proceeding introduction was made all the more painful by how oblivious Brex seemed to be to the awkward dynamic the rest of us shared.

"Will you excuse us?" I asked. "I believe Edward wanted Clara for…"

I trailed away when I realized Brex and Georgia were far more interested in flirting than hearing my excuse. I whisked Clara through the adjoining morning room to the first private room I could think of. It was an office of some sort, likely unused, since none of the family officially occupied this residence at present. The drapes were pulled, allowing only slivers of daylight to break through.

Shutting the door, and locking it as Belle had suggested, I rounded on her. "When did you meet Georgia?"

"A few weeks ago." Clara rubbed her arm, and I noticed her lower lip had begun to quiver. "Who is she?"

"An ex." It was what she was expecting to hear, and mostly true.

"Does she know that?" Clara asked. A single tear glistened on her cheek.

I instantly softened, folding her into my arms. "Poppet, she's a part of my past. I'm sorry you met her that way."

"She's gorgeous," Clara said softly.

"Is she?"

"You know she is." Clara wiped her cheeks and turned her head away from me.

I supposed she was, but Georgia's looks had never been important to me. "In case you failed to notice, I'm rather obsessed with you. I doubt I'd notice if every woman in that room was naked."

"I know I'm being silly." She sniffed. "It's not just her. We all have pasts. I'm overwhelmed. There's so much to learn—who to curtsy to, what title belongs to whom. I can't keep any of it straight, and it makes me think..."

She trailed away.

I drew her closer. "Yes?"

"That I'm going to be a terrible wife. I wasn't cut out for this, X," she confessed in a whisper. "What if I curtsy to the wrong person or forget to address someone? Did you know there's an entire blog devoted to chastising me for breach of protocol?"

"You seem to be under the mistaken impression that I give a damn about any of that." My hold on her tightened. "You could walk into that room and flip everyone off. Your place isn't to impress them. They should—and they will—bow to you."

"Bow, huh?" She laughed a little and tugged at my tie, even though tears continued to well in her beautiful eyes.

"Clara Bishop"— my hands dropped to brace her waist — "you're going to be the Queen. Everyone's place is at your feet."

"Everyone's?" She raised an eyebrow. "I think their place is at your feet, Your Highness."

"But my place is at your feet. Or have you forgotten that?"

Her fingers twisted around my tie, her chest heaving slightly as our bodies urged closer. "I thought that was my place, X."

"Sometimes." I began to draw her skirt up, savoring the

slow reveal of her stockings. "Sometimes I wish you on your knees, Poppet. But you are my religion. I worship your body, so yes, my place is at your feet."

I bunched her skirt in my hand and stepped back to admire the delicate lace garter belt and sheer stockings that complimented her curves. I pressed my palm to her thigh and she responded instinctively, spreading wider to grant me the access I craved. My cock strained against my trousers, but this wasn't about me.

Dropping to one knee and then the other, I hooked a finger around one of the satin straps holding up her stockings and plucked it loose. A strangled cry of anticipation escaped her lips as I unhooked the others and drew her knickers down her hips.

"These are pretty, Poppet." My voice was hoarse as my hunger for her grew. "But unnecessary. Step out of them for me."

Clara did as she was told. I shoved the scrap of lace in my pocket.

"I'll hold onto them for you," I promised her. "It's better if your cunt is ready for me."

I drew a finger down her seam, and she shuddered. Her responsiveness was my drug, it filtered into my bloodstream until I was lost in the haze of her. Her scent. Her softness. She grew wetter as I continued to run my finger along her folds, and I had to reach down and adjust myself.

"Yes, please," she moaned, already lost to me.

"Long live the Queen," I whispered, dropping a trail of kisses from her belly button down, curving to reach her inner thigh. I breathed her in until my mouth watered. Until all I could think about was fucking her with my mouth until she couldn't hold herself upright.

My hand slid up to spread her open, revealing the delicate pink spot that was my favorite place in the whole world. My lips closed greedily over her cunt, sucking relentlessly until I'd drawn her clit out. I swirled my tongue over the engorged nub, a rush of testosterone washing through me as she whimpered. Her hips circled against me and my hands flew to her ass, encouraging her to rock against my mouth.

I wanted to devour her. I wanted to turn her inside fucking out on my tongue.

"Fuck my face," I ordered her in a muffled voice, my mouth still full of her.

But she got the message.

"Oh god, yessss." Clara pitched against me, my hands rolling her toward me until she lost control, bucking hard as my tongue stroked inside her. Her hands wove into my hair and yanked as she melted over me. Her thighs snapped closed on my face, but I wasn't finished yet. Slowly I licked, savouring her taste and the way she quivered on my tongue.

"Stop," she pleaded. "Please."

I kissed her trembling sex softly as I pried her legs back open. Straightening, I gripped her hips in my hands and waited until she looked down at me. Even in the room's low light, I could see the dark flush colouring her skin as she shyly met my eyes.

"When you go back out there and from this day forward, remember this," I said, my voice thick with arousal, "you've brought me to my knees. You've brought me to my fucking knees, Clara."

I nuzzled against her stomach, holding her steady until her shaking subsided.

"Can you stay upright?" I asked when she was still.

"You're getting cocky, X," she said, but when she let go of my hair, her hands dropped to brace themselves against the desk.

I smirked, pushing to my feet. "Wait here."

A moment later, I returned from the attached washroom with a soft towel.

"Don't want me walking around with wet panties?" she asked with a wry smile as I carefully dried her.

"Do you really think you're getting those back, Poppet?" I patted the slight bulge in my pocket. "I would have stayed down there until I'd licked up every bit of you, but you have a curious habit of just getting wetter."

"Imagine that." Reaching up, she fisted my tie and drew me closer. Her nose wrinkled. "You smell like..."

"Glorious, isn't it?" I couldn't keep myself from winking at her.

"But all of those people." She shook her head. "Every single person out there is going to know that..."

"That I'm the luckiest man on Earth?" I finished for her.

"X!"

"I happen to love smelling like you, and I happen to love knowing everyone will know that I just took you. I want them to know I can't keep my hands off of you. I want every man out there to be jealous." I tipped her chin up, forcing her to meet my eyes. "I want them all to know you're mine."

"They don't need to know I belong to you," she whispered, "as long as you know."

I gathered her in my arms, planting a kiss on her forehead. "I know, Poppet."

And God help me, I belonged to her.

AFTER I CLEANED MYSELF UP, we slipped back toward the
party, stopping several times to steal kisses before we reached
the guests.

Edward, looking dashing in a navy suit, caught us at the
door. "Shameless," he said with mock reprobation, "if you
two are going to be constantly mating, you should have your
own nature show."

"I'll get the BBC on that," Clara said dryly.

"Tori and Bennett have been looking for you," Edward
said.

"Are you trying to steal my fiancée?" I asked as he pushed
her playfully toward the corridor.

"I'm trying to save her from your insatiable sexual
appetite," Edward said, dragging her away from me.

She cast an apologetic look at me, shrugging a little. Once
she was my wife, Edward was going to find it much harder to
pry her from me. The thought did nothing to alleviate the
situation in my trousers. But despite that, I felt lighter than I
had in weeks. Clara and I had holed up for much of the last
few months, caught up in each other. Unfortunately, these
types of events were only going to become more common.
But despite the fears she'd expressed to me, she had nothing
to worry about. She'd charmed everyone. Edward already
loved her like a sister. I had to believe the rest would fall into
place. I chose to believe it.

A waiter paused with a tray and I took a champagne flute from it, nodding my thanks. Taking a sip, I swallowed with a gulp as the slow chill of delayed recognition traveled over me. Whipping around, I ran into a man behind me. Muttering an apology, I darted through the crowd, searching for the waiter.

His back was to me and I bolted for him. Grabbing for his shoulder, I seized a hold of him. His tray crashed to the ground as I hauled him around.

"Hey, watch it, mate!" The stranger glared as I dropped my hold on him. His expression shifted to one of horror when he realized who I was. "I'm so sorry, Your Highness. It was my fault."

"I'm sorry," I stumbled over the apology, feeling stupid. Bending to help him pick up the tray, I saw the remains of an assortment of crudités. "Weren't you serving champagne?"

"No, just these," he replied as he scooped them back onto the tray.

Bounding back to my feet, I scoured the crowd from him, but I knew it was too late.

Daniel had slipped through my fingers again.

CHAPTER SEVEN

ALEXANDER

Scanning the crowd I tried to control my panic. My whole body was on alert, every impulse focused on finding Clara. When I finally spotted her, I took a deep breath and shot off a text to Norris.

But I didn't take my eyes off of her. Each second stretched into an unbearable eternity, only serving to intensify my protective instinct. The longer it took for Norris to report to me, the more I wanted to go after Daniel myself. But that would mean letting Clara out of my sight—and that wasn't going to happen.

Norris appeared across the room and I beckoned for him to join me.

"Perimeter is secure," he whispered, his lips barely moving. He understood the importance of keeping this quiet. If the press discovered Clara was being stalked, they would have a field day. The attention could force Daniel further into hiding, or it could fuel his mania. With the psychopathic behavior her ex-boyfriend had shown so far, I didn't dare find out what direction he would take. "And I put a man on her."

I searched the crowd surrounding Clara and finally spotted the undercover security officer casually tailing her as she chatted with her former co-workers, Bennett and Tori. Clara laughed, and though I couldn't hear it from this distance, a bit of the pressure sitting on my chest lessened. As I watched her, she bent and placed a hand on Tori's belly. A moment later, her face lit up. A strange sensation came over me at the sight, but I didn't have time to question it.

"Follow me." Disposing of my champagne flute on a nearby side table, I manoeuvred through the crowd until I spotted her. The momentary lightness that had overcome me when I saw Clara evaporated, replaced almost instantly by a heavy weight—the burden of the past.

Georgia leaned against the wall, her head angled flirtatiously as she giggled at whatever Brex had just said to her. I had to give her full props for her performance. I also made a mental note to warn Brexton. He might still be a ladies' man, but Georgia Kincaid was as far from a lady as they came.

I strode up to Georgia and caught her elbow. "I hate to interrupt the foreplay, but I need to speak to you."

"Excuse us." She flashed a dazzling smile over her shoulder as I directed her toward the hall. As soon as we were away from the party, she yanked her arm away and cast dirty looks at Norris and me.

"You aren't much of a host, Alex," she said.

"Don't call me Alex." I couldn't meet her eyes. I didn't want to.

She leaned toward me, tilting her head to catch my distant gaze. "I have other things I can call you if that's what you still prefer."

"That won't be necessary in our current arrangement."

My stomach clenched as an unbidden image of Georgia on her knees swam to my mind. I shook it away, but the feeling of self-loathing that accompanied it didn't dissipate. "I presume Hammond sent you for a reason."

"I'm not delivering jewelry," she confirmed. Georgia crossed her slender arms over her chest and waited.

It was a smart move. No one would guess what this beautiful woman really was. That didn't mean I liked having her here.

"So he assigned you," I murmured, rubbing the back of my neck as I digested this new information.

"He's sentimental," she said flatly. "Is there a reason for this little rendezvous? Not that I mind a reunion."

"I spotted the mark in the crowd. My men are looking for him, but I want you to find out how he got in here. And I want you to find him."

Georgia shrugged as if I'd just asked her to show me to the loo. "And what should I do with him when I have him?"

"I'll leave that to your discretion." I didn't want to know what she did to him once she found him. Not purely because of the potential legal issues.

"Excellent. As you know"—she trailed a finger over my buttons—"I can be very discreet."

I caught her wrist and jerked her hand away. "Then be discreet."

"Your father would be thrilled to know he did such a number on you." She didn't bother to hide her disgust from her voice. "Does she even know?"

It wasn't any of her business. Not anymore. But I answered anyway. "She knows."

"I didn't know she had it in her." Georgia smirked, obviously impressed. "Then again you can never really tell, right? It takes all kinds. Maybe later she and I could chat—girl to girl. Sub to sub."

"Clara isn't my sub. I'm not in the lifestyle. I never truly was." Georgia took a step forward and lowered her voice, so that Norris couldn't hear. "I have a scar on the back of my left thigh that says otherwise." She moved away from me, adding, "Neither am I. We were young. Impetuous."

That wasn't the word I would choose to describe our former relationship, but I wasn't exactly interested in a trip down memory lane.

"Well, I have a crazy asshole to hunt down." She winked at me. "But later, you're giving me Brexton's number."

Like hell I was. I pressed my lips into a thin smile. Georgia sighed and sauntered back to the party.

Norris moved to my side and cleared his throat as we watched her walk away. "Miss Kincaid." He let her name hang in the air without further comment.

"I should have suspected Hammond would pull something like this," I said disdainfully.

My old friend said nothing. He'd already made his feelings on asking for Hammond's assistance known. Jack Hammond was the last man that I wanted to owe, but I didn't have another choice. Not when Daniel had eluded my own teams for over five months.

Norris pressed a hand to his earpiece, listening intently. When he turned his attention back to me, his expression was grim. "The sweep is complete. We've found no trace of him."

I sucked in a breath. Daniel had managed to evade me again at one of the most heavily secured private events of the year.

"Speak to the caterer," I advised Norris, "and find out if Daniel was actually on the wait staff this evening."

Norris nodded, then paused. "We will contain this situation."

"Will we?" I shook my head, frustration getting the better of me. "Clara is too accessible until this wedding is over. There are too many opportunities for him to get to her. Six weeks."

"And after the wedding?" Norris asked.

"It's been a while since the Royal family did a goodwill tour of America." If I had to cross the Atlantic Ocean to remove this threat, so be it. "He'll never make it through customs."

Norris said nothing, but I knew what he was thinking. Daniel wasn't acting alone. Someone was backing him, providing him with help to stay hidden from the teams I had searching for him. It was why I'd been forced to bring in Hammond in the first place.

"And until then?" Norris asked. "He's making his presence known. I don't have to tell you he's sending us a message."

He was right. The threat was clear. Daniel was practically taunting us, and we were no closer to catching up to him. It was inexplicable. The man had no former ties to military or police. He'd taken a mathematics degree at Oxford. Yet he'd managed to evade us at every turn. "Now"—I straightened my tie—"I speak to my father. Arrange it."

. . .

I sipped my bourbon. It burned down my throat, scalding away the sour taste of the last few minutes. Dropping into a leather cigar chair, I slowly took in my surroundings. I hadn't been in this room since I was a child. Then it had been my father's study. It hadn't been used by anyone in years, not after my grandfather's passing when my family had made the move to Buckingham.

Clarence House had been my childhood home. It was the only one of my family's residences that truly held any pleasant memories for me. Happiness haunted its halls, a ghost always on my periphery that seemed impossible to catch.

Abandoning my drink, I moved to the large oak desk on the other side of the room. Riffling through its drawers, I finally found it. I took the picture of my mother out and carried it back to the chair—and my drink.

I'd lived without my mother for long enough that her picture usually only produced a mild ache of regret. Looking at her now, I saw myself reflected in her. Dark hair and brilliant eyes set against honey skin. I'd been blessed that I'd taken after her in the looks department. But it wasn't only myself that I saw in her.

I saw Clara.

She had been our family's rock—its center. We'd been off-balance since the day she died. I'd been young enough to not lose all faith when my mother died—she had been a piece of my life. Now Clara filled that missing part of me. I'd finally found my center again in Clara and the thought of losing her was impossible to consider.

"I assume you have a reason for hiding from your own

party." My father crossed to the bar cart and poured himself a drink. "And for calling me away from the guests."

"I had no idea you were enjoying yourself so much," I said dryly. "It's particularly surprising given how much you fought Edward on using Clarence House as the venue."

"Clarence House is an official Royal residence," he reminded me. "I was simply adhering to protocol regarding its use. If the house were occupied by one of my sons, it wouldn't have been an issue."

It was so like my father to play wounded, but I knew it was merely a trap to lure me closer so he could attack.

"All the more reason it should never have been an issue." We took sips from our respective glasses, staring at one another over the rims. His eyes darted to the photo I'd left propped on the side table.

"It's a shame she couldn't be here," I said.

"Your mother would not have approved of this situation. She adhered to tradition."

"She loved you," I said quietly. "God knows why, but she did. She had no interest in tradition. Her only interest was in this family."

"What do you want, Alexander?" he asked finally. "Or can you bring yourself to ask anything of me?"

"Can you bring yourself to give me anything?" I countered.

A muscle in his jaw tensed as he shook his head. "You know the expectations."

"Let's not pretend that this is about anything but wanting me to grovel. You have no intention of approving our marriage. That much is clear."

"Now we get to it." He rested his drink on the arm of the

chair, relaxing a bit. "No, I do not, and yet, you continue with the charade."

"The invitations have been sent," I reminded him. "In six weeks, I will make Clara my wife."

"In six weeks you will stage a mockery not only of marriage but of Clara. The crown will not recognize her as your wife." His words cut, but they didn't sting. I'd long since become numb to the damage my father inflicted.

I cleared my throat and forced myself to speak. "The threat to Clara's safety has increased. My personal teams are managing it, but I'd like the assistance of the King's Guard."

"This is what you choose to ask for?" He snorted, a caustic smile flashing over his pale face. "The King's Guard ensures the safety of the Royal family. Clara is not a Royal."

My fist slammed into the side table. "She will be in six weeks."

"No, my son"—he stood and glowered at me—"she won't be."

My jaw locked with the effort of restraining myself. "When will this punishment end?"

"That is up to you. I'm not punishing you, Alexander."

"Like hell, you aren't!" I roared.

"Expectations aren't punishment," he said with meaning. "The sooner you understand that, the better. You might think it's acceptable to play house and stage elaborate public spectacles to undermine my authority, but I assure you that they will do nothing to affect my opinion of this situation. Your future is on the throne. You belong here. Until you understand that, I can't condone your marriage—for the sake of the monarchy."

"Sod the monarchy," I growled.

He grimaced, glancing at me before turning his back and disappearing from the room.

Realization settled heavily over me. There was only one way to ensure the highest level of security for Clara. I stood and headed after him before I lost my nerve.

Rounding the corner of the morning room, I beckoned for a waiter. Swiping a champagne flute from his tray, I lifted it and called out over the crowd. "Pardon the interruption."

A hush fell in ripples over the crowd as the guests turned their attention to me.

"Clara?" I said loudly. I needed to see her, needed to remember why I was doing this.

In the far corner, the room began to part—and then she appeared. Her smile was tentative as if she suspected I was up to something, but it gave me the final reassurance I needed.

"In a little over a month, Clara Bishop has agreed to become my wife. I can only assume because she has no clue what she's getting into." I paused, waiting for the guests' laughter to quiet. "If she does know then I can only assume that, by some miracle, she thinks I'm worth the hassle." This time I didn't care about the laughter, I turned my full attention to her. "Thank you for your trust and for your love. I can only hope to prove that I deserve it. You haven't made an easy choice."

Her smile twisted at the corner in wry acknowledgment of the fact. Taking a deep breath, I looked back across the room. "I recently spoke to my father about the challenges marriage will bring. He reminded me that we can't always predict the future, but we can choose who we face it with. If

Clara and I face the changes the future brings together, I know we can meet any challenge."

My eyes landed on my father. Even across the room I could see the tick in his jaw at how I'd twisted his words.

Wait for it, I thought. He was going to like this even less.

"So I'm thrilled to announce that the first of these many changes will be a change of residence." I glanced briefly to Clara whose eyes widened.

I was going to pay for this later. Extending my hand to her, I waited for her to join me. She crossed the few final steps to reach me and took my hand uncertainly. I leaned in to kiss her cheek, turning my head quickly to whisper, "Do you trust me?"

Her fragile hand knit tightly through mine and squeezed.

"In a few weeks, we will officially take residence here. As some of you may know, I grew up here, and I'm pleased that Clarence House will be our first home as husband and wife." I turned to Clara and took her hand. "And I hope that my fiancée likes her wedding present."

Clara popped onto her tiptoes and gave me a quick kiss. Pulling back, her eyes questioned me, but she didn't press me for answers. Not now. Instead she returned her attention to our guests, graciously accepting the sudden outpouring of congratulations. The crowd threatened to swallow her, but I kept my hand locked on hers, nodding politely at the well wishes directed at us.

It didn't escape my attention that my father was not among the crowd. I'd made my move, sacrificing my pawn—my freedom—and moving ever closer to the grasp of the King.

CHAPTER EIGHT

Boxes were piled throughout the entryway of number 19. I blew out a frustrated sigh. It seemed impossible that in the short time we'd lived here we'd accumulated so much stuff.

Alexander had thrown me for a loop when he announced our move to Clarence House. Putting aside the fact it was actually a palace and not a house—something I couldn't comprehend—it was furnished with objects I'd be afraid to touch let alone sit on.

The weeks had flown by in a blur of dress fittings and appointments, but somehow I'd managed to sort nearly all of our possessions in time for the movers to descend upon us this morning. Alexander had taken the morning off from his meetings to finalize tomorrow's plans. I hadn't questioned his decision, knowing that taking an official residence was inevitable.

That didn't mean I was prepared for it.

Uncapping a marker, I listed off the contents of the box I'd finished packing. Most of these things were going into storage. It was silly to keep them, really—they were just going to collect dust. But I couldn't bring myself to let them go either.

An arm slipped around my waist and I relaxed against Alexander's firm body.

This was why I was doing this.

He was why.

Did anything else matter?

"I think we're ready," he said, his lips brushing the top of my head.

"Are we?" I whispered.

"Don't tell me you're having second thoughts?" I heard the smile in his voice that I couldn't see.

"Do you ever think about just running away? Buying a little cottage on the coast and growing old together?"

It was a wistful fantasy but Alexander tensed behind me. I'd hit a nerve without meaning to. Sighing, I twisted in his arms to face him.

"I know what I'm getting into," I reassured him. He'd made it clear the night he'd proposed. We'd looked out over the glittering expanse of London and he'd warned me. That didn't mean that part of me didn't wish things couldn't be different. Simpler.

"Do you?" he asked, his blue eyes searching mine for the answer to the unspoken question.

"I do." I had known. I still knew. But I also knew what he really needed to hear. "I'm happy."

"I wish I didn't have to put you through all of this." He kissed my forehead. "I wish we could run away and buy some rings. Disappear into that quiet life by the sea, but..."

"Where's the challenge in that?" I asked.

"Something tells me you'll always challenge me." The crooked grin I'd fallen in love with carved across his lips, making my heart pound.

I smacked his chest, pretending to be offended.

"Do that again and I'll have to spank you," he warned me, a playful glint returning to his eyes.

"Promise?" I asked breathlessly.

"Actually"—he drew out the word—"I can't help thinking of all the places we never christened."

A giggle broke past my lips. "Like where, X?"

We looked around. Barring the mountains of boxes, I had very pleasant memories of most of the surfaces in this house—furniture, floors, and walls included.

Alexander gripped my hips and placed me on top of a couple of boxes. "Here."

"That's cheating—"

His lips cut me off. I melted against him, my arms braiding around his neck and drawing him closer. My fingers wove through his ink-black hair as his tongue slipped inside my mouth. I sucked it slowly, wanting more of him.

Needing all of him.

He broke away, his face staying close to mine, as we struggled to catch our breath. "I thought of somewhere, Poppet."

"Is this your way of buying yourself time?" I asked. "Kiss me until I forget what I was accusing you of."

He smirked. "That depends. Did it work?"

I furrowed my brow thoughtfully, but before I could respond, he scooped me into his arms. Wrapping my legs around his trim waist, I relished the contact as our mouths found each other again. I wanted my mouth on him. I wanted to lick across the ridges and valleys of his abs. I wanted to kiss the scars that marked his beautiful body.

But most of all I wanted to be possessed.

And then I was weightless, landing on the sofa with a soft thump.

"Huh." I ran a finger over the tufted back of it. He had actually managed to find a place we hadn't made love. "Do you have some type of homing beacon for places you need to fuck me?"

"Poppet, you are the only thing on my radar." He bit his lip, his gaze raking down my form like he was planning how best to devour me. "Now about all these clothes."

He bent down and plucked open the button of my jeans. My ass lifted automatically as he slowly drew them over my hips.

"I love when I find your cunt naked." He dropped my pants to the floor before placing a palm on the inside of my knee.

I dropped my legs open at the gentle command. The delicious sensation of being bared to him overtook me, building my desire into a frantic need. His eyes hooded as he rubbed the rigid outline of his cock. My hand slipped down to caress the slick, swollen mound between my legs. "You do this to me. When you claim me with your eyes, you make me want to fuck myself for you."

"Show me," he ordered. He abandoned his erection and hooked his shirt, drawing it over his head in one swift motion. His gaze didn't waver as he unbuckled his trousers.

I drank in his body, something primal stirring within my core as I circled my finger over my clit. He awakened my darkness—my own sensual brutality—that captivated me. I was air and he was fire, consuming me until every inch of my body burned for him.

I couldn't bear to look at him, overwhelmed by the raw power he radiated. Closing my eyes, I shuddered as my fingers danced across my throbbing clit.

"Look at me," he demanded.

I shook my head, losing myself in the moment—and knowing exactly what would happen if I disobeyed. I wanted to drive him wild, drive him to the point where his careful control cracked and he claimed me.

"Sit up," he growled as his hand pushed under my ass, knocking my fingers away from my trembling sex. He didn't wait for me to comply, instead he adjusted me himself. Dropping to the couch, he stroked his cock, drawing a bead of creamy pre-cum to its tip. Before I thought about what I was doing, I'd bent to lick it off.

"Your mouth is so hot and wet," he groaned as I swirled my tongue over his crown. My mouth moved to cover his shaft, but he held it back. "I can see how bad you want this, but you can't tease me like that. Show me what's mine and then take it away."

I whimpered, my hips shifting with the weight of my arousal. I'd been so close and then he'd stopped me, left me to suffer the glorious agony of dissatisfaction.

"Stand up."

I rocked onto the balls of my feet, my thighs pressing against the ache at my core. Alexander lay down, his fingers moving swiftly over his cock. I moved toward him, my cunt slick and ready to sheath him.

"Did I say you could have this?" he asked, drawing my attention to the object of my hunger. He dropped his hold on it, letting his cock fall heavily across his abdomen, the tip grazing the edge of his navel. He beckoned me with his index finger. "Come here."

I stepped closer and he hooked an arm around my ass, dragging me to him. I stumbled forward as he guided my legs back onto the couch. But before he could snare me, I pivoted, dropping to my hands. My ass hovered over his face as I knelt over him. His hands kneaded into my hips, rolling me back until his tongue breached my sensitive seam. A moan cascaded from me as a ripple of pleasure shivered through me.

"I'm going to make you feel so good." He coaxed two fingers inside me. His lips closed over my frayed bundle of nerves until they sang with near release. The heat of his mouth withdrew as his fingers pumped harder in and out of me. "This sweet cunt is mine."

"Yours," I gasped as he drove me toward the edge and backed away again.

My pleasure belonged to him. I was at his mercy. I longed to please him. Dipping forward, I grasped his cock in my hand and brought it to my mouth. His masculine scent flooded my nostrils, and all I could think of was sucking him until he was empty. Plunging my mouth over his shaft, I sucked him in a frenzied rhythm. I wanted to take him with me—wanted him to spill over my tongue as his mouth claimed me. I cupped his balls and squeezed gently, earning my mouth a hard thrust.

Alexander slammed my ass down on his face, devouring me as I hollowed my cheeks on his cock. But despite his impatience, his tongue circled and darted skillfully. Each movement precisely focused. Each stroke forging a trail of ecstasy.

His thumb dipped between my legs, coating its pad with my arousal, and then I felt it press against the pucker of my ass. I grunted as he pushed it past the tight coil of muscles. I was full, near my breaking point, made fragile by his total domination of my body.

I writhed against him, rocking hard against his fingers and tongue—wanting more, wanting him deeper. His arm hooked around my thigh, holding me captive to his assault as his other hand caught my engorged clit and pinched.

A scream ripped through my throat, and I choked against his cock. Tiny explosions quaked through my body, my orgasm erupting over him. I fought to keep my own over him as the first spurt hit the roof of my mouth. I swallowed against the streams, even as my body sagged, boneless, against him. When he finally stopped coming, I collapsed onto him, my hand still gripping his undiminished erection.

Alexander pressed a kiss against my inner thigh. His palm massaged my ass cheek, giving me a moment to rest before he shifted from under me. Kneeling on the cushions, he opened my legs and angled the head of his cock at my sensitive entrance.

"No," I moaned. "I can't. I can't..."

"Shhh, Poppet. You know what to say if you want me to stop."

Brimstone. My safe word floated to mind. I hadn't used it in months, even as his expectations of my body grew more demanding. Although I'd grown more fearless, he still continued to remind me that there was always a way to stop him.

I just never wanted him to stop.

He waited, and I moaned another no, even as my hips

bucked closer, my sex flowering open despite the tremors still rippling through me. "That's right. Spread for me."

Alexander leaned over me, his strong arms bracketing my body as he sank inch by exquisite inch inside me. He moved slowly, sliding and retreating. My fingers clawed into his biceps, grasping for leverage, but he continued his leisurely pace. His gaze pierced through me as his hips rocked and circled me toward another release. I felt full—whole in a way only he could complete me.

My sex tightened and my head fell back as the pressure at my core mounted.

"Look at me," Alexander said. "Keep your eyes open. I want to see what you're thinking when you come."

Our gazes locked and I fought the instinct to drift away. Sweat beaded over Alexander's brow, his jaw constricting from the effort of restraining himself. "Just like that, Poppet. You're so fucking beautiful when you come. Show me how it makes you feel when I'm filling you. Show me you love me."

He pressed deeper, his length massaging with patient strokes against the sensitive spot only he could reach. Bliss expanded through my limbs. I unfolded as I arched into him. I held nothing back, revealing everything.

CHAPTER NINE

I paused in the doorway of the bistro to scan the tables. I was late thanks to the discovery of two more places we'd never made love. I'd dressed in a rush, opting for a simple wrap dress and my favorite Louboutins. Favorite because I could stay upright in them despite the fact my legs were still shaky from this morning.

Edward waved to me from a table near the outdoor patio. Smiling at the maître d', I pointed to my companion and continued. As I navigated the dining room, the murmurs of the patrons seemed to swell behind me. I shouldered my purse and did my best to ignore it.

"She makes an entrance wherever she goes." Edward stood in greeting, waiting for me to take my seat.

"Don't remind me," I said, lowering my voice. "Apparently this is lunch and a show."

"You do eventually stop noticing," he promised me.

I hoped he was right. For now, though, I decided to live in the moment. How often did I get to meet up with one of my favorite people for lunch?

Priorities, I told myself firmly.

We ordered quickly so we could focus on catching up. In the whirlwind of the last few weeks, I'd spent less time with Edward than I'd have liked.

"Dare I ask how the wedding is coming?"

"You just did." I curled my lip.

"That well, huh? At least the world is ready."

"I also have a countdown going," I assured him. The thought of the number of media outlets currently guessing about everything from my dress to how I would wear my hair was mildly disturbing. Truthfully, even I didn't even know what I was doing with my hair.

I didn't care.

"One week," we said together.

Saying it out loud sent a flutter of butterflies whirling through my belly. I rubbed it absently, wishing that I could control my anxiety a little better.

"Speaking of." Edward reached into his pocket and drew out a black jewelry box.

"Oh! David's ring?" I asked, grabbing for it.

He snorted. "That's your ring."

"Oh my God." I gasped.

"You forgot!" Edward accused.

"I didn't forget," I hedged. "I simply put it on the back burner."

"Anything else you want to sell me?" he asked.

"My head is in so many places I'm forgetting things left and right. Sometimes"—I dropped my voice—"I forget to go to the loo. I need to and then I forget halfway there and go to the next appointment."

"One week," he repeated soothingly.

"Hope for your brother's sake that I don't lose my mind before then," I advised him as I pried open the jewelry box's lid. My breath caught when I saw it. It was as simple as I remembered. Masculine without being flashy. But there was something about seeing it—about knowing what it represented—that knocked the wind out of me. Plucking it from the case, I turned it over in my palm. No beginning. No end. Just like us. My eyes landed on the delicate promise engraved on the interior band and my heart leapt.

For always.

Two simple words to say so much. He'd asked me to marry him with those words. Next week I would give him my final answer. My promise.

I blinked against the tears welling in my eyes. Carefully putting the ring back in the case, I wiped away the evidence of my sudden surge of emotions.

But Edward had already retrieved the handkerchief folded in his pocket. I took it gratefully and blotted my eyes.

"Do you see this?" I asked him. "I'm going to be one big blotch next Friday. Literally everything makes me cry."

He laughed and I shook a finger at him.

"No, really. Spill your water. I'll cry." Making fun of myself lightened my mood and soon I was laughing with him. "Distract me, please."

"Gladly, Your Highness."

"I am not a *highness*," I stopped him. "That is not the best way to distract me."

"As you wish," he teased.

I groaned and slouched back in my chair. "So where's David's ring?"

Edward squirmed in his seat, his eyes darting out over the

crowd. Either I was dealing with a case of cold feet or he had bad news. My heart sunk as I remembered he'd set up today's lunch. Still, he wasn't crying.

"Change your mind?" I asked, giving him an out. If David had refused him, he could claim a change of heart. I'd let him.

"Not exactly." He inhaled deeply, finally releasing his breath when a familiar figure appeared at the table.

"David!"

"Hi, hon," Edward said as his better half took the chair next to his and leaned in for a quick kiss. With his laid-back style, David complemented my fashion-conscious future brother-in-law. I watched them, feeling the lump in my throat growing. I'd never seen either of them so relaxed before. David lounged casually back, his eyes bright against his coffee skin. A few months ago, they wouldn't have sat next to each other.

"Oh, we've made her cry again," Edward said. David shifted forward with a worried look passing over his hand-some face.

I picked up his handkerchief, embarrassed, and waved off David's concern. "Stress."

"I am not looking forward to that," David said. "Are you going to be like this?"

I swallowed against my tears and stared at them. "Wait a minute! Show me your hand."

David held up his left hand smugly, displaying the sleek engagement band Edward and I had picked out a few weeks ago.

"I can't believe you've been sitting here all this time, and you didn't say a thing," I accused Edward. Jumping up, I gave them both a hug.

"It's my fault," David said. "I wanted to be here."

"You're the first person we've told," Edward added.

"Me?" I squeaked.

"Don't cry again!" Edward laughed as I began to do just that.

"I can't help it," I said. I'd been there for the transformation of their relationship. Now I was here for its evolution.

"You're the reason we're here," David said softly. Our eyes met and in that moment I knew Edward wasn't just getting married, he was growing our family.

"Yeah, if your sister hadn't kissed me at that party," Edward joked.

David smacked him on the shoulder before I could.

"Seriously, Clara, you and Alexander—you showed me I didn't have to choose blood over love." He clasped David's hand and brought it to his lips. "Thank you."

I clutched the handkerchief, joy flooding through me, and waved it at them. "Stop making me cry! And tell me how he proposed."

David flashed a dazzling display of white teeth. "Well…"

AN HOUR LATER, I tore myself away from the happy couple so I could make yet another appointment with the wedding coordinator. I'd surreptitiously tucked a roll into my purse at lunch, having been too busy talking to finish my food. Grabbing it, I smiled at Norris as he opened the door to the car.

"I thought you just had lunch," he said.

"Most brides diet, I eat carbs." I grinned deviously at him.

It was yet another measure of how much Alexander had changed me. There had been a time when I would have stopped eating just to feel in control of something. I didn't have that urge anymore. If anything, it was the opposite. I was always hungry. Of course, my body probably had a hard time keeping up with all the sex.

Ducking into the car, I glanced back at the restaurant, my mind drifting to David and Edward. But as soon as I did, my light mood evaporated. My hand flew out to stop the door from closing.

"Miss Bishop?" Norris stood aside as I climbed back out of the Rolls-Royce. "Did you forget something?"

I shook my head. Norris turned to look at what had caught my eyes, and I felt his body go rigid next to mine.

"I think you should get in the car," he suggested gently.

"I bet you do, Norris." I shot him a look that dared him to stop me.

He moved to the side with a sigh, allowing me a direct line of sight to the woman who'd caught my attention.

Georgia Kincaid.

She was impossible to miss as she casually sipped a glass of red wine, a pair of large black sunglasses perched on her nose. Somehow I'd missed her, even though I'd been dining steps away from her.

Meeting your fiancé's ex once: bad luck.

Running into her a second time: coincidence.

A third time?

Georgia Kincaid was following me, and I was going to find out why.

CHAPTER TEN

Striding across the sidewalk, I set my shoulders and prepared myself for the inevitable confrontation. This was the third time I'd run into Georgia Kincaid, and not a single bone in my body thought it was a coincidence. Georgia pushed down her sunglasses and smiled as I approached.

"Clara, how lovely to see you," she gushed. "An unexpected surprise."

"Is it?" I asked pointedly.

Georgia blinked. A moment later the smile vanished from her face and she gestured to the seat across from her. I hesitated, but something told me that she was even less into playing games than I was. I sat down, crossing my arms over my chest and waited.

"Don't stop now," she urged. "There was an accusation in there somewhere, and I'm dying for you just to say it."

"You're following me."

She shrugged. "Lots of people follow you, Clara. Photographers, reporters, *stalkers*."

"Are you stalking me?" If she wanted me to be direct, I could be.

Georgia laughed and lifted her wine glass. "No, you're just the bait."

"Then tell me what I've done to earn the pleasure of your attention," I snapped.

"I believe that's a question for Alexander."

My stomach flipped over, and I fought against the urge to slap her. "What are you implying?"

"Not what you think, apparently." She took a sip and set her glass back on the table. Leaning across it, she pulled off her sunglasses and studied me. "I've been engaged by a mutual friend to ensure a certain problem is dealt with."

Somehow she managed to say everything while admitting to nothing. I was obviously out of my league with her, but that wasn't going to stop my pushing for answers. "Who is your employer?"

"That's the wrong question," she chastised me. "What you want to know is who engaged my services. But I think we both know the answer to that question."

"Alexander," I breathed before clamping my mouth shut. Information was currency here. I was sure of that.

"Your fiancé is concerned for your safety, and frankly, he should be."

I shook my head, trying to process the jumble of thoughts. "But what does that have to do with you?"

"I have a particular set of skills." She shrugged as if this was an answer.

"Skills?" I repeated.

"It's best to say I lack a certain moral decency that infects most people."

In that moment, part of me screamed *run*. I had no business sitting here with a woman who considered morality a blight. But I couldn't bring myself to leave. If Alexander couldn't be bothered to tell me everything, I'd have to find the answers on my own.

A few of the pieces were already falling into place. "You're here because of Daniel." The statement was simple enough, but the implications staggered me. Maybe Alexander couldn't keep me safe. Of course I knew how far he would go to protect me. I never considered it might not be enough, that he might have to resort to using someone like her.

"Don't bother being offended on his behalf. Someone has to clean up the scum, Clara."

"And that's your job?" I asked, not caring to hear her answer.

"Ah yes. Sit in your ivory loft of privilege and judge me," she said flatly. "Be as horrified as you like. In the end you'll be glad I'm so good at what I do."

I swallowed against the lump in my throat.

"I suppose it's easy to judge when you don't have to know the details," she purred.

"What are you going to do to him?" I whispered.

"Don't trouble yourself," she said dismissively. "I'll do my job. You'll walk down the aisle, and everyone lives happily ever after."

"Everyone lives, huh?" I laughed dully.

"As far as you are concerned." Her finger traced the rim of her wine glass. "Now ask me what you really want to know."

"I'm not sure I follow." The dread creeping across my

skin suggested otherwise. But after the shock of what I'd just learned, I wasn't positive I could handle any more.

"You're a smart girl, Clara. Don't play dumb," she said, an edge of distaste coloring her words.

"What is your relationship with Alexander?" Finally, I had asked the question I wasn't sure I wanted answered.

"I have no relationship with Alexander," she assured me, tacking on, "anymore."

"We're strong women. Lies don't become us."

"I'm not lying. And once again you're asking the wrong question."

I didn't have to search for the right one. "What were you to him?"

"Now we're getting to it." A delighted smirk played over her stunning features. "Alexander assured me that you knew. Was he lying?"

My eyes shut and I inhaled deeply before answering. "He told me that you had a relationship. You're his ex-girlfriend."

"I know Alexander isn't sentimental enough to call me his girlfriend, even in the past tense." She raised an eyebrow.

"I believe I called you an ex-girlfriend," I clarified.

"And he didn't correct you?" she asked. "Interesting."

"I don't have time for this." I stood shakily and nodded to her. My body was already preparing for the confrontation I knew was coming. My issue wasn't with Georgia Kincaid. It was with the man I was about to marry.

She held up her hand. "Please sit."

I considered it for a moment before returning to my chair. Whatever was brewing inside of me would keep. Of that much, I was certain.

"I had hoped to run into you," she admitted. "I thought a little girl talk was in order."

"Is that what we're calling this?" I asked. "You didn't strike me as a woman who played games."

"Then you've misread me. I *love* games. Almost as much as I love to play." She left the final word hanging in the air.

My hand flew to my mouth as I swallowed back a rush of stomach acid. I didn't need her to explain what that meant.

"You?" I asked, trying to wrap my head around the idea.

"I know." She licked her lower lip, making her red lipstick glisten. "I don't seem like a submissive. But then again, neither do you, my dear."

"That's because I'm not," I bit out.

"I do remember Alexander saying he wasn't in the lifestyle," she recalled. "Or at least claiming he wasn't. But I'm not stupid. Everything about a man like Alexander craves dominance. He was born to it. The most natural Dominant I've ever met, actually."

"Enough," I cried, drawing the attention of a few surrounding tables.

Georgia shot me a look and mouthed one word. *Discretion.*

"You're advising me to be discreet?" I could have laughed if I didn't feel so sick.

"I prize discretion over all things. You are one of only a few people who know about my former relationship to your fiancé." Her hands folded together. "That is why I was assigned to handle your problem."

"I don't want you to handle it."

"Don't let your emotions get in the way," she advised me.

"As I said, I am discreet. I'm surprised you even noticed me here today, but then again maybe I'm not."

"Why?" I asked.

"You've wanted answers from me since the moment we met. You were looking for me, Clara. You just didn't know it." Her head tilted to someone over my shoulder, and a moment later, the waiter appeared. "The check, please."

"I didn't..."

"You didn't want these answers," she finished for me. "Regardless, I operated under the assumption that Alexander had been truthful with me. He'll be displeased that you know. His urge to protect you is very strong."

"I know." I'd seen that at every turn. But how was I supposed to overlook this? I sat silently as the waiter reappeared with the bill.

Georgia drew out her wallet and tossed down a few pound notes. "Perhaps you should reconsider submission. It's based on trust."

"I trust him." But I couldn't quite make myself believe my own words.

"I trusted him," she said softly. "He didn't break that trust. Maybe he needs you to trust him more."

The insinuation in her words chilled me, and for some reason I found myself asking her the question that occupied my darker thoughts. "Do you think he can be satisfied without that?"

"If you have to ask, I feel like you already know the answer." Georgia pushed to her feet and grabbed her purse. "Please believe me when I tell you that I hope you work this out. My experience with Alexander was limited, but he's a good man. When you're ready, don't be scared."

She left me then and I stared out over the bustling London street. Dozens of people strolled by on their way to jobs and meetings and appointments. Off to meet lovers and friends. I was surrounded by a sea of people, and I'd never felt more alone.

CHAPTER ELEVEN

My knee made hard contact with a moving box as I stumbled into the house.

"Fuck!" I screamed.

I'd gone to my appointment with the publicist and listened half-heartedly to her explain the protocols I'd be expected to know when I married Alexander in a week. The whole time questioning if I needed to be there. One week. In a week I was supposed to make vows I was no longer sure of. Not because I wouldn't mean them, but because for the first time in months I questioned if I could be the wife Alexander needed.

Georgia's words echoed in my mind as I rubbed my smarting knee. *He's a good man.*

A good man who had hired his ex-sub to murder someone. I'd read between the lines. I understood exactly what Georgia had been brought in to do. But the thought that scared me—that made my blood turn to ice—was that I cared more about his other secret.

I'd met his submissive, and he hadn't been up front with

me. If he'd kept their relationship a secret, was he capable of...

I shook the thought from my head.

Alexander was faithful to me. I was positive about that. But Georgia had seen a side to him that he'd only shown me in carefully timed glimpses. Even in his most dominant moments, even in my most submissive, we had been equal. I'd never known true fear at his hands, but she had. He'd admitted to me that his submissive had craved pain and that he had inflicted it.

When the time came, as she suggested it would, could I endure it?

The door behind me opened and he stepped inside, a bright smile flashing over his face when he saw me standing there.

"Last night in Notting Hill," he said. "I thought we could walk down to Portobello and grab a bite."

"It's going to rain. We've packed the umbrellas," I responded flatly.

"I'm certain there's one in the car." He reached for me and I flinched. "Clara?"

Closing my eyes, I searched for the right words, but in the end there was only accusation. "I ran into Georgia Kincaid today."

"Oh?" His expression stayed carefully detached.

"And when I say ran into Georgia, I mean, I confronted her about following me." I planted my hands on my hips, daring him to feign innocence.

"Norris didn't mention this."

"Norris," I spat back, "knows when to keep out of our

business. Something your little friend doesn't seem to understand."

"She's not my friend," Alexander corrected me. He tugged the knot of his tie loose and unbuttoned his top collar button.

I refrained from grabbing the loose tie and strangling him, but only just barely. "Yes, she made that clear. She also informed me about your arrangement."

"Clara." He placed hand on my arm. "Whatever you think—"

"I don't think! I know! You hired a hit man. Woman. Whatever!" I jerked away from his grasp.

His shoulders relaxed, and I knew then that he was relieved. He thought she hadn't told me any more than that. Comprehension crashed into me—he had no intention of ever revealing the true nature of his past relationship with Georgia.

"Oh," I continued, my lower lip beginning to tremble, "she also told me that you used to tie her up and whip her."

Alexander drew a sharp breath. "Clara—"

"I knew I was forgetting something," I said, ignoring him. "We had a lovely conversation about it. She was under the impression that we had all shared our stories."

"Before a few weeks ago, I hadn't spoken to Georgia Kincaid in years."

"And now you've hired her to commit murder," I seethed. "What kind of sick bond do you two have exactly?"

"I asked for assistance. I did not ask for her assistance."

"Yeah, who knew the family jeweler was also the Royal cleaner?" I shook my head in disbelief. "Is this who you are? How far are you willing to go, X?"

"When it comes to protecting you, I will go as far as I have to. No one will touch you and I don't care if I have to get in bed with the devil himself," he roared, anger flaring like the tip of a flame in his blue eyes.

"Call it off," I demanded in a low voice. "Call Hammond and tell him you will find another way."

"I can't do that." He pressed forward, backing me into the wall. "Not until I'm sure this threat has been dealt with."

"Call it off," I pleaded. "I won't have blood on my hands —or yours."

He straightened, an angry tick pulsing in his jaw as he withdrew his mobile from his breast pocket and dialed.

"Hammond, close the show." There was a pause. "I'm certain."

Even as I heard him give the order, my heart pounded. Avoiding one mistake didn't erase the others he'd made. It also didn't erase the danger I'd placed my friends and family in unknowingly.

"Happy?" He dropped the mobile back in his pocket.

"No," I whispered.

"Clara, I needed information. There was no standing order." His words reeked of excuses.

"That's not what she said."

"Whatever Georgia told you, please trust that I am acting in your best interest."

"How can I trust you, X?"

"What else did Georgia Kincaid say to you?" His voice was measured, but the demand was clear.

She told me something I didn't want to hear. She told me exactly what I'd feared to be true. I tried to meet Alexander's eyes and answer his question, but in the end, I couldn't. "Sorry, X."

I sidestepped him and reached for the door, but his hand shot out to hold it closed.

"Does it really matter?" he asked. "She's in my past."

I laughed hollowly. "If you have to ask that, then you already know the answer."

Alexander's hand dropped, allowing me to open the door. "Where are you going?"

"I don't know," I answered honestly. "But don't follow me, okay?"

"I can't allow—"

"You can," I stopped him, "and you will."

I darted out the door and to the street, hailing a taxi before he could send for Norris. Part of me wanted to believe he'd let me go, that he'd give me a chance to think.

And part of me watched out the window as rain began to fall, hoping he was right behind me.

RAIN DANCED ACROSS THE THAMES, making the lights of London sparkle with a frenetic energy. I clutched the stone rail until the rough surface had nearly rubbed my fingertips raw. Turning my face to the charcoal sky, I let the downpour shower over me. A chill ran up my neck but I couldn't bring myself to choose a direction. If I turned left I'd be heading toward the Westminster Royal, the hotel where I'd naively fallen into Alexander's bed. To the right, the London Eye sat stalled due to the weather. The ghosts of our relationship were all around me. Alexander was at the heart of this city to me, which made it impossible to escape him.

"Clara!" My name carried over the wind, held aloft by the desperation buoying it.

I pivoted toward his voice instinctively. Passing umbrellas broke my line of vision, allowing flashes of him. Alexander stood on the other side of the bridge, his hand still gripping the roof of the Rolls-Royce. It seemed impossible that I could hear him over the rain shower and passing traffic.

Alexander darted across the traffic, narrowly dodging an oncoming taxi, which set my heart racing. Apparently, he was all about stupid decisions lately. I was too wet to move—too wet to care. By the time he reached me, the white shirt under his open suit coat was soaked through. It clung to him. But it didn't only display his muscles—his scars showed through. He halted a few steps before me and we stood as heaven cried over us, neither of us speaking.

"How did you know where I was?" I demanded. "Are you tracking my phone now?"

"No," he panted. "I just knew."

"Bullshit," I accused. In a city of eight million people, no one was that lucky.

"I went to where we began," he called over the storm. "Where I asked you to marry me. I went to where I would have gone."

"I don't know why I came here," I admitted, a shiver rolling through me. Alexander took a step towards me and I backed away.

"You were looking for us."

"Maybe you're right. All I've found lately is more questions. More secrets."

"Georgia means nothing to me," he said. "I didn't tell you because that man is gone. He was broken, Clara. *You* healed him."

I shook my head, rain drops spilling from my lashes. "I changed him."

"And that's a bad thing?" He took another step toward me, pausing like he was approaching a frightened animal.

"People don't change like that. I can't ask you to be someone you aren't." I thought of Georgia's warning—that what was enough for Alexander now wouldn't satisfy him forever.

"Like hell people don't change." Alexander took another step, bringing his body within inches of mine.

Awareness prickled over my skin giving way to the physical reaction his presence always induced, but I couldn't feel it. I sensed it—my nipples pebbling, my core tightening—but I was numb.

"I don't want you to change." I stumbled on the words, trying to find a way to explain even as my heart broke. "I love you, but I can't give you what you need. Not completely. Someday you'll resent that, X. And this might kill me now, but I won't survive when you finally leave."

"I'm not leaving," he said, his voice hoarse with all the things he could never express to me. "I don't want that life, Clara."

"Did it fulfill you? Did it satisfy you?"

His head fell forward, rain dripping from his hair. "Yes. It did."

That was all I needed to know. Choking down a sob, I forced myself to turn. My arms wrapped around my chest protectively, but I couldn't hold onto the last pieces of my shattered heart. His hand grabbed my upper arm and spun me around, pressing me into him. Our eyes met and I couldn't look away.

"It *did*," he repeated. "But it never could again. It soothed a part of me that was empty for only one reason, but it could never fill the space. Nothing but you ever will."

My hands found his face, and I held him there, so close that I tasted the sweetness of his breath on my lips. "Why?"

"Because you found me, Clara. I was lost, and you gave me a home. Let me stay," he whispered as his face angled over mine. His hand cupped my chin, blue eyes searching mine for permission.

He wasn't demanding it. The arm bracing me against him was loose. I could slip away, disappear under the cover of the stormy night sky.

But I already knew that no matter what path I took—no matter how far or hard I ran—all roads led back to him. I may have given him a home, but he was my shelter. My protector.

I couldn't deny that any more than I could deny the ache in my chest. What if his past continued to intrude on our future? What if mine did? It no longer mattered—I loved him, and I'd promised him nothing in his past could change that.

Lighting cracked overhead, but neither of us flinched. So long as we were here—so long as we were united—no act of God or man could tear us apart.

I guided his face to mine, our lips meeting softly. Rain washed over us, cleansing us of our pasts and our mistakes. The choices the future forced would be ours alone.

Alexander's hand fell away as he bent and scooped me into his arms. I clung to him even as he broke away. When we reached the edge of the sidewalk, he murmured, "Trust me, Poppet?"

I looked into his eyes and knew that I did. It was inexplicable and reckless, but even though I had questions, I trusted him. I nodded.

"Then hold tight."

My arms locked around his neck as he dashed across lanes of traffic. Fear thrilled through me, but the rush of it faded almost instantaneously. He had me—what did I have to fear?

I didn't miss the reproachful look on Norris's face as he opened the back passenger door for us. I scrambled into the back of the car and Alexander slid in behind him. In moments, he'd gathered me into his arms.

Alexander brushed kisses over my forehead, my cheeks, across my nose. Silent apologies. I closed my eyes and accepted the offering. Melting against him, I listened to his steady heartbeat. My own heart beat for that rhythm.

"Being with me will always be dangerous. There will always be security, because there will always be threats. I only want to protect you." He hesitated. "I wish it could be otherwise."

"I know," I whispered. "But I need you to stay open."

"I can't promise you there will be no darkness, Clara." His face nuzzled against my neck, inhaling deeply. "I am not a perfect man, but you have all of me. Never doubt that."

"Can I ask you for something?" I said shyly.

He tilted my chin up. "Anything."

"Take me for coffee." It was a simple request, but my voice broke as I asked, knowing it was laced with meaning.

Coffee was normal. Something we weren't very good at it, but if we were going to make this work we needed normal.

"You're soaked and cold."

"I don't care," I whispered.

He leaned forward and rapped on the glass. The partition separating us from Norris descended.

"Coffee?" It was more of a question than an instruction.

Norris's smile flashed in the rearview mirror. "I know just the place, sir."

The car edged over a lane before pulling to a stop in front of a small café. A neon sign flashed 24 *hours*.

"I have to admit this is a first for me," Alexander said as he swung open the door.

"Really?" This delighted me. "I've never been around for one of your firsts."

He paused, turning back to me and catching my hand. "You have been all of my firsts."

As I followed him out of the back seat he slipped his suit coat over my shoulders.

"It's wet," he said unapologetically.

"It doesn't really matter." I couldn't possibly be any more drenched. I clutched it shut over my collarbone, breathing in the scent of him.

He shook the rain from his hair, which fell over his forehead in dark gashes, sending rivulets streaming over his face. The drops caught in the lashes that framed his smoldering eyes. He was fire in the rain. Impossible. Magnificent. *Mine*.

He crooked his arm. "Can I buy you a coffee?"

"Just one?" I teased.

"I wouldn't want to keep you up all night."

"Are you sure about that?" I trailed a finger over the inside of his wrist.

Alexander held up a finger and called to a passing waiter. "A pot of coffee, if you will."

The waiter nodded, looking a little confused as he headed back to the counter. No doubt he was wondering if his imagination was playing tricks on him.

Alexander and I slid into a booth, our hands finding each other's across the table. It wasn't exactly normal, but it was a start.

CHAPTER TWELVE

I t is an irrefutable fact that the more a girl has on her to-do list, the faster time flies. Apparently that went double for women who were planning weddings. I'd been concerned I'd be bored after I left Peters & Clarkwell, but now I realized I didn't have time to be bored. Especially not with my mother breathing down my neck about last minute decisions and the hundreds of new etiquette rules I had to follow. It made me wonder exactly why anyone would use the term 'blessed' in regards to marriage.

It also provided me with some distraction from the fight Alexander and I had had last weekend. We'd spent the last few days breaking in our new quarters within Clarence House, and somehow I'd found that despite my anxiety over everything, I was happy.

Ducking out of a final meeting with the florist I'd managed to keep off my mother's radar, my phone rang. I dug it out of my purse, pleased to see it was one of the few people I had not placed on my mental block list.

I slid accept to take my sister's call. "Are you calling to talk to me or to relay a message?"

"I should be employed as your secretary," she said, not bothering to hide her annoyance at becoming the communications gopher between me and my parents. "I have about a dozen messages I'm supposed to relay, absolutely none of which are important."

"When are they ever?" I asked as I slid into the back of the Rolls-Royce that had magically appeared amidst the afternoon traffic.

"She's going to drive me crazy. *'Tell your sister that her cousin Elise won't be able to make it. Tell your sister that Elise just called to say she moved her meetings and is flying in. Tell your sister to remember to offer a gluten-free cake option. Tell your sister it's too late to change the cake and she hopes no one has an allergy.'* Honestly, the only thing I want to tell you is to run while you have the chance."

"I'm sorry." My apology was sincere, although I couldn't help but be glad she was bearing the brunt of my mother's last minute panic. There were already enough other people panicking around me.

"I didn't call to pass on her ramblings," she said dismissively as though this was all completely normal—and to some extent it was considering our mother's penchant for drama. "Where and when? And what should I wear? I don't think I've ever needed a night out so badly in my life."

"We're meeting at CoCo's for dinner first. Belle booked a private room and then we're going dancing, so nothing formal," I advised, choosing to skim over the number of ridiculous security procedures Alexander had insisted on for the evening. I'd grown used to having a constant shadow, but it didn't mean I liked it. I also didn't want to draw any more attention to the presence of security this evening. I wanted to be carefree for once.

"I still think we should have gone away for your hen night." I could almost see Lola's pout as she spoke. It looked something like our mother's without the added weight of years of disappointment. "I can't believe Alexander was so against it."

"I'll see you at six," I said, bypassing her complaint and hanging up. It was hard to explain to someone who wasn't in love why it was so difficult for us to be apart. Of course, we were a little more dependent on each other than most people, and we'd spent more time apart than we'd have liked of late, given the increasing responsibilities he'd taken on for the crown. I slid my phone back in my purse and turned my attention to the street.

I missed being able to walk around London. With the number of foreign dignitaries already arriving for the wedding and the number of meetings and rehearsals planned for the next few days, security had increased to the point of suffocation. But as I gazed out the window I caught glimpses of my face—flashing on TV screens in shops, on magazine covers at the corner stand, and, in a surreal twist, plastered all over souvenir items sold by street vendors. I shrank back when I spotted a rather burly man wearing a t-shirt with a poorly photoshopped picture of me clad in a bikini on the front, grateful for the darkly tinted glass of Alexander's personal vehicle.

This wasn't my life. It couldn't be.

Part of me didn't want it to be.

A familiar mix of dread and elation churned in my stomach. In three days I would marry the man I loved. It was more than I'd ever dreamed. What was difficult to swallow, was that in three days I would officially be granted a title—or so the tabloids claimed—and then promptly given the keys to Clarence House, the personal residence of the Prince of Wales. Because Alexander was the Prince of Wales. He had titles. Multiple titles. How exactly was I supposed to absorb that?

"Norris?" I called to the front seat.

Two alert eyes found mine in the rearview mirror. "Yes, Miss Bishop?"

I suppressed a sigh that he continued to insist on being so formal with me. "Do they give public tours of Clarence House?"

"If they can charge for admission, they'll give a tour of it," he said with a laugh.

"Great," I grumbled, "I'm going to be living in a museum."

"It could be worse," he said and though I couldn't see it, I knew he was smiling.

"How?" I challenged him, a grin tugging at my own lips.

"You could still be living with your parents."

I shook my head in mock-horror. Maybe Norris wasn't so formal after all. Maybe I just had a bad habit of being too quick to make assumptions about people. The world wasn't nearly as worked up about my wedding as I was. Maybe none of this was that big of a deal. I'd almost managed to convince myself I was right when Norris turned the corner near my old flat. I'd almost managed to believe that my life might not be changing as drastically as I fear. Yeah, *almost*. And then I saw the pile of signs and flowers and other tokens piled near the building's main entrance.

Not only was my entire life about to change, it had infected my past as well. Clara Bishop only existed in the context of Prince Alexander, and even as I clung to who I was, I felt pieces of myself slipping away. Everything about my life—past and present—was an open book. I was to be read and studied and analyzed. It was overwhelming, and one thing was certain: I needed a night out even more than my sister.

AUNT JANE OPENED her door with a large glass of red wine in hand and held it out, but I waved it away. Between the ride to my old flat and tomorrow's schedule, my stomach was churning. The last thing I felt like was a drink.

"No thanks." I groaned and slumped at her kitchen table, instantly feeling at home in the cozy apartment. She'd updated the space to complement the pre-war architecture and then filled it with trinkets and pieces from her travels. The strange mix of elegant and eccentric was as warm as Jane herself. "I think I'm going to throw up. Did you know you can buy a Clara doll with interchangeable fashion items?"

"I won't tell you the Clara paraphernalia I saw the other day. It would make you blush," she said conspiratorially, pouring the wine she'd offered me into her own glass.

"Not bloody likely," I promised her.

"It made me blush," she said pointedly.

Okay, I had to admit *that* was a feat. It was impossible to imagine ruffling Jane. She'd been game for all of Belle's hen night plans, including hitting the club. I had to admit that between her messy pixie-cut, black crepe tunic and leather pants, she was going to fit in better than me. Belle had the same knack for fitting seamlessly into any situation. Maybe it was shared genes, but part of me wondered if it was their pedigree. Their family were aristocrats and came from old money—unlike my own. Perhaps that helped them feel more comfortable in their own skin. Or maybe I had just never managed to get comfortable in my own.

"What have I gotten myself into?" I asked in a soft voice.

Jane settled into the chair across from mine and took my hand. Her gray eyes that usually sparkled with mischief grew serious. "Do you love him?"

I nodded, a lump forming in my throat as I considered how much. "I can't imagine my future without him."

"Then it doesn't matter who he is or what people think. Relationships are hard for everyone, even people who don't live their lives on the front page. They take work and commitment. Are you willing to fight for him?" she asked.

"Yes." I'd already fought for him, and I wasn't about to give him up for anything.

"And he's willing to fight for you?"

Despite the tears threatening to show themselves, I smiled and nodded. I had no doubt Alexander would fight for me, too. We'd overcome so much in our short relationship. I sensed there were more obstacles ahead, but I could face any of them with him at my side.

"If you're both willing to work and willing to fight for each other, then you'll stick together even when things get tough. Just remember this: at the end of the day, he's a man and you're a woman, and you chose each other. You're commitment to one another is all that matters. The rest is just background noise."

She squeezed my hand and I squeezed back.

"Now get upstairs," she demanded, tossing her head toward the door. "I'm not going out with you if you're planning on wearing that."

"And what is wrong with what I'm wearing?" I asked, deliberately baiting her. The navy dress coat, while chic and appropriate for appointments, wasn't club attire.

"You aren't the Queen of England yet," she said flatly. "Tonight you're just a twenty-something hitting a bar."

And that was exactly what I needed—to blend in, to get lost in a crowd, to dance mindlessly.

To forget for just a few hours that my whole world was about to change.

"WHAT IS THIS?" I asked suspiciously when Belle tossed a pink shopping bag in my direction.

"A little something sexy," she said, shrugging innocently. She flopped onto her bed and waved her hand. "Open it."

"I didn't expect presents." Apparently I had a lot to learn about hen nights before it was my turn to plan Belle's in a few months.

"Of course!" Belle giggled, tossing her blonde curls over her shoulder. She looked like she was about to burst with excitement.

Discarding the paper wrapping, I drew out what could best be described as a collection of straps held together by very little fabric. I held the lingerie up. "Oh, they're panties!"

"Knickers," Belle corrected me, wrinkling her nose. "Your American is showing."

It was an innocent reminder, but it set off alarm bells. I inhaled deeply, trying to steady the race of my pulse.

"You look ill," Belle said. She sat up and patted the bad next to her.

Dropping down next to her, I crossed my legs and unleashed a torrent of anxiety. "I am American. I mean, not *legally*, but let's face it, I was raised in America. For every person who doesn't care about that, ten more do, including Alexander's father. I'm never going to fit in."

"And that's why Alexander loves you," Belle reminded me gently. "And why I love you and Edward loves you. You're our Clara. We don't care where you were born."

"Yeah?"

"Yes. Although you have to stop saying panties. Promise me." Belle held up her pinkie.

Rolling my eyes, I hooked my little finger around hers and we shook.

"I think you're going to be just fine."

Belle bounded up and threw open her closet door. She whirled around and studied me for a minute, her eyebrows knitting together. A few minutes later she'd produced a sequined top and high-waisted leggings. "Comfortable but sexy. You need to be able to dance your ass off."

"I do, huh?" I inspected the outfit for a moment. I'd spent the last few weeks polishing my wardrobe to look more...royal. Standing I slipped out of my dress coat and slid the top over my head. Tugging it down, I frowned when it barely stretched over my boobs. "This one is a no go."

"I didn't think your tits were that much bigger than mine." Belle disappeared back into her closet.

"I guess they are," I said dryly.

I pulled the shirt back off, and then unfastened the garter belt I wore. Rolling off my stockings I glanced at the sexy knickers Belle had given me. I shimmied into them, smiling when I realized the bands intersected to create several sexy crosses.

Or Xs, I thought. I considered waiting to wear them for him, but if I had to spend a night away from Alexander, I didn't mind the sexy reminder. Plus, they were hot. Just the kind of thing that a carefree bride might wear for her hen night. And tonight I was determined to be carefree.

The pants were thankfully a much better fit and I could get away with wearing the Louboutins I'd worn over. Belle reappeared and handed me a red blouse. I put it on and turned toward the mirror. The flowing shirt might not have been sexy, except that it was almost completely see-through.

"Perfect for one last fling," Belle said with approval.

My mouth fell open and I struggled to come up with a response. Apparently my best friend was spending too much time with her Aunt in my absence.

"I'm kidding," Belle said, emphasizing each word. "Tonight it's chicks before dicks, except for Edward," she tacked on.

I studied myself in the mirror, unable to decide if Alexander would love this shirt or hate it.

"Stop," Belle ordered.

"What?" I asked in confusion.

"Thinking about him," she said, holding up a hand so I wouldn't interrupt. "Don't try to tell me you aren't! You get all goofy. Tonight it's my time. If Alexander is going to steal you from me, I get one night."

"As long as I get one before Philip steals you." I smirked.

Belle shrugged, turning away from me, to dig through her cosmetics bag. "Now, sit down and let me finish your camouflage. Those reporters aren't going to recognize you."

"Is everything okay?" I asked as she lined my eyes.

"Fine." But her response was too terse to be believable.

"What's going on?"

Belle paused, mascara tube frozen in place, and shook her head. "Seeing you and Alexander together, I...Philip and I aren't like that."

"Like what?" I asked.

"For starters, Philip and I don't shag like rabbits all the time. Don't deny that you two do! I saw you coming out of that room at the engagement party. Alexander can't keep his hands off of you."

"And Philip doesn't..." I trailed away, uncertain if I should press for more information.

"Not like rabbits," she said ruefully.

"You've been together longer." But we both knew it was an excuse.

"Alexander should be studied for science," she told me. "It's inhuman."

I blushed, shaking my head in confusion. "How—?"

"Thin walls." She tipped her head toward the hallway that led to my old bedroom. Her face grew serious. "Just answer one question for me: is he the one?"

"Yes," I said without hesitation.

I wanted to ask her if Philip was the one, but something

about the look on her face shut me up. She remained quiet as she finished my makeup, but her silence spoke volumes.

WE'D BEEN OVERDRESSED for dinner at CoCo's, but Tori's presence had made up for that. She was a ball of energy, spilling office gossip and showing off ultrasound pictures. Now that the wild portion of the evening had commenced, I missed the cozy restaurant and easy conversation. Clubs had never really been my scene, but I had it on Belle's authority that dancing and drinking were required hen night activities.

I tugged at my practically sheer shirt, cursing myself for being talked into wearing something so revealing. But Belle was right—I didn't look a thing like the Clara Bishop currently gracing the cover of *Time* magazine. She'd outdone herself this time, straightening my slight waves into a curtain of sleek mahogany and lining my eyes until they were smokey and sultry. It was a pity Alexander wasn't invited. I could hardly imagine what he'd think of me.

Or do to me, for that matter.

"We should just wait in line," I suggested as we pulled up the back entrance of Brimstone. "Nobody will recognize me."

"But they'll recognize him." Lola jerked her thumb toward Edward, who shrugged.

"Sorry," he said, sounding anything but apologetic. He'd opted for a slim-fitted black suit and plaid bowtie. His black curls were smoothed back and without his usual horn-rimmed glasses, he looked more rockabilly than royalty. But that did nothing to cover his familiar face. Few people were blessed with the genes Edward shared with his brother. There was no doubting who he was.

"If they're going to recognize him, then why bother at all?"

"Stop worrying and have fun," my sister ordered me. "I've escaped from our mother's clutches for the evening."

On cue, her phone began to ring. Lola huffed as she slid it out of her clutch. She was perfectly polished as usual down to the gold clutch and hoops she'd paired with an elegant black jumpsuit. It was an outfit only someone like my sister could pull off.

"Guess who?" she asked flatly before she hit silent and dropped it bag in her bag.

Going in through the back *seemed* like a great idea, but if the paparazzi were camped out, they'd be all over the rear exit. To my surprise, Norris opened the door to the limousine. He helped me out of the back seat and I was even more shocked to discover the back alley was completely empty.

"Alexander has ensured that your entrance will be private," Norris explained as I looked around.

Of course he had. Alexander thought of everything. We slipped inside, and my heart sank when I spotted two more private security guards by the door. No doubt the place was crawling with undercover agents.

As Belle sauntered inside, it occurred to me that my group might be hard to miss regardless of security measures. It would be hard to ignore Belle's tousled blonde hair or her long legs that streamed past a sequined dress that swung just over her ass.

Belle looped her arm through mine and dragged me down the hall and into the pulsating heart of the club. A strange sense of Déjà vu came over me as we stumbled onto the dance floor. I'd been here with her before. In fact, the two nights I'd found myself at Brimstone were burned indelibly in my brain. Closing my eyes I could perfectly picture the club's flaming murals. I swore I felt the heat of them on my skin. My eyes opened, flashing to the catwalk overhead and beyond that the mirrored windows that overlooked the dance floor. The hair on the back of my neck stood up. Was he in there watching me?

Our circumstances had changed completely since the last time I'd found myself alone in that room with him. That night we'd been caught in a relationship tug-of-war. Neither of us had won then. Now might be a different story.

Well, if he was watching, I might as well put on a good show.

Catching Belle, I hooked an arm around her waist and rocked against her. The music took over and we twisted and writhed to the beat until sweat beaded across my forehead.

Belle nudged me and nodded toward the center of the floor where Aunt Jane had two much younger men grinding against her. I swallowed back a laugh and let the beat carry me away. I felt it in my blood, allowing it to overtake me. There was only one other thing that enabled me to lose myself like this. I pushed the thought of Alexander away.

"C'mon," Belle called, her voice getting lost in the music.

We sauntered off the floor, leaving Aunt Jane to her prey. Belle led me across the dance floor toward the private rooms above. I guess Alexander wasn't here this evening, even if his ghost was everywhere. As soon as we were behind the hidden door, she collapsed onto the couch. I tossed her a bottle of water.

"Hydrate," I ordered her.

Edward stood behind the bar, mixing drinks. Lola was perched on a barstool. I studied them for signs of awkwardness.

"I see we lost someone."

"Aunt Jane has met a new soul mate," Belle confirmed. "Or two."

Edward brought us over drinks and raised his. "To the end of Clara's single life—and the impending death of ours."

Belle stuck her tongue out at him, but I clinked my glass. Taking a sip, I gasped.

"Too strong?"

"Is the paint peeling?" I asked, abandoning the drink of the table. "I'm going to run to the loo."

Belle and Edward exchanged a look.

"I'll come with you. Give me a sec." Belle pushed herself up, but I shook my head.

"I'm a big girl, and we all know this place is crawling with security. Enjoy your paint thinner."

I darted out the door before either could stop me. The club's music pounded through the hallway as I searched for a bathroom. There had to be one up here for the VIPs. A prickling sensation on the back of my neck froze me in place. I wasn't alone.

Stop being silly.

"I really don't need an escort." I whipped around, planting my hands on my hips. I expected to see Belle or Edward behind me.

But it was him.

CHAPTER THIRTEEN

The music faded as our gazes locked across the dark corridor. The low spark inside me that had started on the dance floor ignited. Alexander had dressed down, no doubt to avoid unwanted attention. But seeing him in a loose grey t-shirt with jeans hanging suggestively on his trim hips had the opposite effect on me. I was riveted to him, unable to move and frantic to get to him. He prowled toward me, his face cast in shadows from the low lighting. His eyes were dark, glinting with the hunger I felt.

He didn't speak as we met. Instead he took my hand and led me toward the end of the hallway. We were alone and surrounded, cloaked by the privacy afforded to the club's most important patrons. He stopped and placed his hand against the wall, his expression unreadable. A moment later, I was being pulled into another private room.

Alexander had me against the wall. His hands caught my wrists and forced them over my head as he leaned into me.

"Do you remember the first time we were here, Poppet?" His stubble grazed my jaw, sending shivers cascading down my neck. "I wanted to pin you against the wall and make you beg for my cock."

I whimpered, recalling all too clearly that night. I had thought then that it was impossible to want him more. Now I knew better. My craving for him had grown every day since. My body fought to get closer to his, desperate for nothing to be between us.

Alexander kept my hands pinned above my head. He dipped lower, sealing his mouth over my breast through the thin fabric of my blouse and bra. My nipples stiffened as I felt the wet heat of his tongue. He drew back and hovered over the other breast.

"You wanted it," he recalled hoarsely. "You wanted to beg, didn't you?"

His hips rolled, teasing me with the promise of his cock.

"Yes." My eyes opened meeting his directly. "But not as much as I want you today."

"You said no that night and then you walked away." The grind of his hips grew more impatient. "I didn't know then why I went after you."

Neither did I. Alexander could have walked downstairs, snapped his finger, and had a dozen women appear. But he had chosen me. A gush of arousal warmed my cleft at the thought.

"You were a challenge," he admitted gruffly. "This gorgeous woman with the most fuckable body I'd ever seen, who was also smart enough to walk away from me? That was so sexy."

I bit my lip as my body remembered how it had felt. A switch had flipped that night, casting a light on a side of myself I never knew existed.

"Would you have come back to me?" he asked in a low voice.

"I'll always come back to you," I whispered.

Alexander groaned and shifted his weight, crushing me against the wall as his lips captured mine. I lost myself in the kiss. The past, present, and future merged seamlessly with one another. Everything had truly begun here. And even as he reminded me of the past, the only thing on my mind was the life I would spend with this man.

His lips ghosted across my ear. "I'm ready for you to beg now."

"Please," I breathed, writhing closer.

Alexander dropped one hand without releasing me. His eyes locked on mine, holding me captive with his gaze. Need surged within me and I arched toward him. Seizing my waist band, he shoved my tight pants down to my feet. His finger-tips traveled over my navel and stopped when he reached the first intersecting band of my panties. A curious grin curved across his face as his finger slipped under the elastic.

"What is this?" he asked.

"See for yourself," I suggested. I already knew the effect the lingerie would have on him.

His eyes dropped and a low growl rumbled through him as he drank in the black straps that crossed and intersected in a series of x's that left little to the imagination. Following the intersecting bands, he traced an x.

"X marks the spot," I said.

"Such sexy knickers for a night out with the girls."

I crooked an eyebrow, an odd sense of satisfaction rolling through me at his jealous tone. "You told me to always be ready," I purred. "I'm ready."

He released his hold on my other hand and twirled his finger. "Turn around, Poppet."

I pivoted slowly, loosely bound by the pants around my ankles. I wanted him to get the full effect, particularly the criss-cross that formed a perfect x over my tailbone and narrowed into a thong.

He stepped closer, his palms caressing over my hip to my tailbone. "This reminds me of ropes and scarves. It makes me think of how your wrists would look bound together."

His fingers descended farther and I gasped as much from the suggestion of being at his mercy as from his intimate touch.

"When I have you home, I'm going to tie your wrists together and spend all night making you come." His strong hands cupped my ass cheeks, spreading them as he knelt behind me. His tongue danced over my soaked panties. "As much as I like these..."

He yanked my underwear down to my ankles.

"Put your hands behind your back," he ordered.

I obeyed, already savoring his dominance. A hand closed over them, gripping them tightly. Alexander urged me forward until my knees bumped against the arm of the room's sofa. With a shove, he pushed me over it. He paused and my ass squirmed trying to make contact with him.

"Patience," he murmured, stroking down the crack of my ass with his finger. "Were you this wet for me that first night?"

"Yes," I moaned.

"Tell me what you want. What you need."

"I need to be fucked."

"And I'm here to give you what you need." The hand

caressing my bottom disappeared, replaced a few moments later by the warm, velvety tip of his cock. Alexander rubbed it down the length of my slit. My legs tried to widen in welcome, but the leggings around my ankles prevented it. I was restrained in all the right ways, dying for him to release me in the only one that mattered.

He pushed forward, stretching me over his wide crown, and paused to allow me time to adjust.

Yes, please.

His grip stayed locked on my arms as he slid in, sheathing himself entirely. I couldn't contain a cry as he filled me.

"Christ, you feel so good." He groaned, drawing back slowly. "I've been fantasizing about this since you showed up that night in that sweatshirt and jeans. All I could think about was shoving your pants around your ankles and fucking you senseless. And because I've been waiting so long, I have to warn you that I can't take it slow."

"Then don't," I whispered.

"I need to fuck you hard and I need to fuck you now." He slammed inside me, jerking back my arms so that I was no longer braced over the sofa's arm. His pace quickened until I was bouncing against him violently.

"I want to hear you, Poppet" he demanded.

My teeth released my lip, my mouth falling open to spill the screams I'd held inside me. His thrusts matched the pulse of music vibrating through the floor, driving into me with the same primal rhythm as we edged closer to the brink. Conscious thought gave way to impulse as he continued to pummel relentlessly. I erupted in a frenzy of cries and groans, my sex clenching tightly over him.

I was falling.

Falling.

Falling.

And I never wanted to stop.

But as I came crashing down, I felt the heat of Alexander's release. He dropped his hold on me and I collapsed, boneless against the sofa, and he whipped out of me, sending the last hot jet streaming across my tailbone.

"Couldn't help it, Poppet." He bent and kissed my cheek. "X marks the spot."

"That's becoming a bad habit," I mumbled.

"If you don't like it..."

I bit my lip, averting my eyes, but I was unable to keep a grin off my face.

"That's what I thought." He trailed a finger across my lip and sighed. "Wait here."

A few moments later a rough napkin wiped across my backside. Alexander cleaned me carefully before bending down to help me shimmy my pants on. When I was dressed again, I turned into his arms. He tipped my chin up with his thumb, looking serious. "Now, can we talk about this outfit?"

"You don't like it?" I pretended to pout.

"Oh, I like it, Poppet. I'm just not certain I like every man in this club seeing this much of you."

"Too bad, X. Tonight I am the bachelorette. Young and carefree."

"So long as the bachelorette is in my bed in the morning," he said dryly.

"I'll be in your bed every morning," I whispered. "Why do you think I'm celebrating?"

Immediately his mouth slanted over mine, capturing my mouth just as he'd captured my heart. It was a serious kiss—

the kind that often led to more—which is why it took every ounce of self-control I had to wiggle free of him.

"They're going to send out a search party."

Alexander stretched out his hand and I took it, marveling at how such a small gesture could make me feel so loved. He could dominate me, use me, push me to the edge, but he was always there on the other side. My constant. My completion.

We walked back down the hall, stopping just short of the secret entrance to the VIP room I'd left everyone else in. Alexander kissed my knuckles. "Come home to me tonight."

"Can't, X." I shook my head. "Belle plans to keep me out all night."

His mouth twitched into a mischievous smirk. "I could persuade you."

"One night apart," I told him, "and the rest of our lives together."

"You strike a wicked bargain, Miss Bishop." He inclined his head.

"Mr. X, you have no idea how wicked I can be." I danced away from him, blowing him a kiss as I darted inside.

"That was the world's longest trip to the loo," Belle said when I stepped through the door.

Despite the thump of the club's sound system, the atmosphere here was remarkably chill. Of course, they might have all fallen asleep waiting for the guest of honor to reappear. I wasn't about to ask.

"Take a gander at her." Edward shook his head and shot me a knowing look.

"Time to switch locations." Belle pulled out her phone and began texting.

"Wait. What?" I asked, confused.

"You don't think we had contingencies?" Belle snorted and grabbed hold of my arm. "This venue has been compromised."

"I have no clue what you're talking about." I shrugged even as my cheeks grew red.

Lola took my other arm and they marched me out of the room.

"What about Aunt Jane?" I asked, glancing quickly over my shoulder, but the corridor behind us was empty.

"She staked a claim downstairs. You're stuck with us." Despite her slight frame, she made that sound menacing.

"Seriously?" I said. "You don't think this is an over-reaction?"

"Alexander has breached the premises," Lola informed me.

"That's not all he breached from the looks of it," Edward quipped.

Lola squeezed my arm as they escorted me toward the back door. "This is your hen night. No dicks allowed."

Edward cleared his throat.

"Sorry, Edward," Lola called over her shoulder.

"It's okay. I'm not a dick."

"Touché."

My annoyance subsided as I listened to their easy banter. Apparently things weren't going to be awkward between them after all.

Norris stood at the exit. He opened the door as we approached him.

"I think I'm being abducted," I told him as they hurried me out to the waiting limo, but he only laughed good-naturedly. "Rotten security."

"Sorry, Clara, tonight you belong to us. Alexander will have to wait until morning," Edward said as he slid into the backseat next to me. "Don't worry. It's good for him."

I held up my hands. "Okay, I surrender."

Alexander could wait until morning. It would only make our reunion all the more satisfying.

CHAPTER FOURTEEN

P art of me was relieved to leave the club behind. I didn't want to tell the others that I was tired—last minute preparations had exhausted me. Not to mention the recent fight and evening-long make-up session I'd had with Alexander just after. Pushing a strand of hair behind my ear, I peered out the window.

"We aren't going back to the flat?" I asked when we turned the opposite direction on the street.

Belle's lips pursed in disapproval of my question. "We have a whole night ahead of us."

Her attention returned to her mobile, and I tried not to look too disappointed. Maybe along the way I could sneak a coffee or one of those energy drinks. But as hard as I tried to stifle it, a yawn escaped.

"Are you feeling okay?" Edward whispered, so only I could hear.

"The wedding is sucking the life out of me." I clapped a hand over my mouth when I realized what I'd said.

"Don't worry, you aren't scaring me off." He sat back and

draped an arm over my shoulder. "I thought you were used to late nights and very little sleep."

I punched him lightly in the chest. "It's just stress. And my mother."

"This time next week you'll be off on your honeymoon," he said, adding, "even though you still won't tell me where you're going."

My lips pressed together and I shook my head. Alexander had insisted that no one know where we were headed. It was one secret I was happy to keep. But Edward was right. In a week, I'd be married and sunning myself on a private beach in the Maldives.

"Fine, keep your secret." He narrowed his eyes. "Unless it's something terrible like you're secretly staying here. I cannot approve that plan."

"What if I was?" I shrugged. All that really mattered was having Alexander to myself for the better part of a month, away from all the drama and attention. "I want to start this marriage the right way—by focusing on us. It doesn't really matter where we do that."

Edward grimaced. "Yes, it does! Take your pasty ass to the beach and screw in the sun for once. You could both use the Vitamin D."

He had a point. I shot him a coy smile. "My lips are sealed."

"Remind me not to invite you to my wedding."

"Unfair," I cried. "You're invited to the wedding, but the honeymoon is by invitation only. I better get to come to your wedding. You're my only brother, so no eloping!"

"Father would have a fit anyway. Of course, I'll be lucky to get his—"

The car jolted to a stop, stopping him mid-thought. Belle rolled down the window and poked her head out. "Some type of traffic jam."

But her eyes didn't meet mine when she spoke.

"I want to see." I scrambled for the window, but Edward grabbed my waist and pulled me back down.

"What's really going on?" I demanded.

"Just some paparazzi." She shrugged like this was no big deal.

"Let's just head to your place."

Lola frowned. "I hate to break it to you, but they're all over. They're even camped in front of Mom and Dad's."

This was total madness.

"Where are we going anyway?" I asked finally, rubbing my temples as a headache began to form.

"The Westminster Royal," Belle admitted.

Sheesh, had they planned this trip down memory lane? If we wound up at another place where Alexander and I had made love I was going to start looking for cameras.

Tapping the privacy screen, I leaned forward and called to the driver. "There's a private parking garage under the hotel. I'm assuming you're in contact with Norris Echols?"

The driver nodded, his eyes glued to mine in the rearview mirror.

"He'll get you in."

I settled back, only to realize all three of them staring at me.

"What?" I tried to sound nonchalant, but my cheeks flushed.

"I remember when you were my sweet, innocent Clara."

Belle fluttered her lashes and sighed. "Now you've been replaced by a crazed sexpot."

"I resent that remark." But I couldn't quite keep from grinning.

"You resemble that remark," Edward corrected me.

A few minutes later the limousine had managed to navigate through the traffic and past the paparazzi. I flinched as their cameras flashed, taking snaps of the car.

"They can't see us." Edward patted my hand.

I knew that, but I still wasn't used to the attention. I never would be. It was the price to pay for falling in love with a man like Alexander, and even though I'd choose him time and again, it didn't mean I liked the public attention. Or the constant barrage of questions and speculations about my private life, my health, and my past.

I looked over to Edward, who'd grown silent. I was a lot like his fiancé. David and I were both caught between our love for these men and the heavy responsibilities that accompanied a life with them.

Impulsively I lunged and hugged him.

"What did I do to deserve that?" he asked with a laugh.

"Nothing. I just wanted to hug you."

The limousine made it to the underground garage without incident and we piled out of the back. Belle and Lola began walking toward the elevator on the far wall.

"Hey," I called, "that one goes straight to the Presidential Suite."

"You are a wealth of information on private hotel privileges," Lola said as we reached the other elevator. "I have to admit I'm a little impressed."

"Don't tell our mother."

"Deal."

The lift doors slid open, depositing us in the lobby.

"No paparazzi," Belle said with relief.

Of course not. She didn't know how much the Westminster Royal prized their guests' privacy. It was the reason Alexander had once utilized it to meet women. I supposed that fact should have made me queasy, but since our first encounter had occurred in the very Presidential Suite the underground elevator traveled to, it felt a bit hypocritical.

"Why here?" I asked her.

"Why do you think?" she asked blithely.

I was beginning to wonder if Alexander had actually been the one to plan this.

"We're already checked in," Belle said. "The Presidential Suite is taken, but the Honeymoon Suite was open. Alexander sent over some clothes for you."

I practically melted at the thought of changing, but before I could voice my relief, she continued. "But for now, we're hitting the pub."

Forcing a smile, I followed them across the lobby to the attached late night spot.

"Christ, now you've put in a booty call." Edward said as we crossed into the posh bar.

Belle stopped dead in her tracks when she spotted what Edward was talking about. Philip lounged at the bar, his profile unmistakable even in the atmospheric lighting. He swirled a drink in his hand, glancing up occasionally as if he was waiting for someone.

"Hey, I did not call..." The denial died on her lips as a beautiful blonde strolled up and wrapped her arms around Philip's neck. She was dressed in a slinky red dress that dipped low enough in the front and the back to display all her *assets*.

It was the inevitable moment before a car crash. I saw what was about to happen. I knew that I should pull Belle away. But I was frozen to the spot, incapable of doing anything but watch as the truth smashed into us headfirst.

Philip turned, but he didn't see us. Perhaps because his eyes were transfixed on the other woman. Any hope I'd had that we'd seen a friendly act out of context shattered. The blonde tilted her head, leaning down to meet Philip's waiting lips, and I jolted out of my stupor with a shocked cry.

"That bitch!" Belle exploded next to me.

I didn't try to stop her when she stomped toward them, a murderous rage glinting in her eyes.

Pepper Lockwood had it coming.

CHAPTER FIFTEEN

W ords couldn't convey the expression on Philip's face when Belle reached the bar. Pepper, on the other hand, seemed less surprised—and certainly less concerned. My blood pressure kicked up a notch when the bitch pivoted to Philip's side, her arm still draped over him. The possessive gesture was just like Pepper Spray. That girl had a serious problem with trying to claim things that didn't belong to her.

Belle glared at them, her hands clenching and unclenching at her side. "Tell me this is your really poorly planned idea of a surprise threesome before I kill you *with my bare hands.*"

"Annabelle—"

Belle cut him off with a flick of her wrist. "Don't *Annabelle* me. Explain this."

"I thought she was slow, but honestly, Phil, what do you see in her?" Pepper tapped her nails on his shoulder, a malicious smile creeping over her plump lips.

"How long?" Belle demanded, ignoring Pepper.

"It's not what—"

"Do not say 'it's not what it looks like!' For one thing, I have eyes and for another, it's cliché," she added. Her jaw tensed as her eyes flashed back and forth between them. "How long?"

"Phil and I have known each other for years. We were childhood playmates and then we were...playmates." Pepper ran her tongue over her teeth like she'd just devoured something delicious. She turned her attention to me and blinked. "In fact, we reconnected at *your housewarming* party."

Up until this point I'd stayed back, torn between anger and shock, but her words thawed my numbness, freeing me from my stupor. Apparently she hadn't taken my warning seriously. But if she thought that she could get to me through my friends she had another think coming. I'd suffered Pepper for long enough. Without thinking I lunged forward, my hand balling into a fist.

Unfortunately, Edward was faster. He hooked an arm around me and hauled me a few steps back.

"This is not your fight," he said firmly.

"Like hell it isn't," I hissed. There was no doubt in my mind that Pepper had gone after Philip because of Belle's connection to me.

"No," Belle said, her voice eerily placid. "It's mine."

And then her fist smashed into Pepper's nose.

"*And* that's what they mean by the calm before the storm," Edward muttered. He shook his head and jumped between the two women, capturing Belle around the waist and pulling her back. Philip, in typical asshole fashion, watched with his mouth hanging open.

There was something poignant about the way Pepper's

nose sprayed blood all over Philip's suit. Also it was just plain awesome.

"Fucking bitch!" Pepper screamed as she held her nose.

"It takes one to know one," Belle shot back, fighting Edward's hold on her waist.

"We fucked in his bed! In his car!" Pepper's vitriol spewed as freely as the blood spewed from her nose. "We even fucked in your flat on the kitchen counter!"

Edward pushed Belle toward me, but she broke free and got back in Philip's face. She twisted her engagement ring off and held it in front of her nose. "I'm keeping this for damages. I'm glad you two found each other. It's a real match made in hell."

Philip stood so fast that his stool fell over behind him and snatched for the ring. I glanced around realizing that a crowd was gathering. Hooking my arm through Belle's I tugged her toward the door. When she resisted, Lola took her other side. With us surrounding her, Belle straightened up coolly and walked away. We were almost out the door when the first security arrived. The trouble was that I didn't know whose security team it was.

Edward pointed toward the lift. "Get her to the suite and out of sight. I'll deal with this."

"How?" I asked. I'd always suspected that Philip was an asshole, and I wouldn't put it past him to press charges now. I knew Pepper would try.

"Norris," he said quickly, holding his hands up, "and you know, I'm the *Prince of England.*"

"Shit, you can't get involved with this."

He pressed the up button and smirked. "It will only help

my rep. Alexander has been the bad boy for too long. Maybe it's my turn, especially with him settling down."

I was sure David would have something to say about it, but I followed Belle into the lift as soon as the car arrived.

Belle pressed the button for our floor and stepped back like nothing had happened. Lola peeked over her shoulder and shot me a confused look. Just when I was beginning to question how she could be so calm, I noticed Belle's chin quiver. My arms were around her before the first tear fell.

"That bloody knobhead! Pillock! Wanker!" A steady stream of insults followed as I rubbed her back and continued until we arrived at our suite.

I swallowed a sigh when I saw the placard on the door. I'd forgotten that we were in the Honeymoon Suite. I was just about to suggest heading home when Belle's hand lashed out and ripped the sign down.

That worked, too.

"That sodding arse! How could I be so bloody stupid?" she sobbed.

I hugged her close to me. "Hey, your British is showing."

This earned me a small smile.

"And," I continued, "you have a serious right hook. Let me see that."

She grimaced as I gingerly took her hand. Her knuckles were raw.

"I hope this means you broke her teeth," I said, inspecting the damage.

"I broke her nose." That garnered a real smile from both of us.

"I'll go grab some ice from the front desk," Lola said.

I shot her a grateful look. As soon as she was out the door, what was left of Belle's composure dissolved, and she melted into me. A lump formed in my throat and sat there as she cried into my shoulder. I tried to blink back my own tears but there was no way. Not when my best friend was hurting this much. I cried for the future she'd lost, and I cried because of the guilt I felt. But mostly I cried because I didn't want her to cry alone.

"Clara," Belle whispered. "I need to tell you something."

I drew back and nodded. "You can tell me anything."

"No, I can't." She choked a little as she shook her head. "You'll think I'm terrible."

"You just broke Pepper Lockwood's nose," I told her. "Your brilliance has been established. Nothing will make me think you are anything less than a badass."

"I cheated on Philip a few months ago," she confessed breathlessly. "I had no right to be so angry with him."

I swallowed hard on her admission. "That might have been wrong, hon, but it doesn't change that he's been cheating on you."

"That's not the terrible part." She bit her lip, her eyes welling up.

Ice formed in my veins, but I forced myself to speak. "You can tell me."

"I slept with Jonathan Thompson."

"Oh!" I gasped in surprise, trying to ignore the sharp stab of hatred her revelation provoked. Jonathan had been a first class asshole to Belle at university, but it was what he'd done to Alexander that made me loathe him. Not only had he been responsible for the crash that killed Alexander's sister, he'd also let him take the fall for it when Pepper Lockwood leveled accusations against him. That put him neck-and neck with Pepper Spray for the top of my shit list.

"I couldn't tell you after you found out what he'd done to Alexander's sister," she babbled.

"When?"

"Last summer," she admitted. "I ran into him and one thing led to another. You were..."

I was home heartbroken over Alexander. A pang stabbed my center as I recalled that time.

"But also I was embarrassed that I shagged him after the way he treated me at university."

I sighed and gathered her into my arms. "We all do stupid things."

"But maybe Philip sensed it and—"

"No," I stopped her theory in its tracks. "Philip is a wanker, remember? I won't say what you did was okay, but it didn't give Philip a free pass." I clamped my mouth shut before I could add that from the sounds of things, Philip and Pepper were a lot more than a one night stand.

"How am I going to do this?" she asked me, her chest heaving with the effort of holding back tears. "We're supposed to be getting married in six months. Everything is planned. What am I supposed to do?"

I recalled the night that I'd left Alexander. Even now, the pain at that memory nearly knocked me off my feet, but I locked my arms around her. "Tonight, you cry."

We'd figure out the rest in the morning when the sun shattered the darkness.

CHAPTER SIXTEEN

K atherine Paige Couture was on lockdown. The posh bridal shop had practically become my second home over the last few months. But today the curtains blocked curious eyes from seeing inside the shop. Kate met me at the back door, her eyes bright as she guided me inside. Most people had been surprised when I'd chosen her to design my dress. What they didn't know was that Edward had introduced us. Hardly older than me, Kate could have passed for a model instead of a lead designer with her curly brown hair and lithe figure. But her passion lay in the design business, which had earned her an exclusive, albeit small, clientele.

"We've spent all week kicking paparazzi out of here," she explained when I shot her a questioning look.

"I'm so sorry," I apologized. It seemed my marriage was actually becoming the spectacle of the century for all involved.

"Don't be! How often do I get to design a wedding dress for the next Queen of England?" she gushed, pushing a loose curl behind her ear.

The next Queen of England. A dizzying rush clouded my head and I caught her arm to steady myself. "I can't get used to that. One of these days I'm going to get so nervous that I *will* faint."

"As long as you don't ruin your dress." She winked mischievously, reminding me exactly why I felt so at ease with her. "If you're light-headed, I suppose that champagne is a bad idea."

I couldn't argue with that. "Maybe later."

The dressing room was nearly as beautiful as Kate's gowns, managing to be lavish and welcoming at the same time. Warm ivory walls and soft lighting made the space glow. The gold leaf tables and mirror frames added a touch of sophistication.

But the calm atmosphere faded with the arrival of my bridal party. My mother and Lola fluttered into the room with Belle at their heels.

"Two days!" My mother caught me in a hug, pecking me on both cheeks.

I did my best not to look like I was about to throw up.

"Mother has been counting down the minutes all week." Lola shot a save-me-now look over my mother's shoulder.

"It is not every day that a mother marries off her daughter." Mom plucked a champagne flute from a nearby tray and took a dainty sip.

"We're set for the final rehearsal in the morning," I told her, bypassing small talk in favor of direct action. I needed to focus if I was going to keep my sanity. I would give myself a list and not let my mind wander to the cameras and crowds already filling the streets that led from Westminster Abbey to Buckingham Palace. It was the only way to prevent getting caught in a cycle of disturbingly vivid fantasies about all the ways I was going to make an ass out of myself.

"Here are the shoes." Kate bustled into the room with a pair of simple ivory silk pumps.

My mother grimaced, not bothering to hide her disapproval of my choice. "Are those heels tall enough?"

"I'd rather hoped not to fall on my face," I told her.

"Your father is not going to let you fall." She tilted her head and called into the adjoining lounge. "Are you, Harold?"

"Dad's here?" I asked, unable to hide my surprise.

"Of course, he wants to see his little girl in her wedding gown." My mother's voice caught, but she looked away before I could see if she was crying. Tears weren't in Madeline Bishop's emotional repertoire. Sightings of them were rare enough to warrant study.

I couldn't be certain if the show of emotions was maternal sentimentality or if she was strongly clinging to the last shreds of her marriage.

A hush fell over the group as two of the shop's employees cautiously carried my gown into the room, holding it as I undressed and Kate helped me into a corset. I'd seen the dress at various stages, standing through numerous fittings until my feet ached and my skin throbbed from renegade dress pins. But I wasn't prepared for the emotions that swept through me when I saw the final dress.

Decorum dictated a certain level of modesty for a church wedding, but somehow it was still the sexiest thing I'd ever owned. Even if it took four of them to lift it over my head.

"I hope it's not this hard for Alexander to get it off," Belle whispered.

"I have faith in his abilities," I said in a low voice, reminding myself now wasn't the time to fantasize about those skills.

My arms glided through the delicate lace sleeves, allowing the skirt and train to float down. Turning as they arranged my skirt, I drew in a deep, steadying breath. French lace rested gracefully off my shoulders, covering my décolletage where a silk bodice narrowed to my waistline and then widened into a full skirt trimmed along the hem with the same lace.

Thousands of tiny Swarovski crystals glittered delicately in the light. I pressed a hand to my stomach, absorbing the fact I was wearing my wedding gown as Kate began to fasten the zippers and buttons that ran from the back of my neck to my tailbone.

"Oh dear," Kate muttered, heaving a sigh.

I glanced over my shoulder. "Oh dear *what?*"

She yanked the back of my dress tighter, struggling to get the zipper up.

"Breathe in," she instructed, widening her stance for leverage.

I sucked in, contracting my belly against my ribs. Relief poured through me when I heard the zipper slide up, but it was short-lived as soon as I exhaled.

"Is it supposed to be this tight?" I asked, turning to get a side view.

The seamstress frowned, pins jutting from her teeth. She plucked them out and checked her notes. "It's been tailored to your most recent measurements." She sighed and circled me. "We'll have to let it out a little."

"Is that a problem?" my mother said, biting her nails.

Never in all my life had I seen Madeline Bishop risk her manicure. If she had the choice between saving a baby seal and chipping a nail, it was a no-brainer for her.

"It shouldn't be." Kate patted my arm. "There's room in the bodice to let it out, but it's not that bad. We can always adjust your corset."

I swallowed a groan. Said corset was already digging into my ribs, its boning stabbing me every few seconds. There was no way it was getting tightened.

As soon as Kate excused herself, my mother rounded on me. "This gown cost twenty thousand pounds. Every major media outlet has been speculating on it for months."

"Mom!" Lola interjected.

She ignored her, pacing in front of the three-way mirror. "They are predicting millions of television viewers. I'm merely surprised that this is the time Clara chooses to let her weight go."

As soon as she said it, she clamped a hand over her mouth, a look of horror descending over her elegant features. "Clara, I'm—"

I waved off her apology, locking my jaw to stop my trembling chin.

"Let's go see about some tea," Lola suggested, taking our mother by the shoulders and marching her into the lounge off the dressing room.

Belle exhaled loudly when they were out of sight, relaxing against the mirror. "Sometimes I think she actually studies thoughtlessness."

"It comes naturally," I assured her. Gesturing to my gown, I bit my lip. "Does it look terrible?"

"Clara, you look beautiful." Belle straightened to face the

mirror. Her grey eyes sparkled in its reflection. "Alexander isn't going to know what hit him."

I reached back and fluffed my train, allowing all twelve feet to cascade silkily from the raised platform I stood on. "He generally prefers me less clothed."

"Clara's new clothes. *Now that would surprise all the major media outlets,*" Belle said, tipping her nose in an excellent impression of my mother.

I fiddled with my hair, pulling it up and letting it down again. "Honestly, I wish it was all over with. I want to be married to Alexander. I could happily skip the wedding," I admitted.

"Every girl dreams about her wedding."

"I guess," I said absently. "Maybe that would be true if mine weren't a spectacle. If I had my way, we'd have gotten married with a couple of close friends standing by."

Out of the corner of my eye, I spotted Belle's smile tighten.

"Will you please tell me when I'm being a total bitch?" I groaned. "This is probably the last place you feel like being."

"It's okay. I keep forgetting, too." Belle sank to the ground and crossed her legs.

It took some effort but I managed to maneuver around my train and join her. "I should warn you now. I'm not going to be able to get back up without your help, so I hope you're still my best friend."

"No," Belle said sharply.

"Umm, okay. I'm not sure what to say."

"Philip doesn't get to ruin this," she said, completely oblivious to the near heart attack she'd just given me. "This is your wedding, and I am happy for you. I swear I am. But I'm..."

"Hurting," I finished for her. "I want to castrate him for what he did to you. But honestly, I can't imagine getting through this without you, especially if it means dealing with my mother."

"Lola seems to have her pretty well in hand," Belle noted, "which suits me because I want to focus on you."

"Are you sure?" I blinked against the tears swimming across my vision.

"Don't cry," she pleaded, her words hitching slightly. "If you cry, then I'll cry—and oh, sod it! It's too late."

"Alexander knows people who can kill him for you." The joke was out of my mouth before I remembered that it was actually true.

Belle's lip curled, but she shook her head. "I think getting stuck with Pepper is punishment enough. She'll take all of his money and then he'll just be some wanker with a small prick."

"Small?" I repeated.

She wagged her pinky finger, adding, "Aunt Jane is already discussing who I should take as my rebound lover."

"Might I suggest someone with a substantial prick," I whispered.

She laughed at this, wiping away tears with a sigh. "Clara Bishop, you are a fallen woman. To think, a year ago I was begging you to shag someone with wealth and power. Now you're total vixen."

"I took your suggestion very seriously," I assured her.

"I love you," Belle said, her expression growing serious.

"I love you, too." I wrapped my arms around her shoulders, only to hear the sickening rip of lace.

"They can fix it," she murmured, not letting me go. When she finally did, she smiled impishly. "Come on, let's go toy with your mum's blood pressure."

I held out my hands, and she bounded to her feet gracefully. Struggling up from the mass of silk and tulle, I collapsed into her with a giggle.

"Hey, you're getting married," Belle said.

"I'm getting married," I repeated, willing her words to sink in. In a few days I would no longer be Clara Bishop. I would be entirely his.

My father's head poked into the dressing room. "Can I have a moment?"

"Of course." She gave my hand a quick squeeze.

My father grinned sheepishly as she passed, running a hand over his thinning hair.

"You look stunning," he said softly.

A girlish contentment settled over me. No matter what mistakes he'd made, he was still my father, and I wanted his approval. "Thank you, Daddy."

"No. Thank *you*," he said. "I know these last few months have been hard on the family, and I know you've been less than thrilled with your mother and me."

"With Mom?" I asked.

"You've been hard on her." Dad wrung his hands together. "But your mother was doing the best she could. I know that's difficult to understand. I'm not an easy man to live with."

"Mom's not exactly low maintenance," I admitted, unsure whose side I was taking.

"That's the thing about marriage, Clare-bear. Sometimes you mess it up. What matters is how you handle," he added.

"I only want to know you two are going to be okay." I couldn't help but want my parents together. I was their daughter, after all. I couldn't imagine any other scenario for either of them.

"This is going to shock you, but your mother is a very tolerant woman," he told me.

"What about the other woman?"

"I ended that months ago. Your mother and I have been speaking to a counselor." He held open his arms. "I couldn't bear to cast a shadow over your day."

"You won't."

We stood for a moment and regarded each other.

Dad cleared his throat, but his voice was thick with emotion as he spoke. "I hope Alexander knows how fortunate he is. I made certain that he knew I didn't care who his father was. If he hurts my little girl—"

"Dad!" I laughed with shock.

"Let's just say he knows what will happen." He winked at me, drawing me close to him. My head dropped to his shoulder, and for the first time in a very long time, things were right between us.

CHAPTER SEVENTEEN

B elle let out a low whistle as I escorted her to one of the
fifty or so guest rooms my new home boasted. "Our flat
would have inferiority issues if it saw what you left it for."

I snorted. Belle had been here before for our engagement
gala, but then it had been crammed full of guests. Seeing it
after hours, when the staff had largely left for their private
apartments and the place was empty was a whole other experience. I pivoted around, walking backward and gesturing to
the space around us. "This is the aptly named Horse Corridor, because, as you can see, someone liked horses."

Like most of the house, the corridor skirted a thin line
between the garish and the opulent. The walls were papered
in crimson damask that matched the curtains and antique
divans, but the showstopper was the equine portraiture that
decorated the space.

"I imagine I'll have to take up riding," I said thoughtfully.

Belle giggled, her eyes darting across the extravagant
space. "I thought you already had."

If only she knew. Thinking back to the ill-fated country

weekend I'd spent with Alexander last summer, I remembered just how pleasurable riding could be.

"Your cheeks match the drapery," Belle continued to tease. "Thank God Alexander is making you an honest woman tomorrow."

"Follow me," I said, flourishing my arm toward a long staircase at the end of the corridor. I led her up the stairs, pointing out which rooms would comprise my private quarters as we made our way to the guest room I'd set aside for my best friend's use.

"I'll be across the hall," I said as I showed her inside her room.

"What about your private quarters, Your Highness?" Belle dipped into a curtsy.

"Promise to never do that again," I groaned and flopped onto her bed, not quite ready to be alone for the night. Butterflies had begun to circle in my stomach, each second that passed ratcheting up the anxious excitement I'd felt since I had woken up this morning. "I'm sleeping across the hall, because I told Alexander he couldn't see me until morning."

"Will he survive that long without shagging you?" She raised both her eyebrows and tapped her fingertips together. "Inquiring minds want to know."

"It's tradition."

"One of many," Belle said as she inspected her surroundings. She drew a manicured fingertip over the top of nightstand. "They must clean all the time. So how do you really feel about your humble abode?"

"It's...something," I managed.

"That's highly complimentary," she said dryly, dropping onto the bed beside me.

"It's not mine. Not yet. It might be eventually." I already missed the house we'd left behind in Notting Hill. Not only because we'd made it our own, but because it had been our first home. "I feel out of place here. In every room some stuffy portrait glares at me and I get lost at least twice a day."

"You'll get used to it," she said, dropping her voice to add, "especially once you start breaking in all the rooms."

I glanced out her bedroom door to the expansive hall. "That will take forever."

"Not with the way you two go at it. There's even a bet going around about when you two will get caught by the staff. " She pulled her mobile out of her bag and turned on the screen. "I gave it a week, but Edward gave it five days."

I snatched the mobile from her hands only to discover a blank screen.

"You're shameless, Annabelle Stuart," I said, handing it back to her.

"I think that's the nicest thing anyone has said to me." She lay down on the bed, and I rolled over onto my back, resting my head against hers.

"Do you think Philip will come?" she asked quietly.

"His invitation has been rescinded. I also asked Norris to place a shoot on sight order for Pepper."

Belle's lips twisted into a rueful smile. "If only."

"If only," I agreed.

"Hey," Belle said, "you should get some sleep. I hear you have something to do in the morning."

I rocked to my feet with a sigh and blew her a kiss.

"Very regal," she assured me.

I tossed a pillow at her head.

"Sweet dreams to you, too!" she called as I padded across the hall.

The bedroom was a massive reminder that I'd spend my last night as a single woman alone. The few objects that belonged to me were scattered on an antique dresser, but the centerpiece of the unfamiliar space hung from the wardrobe.

My wedding gown stared mockingly at me from within its protective bag. Tomorrow I would put that dress on, I'd be escorted to Westminster Abbey, walk down an aisle, and be married. It didn't seem possible that a year ago I'd been fever-ishly studying and taking final exams.

"How did this happen?" I asked the empty room.

Damn me and my tradition. My strange surroundings only reinforced his absence while reminding me just how far I'd landed from my own league. Maybe it was my nerves kicking into overdrive, but I needed Alexander and the reas-surance his touch provided.

A knock called me from my memories, as if someone had arrived to answer that very question, and I hurried to the door, keeping my hand over the lock.

"Yes?"

"I was informed there's a woman inside who's about to make a terrible mistake, and I came to see if I could talk her out of it." Alexander's muffled voice answered from the other side.

"You can't see me until morning," I reminded him. I had been the one who had insisted on taking separate quarters for the night, wanting to ensure he didn't see me before the cere-mony. That had seemed like a brilliant idea until I'd wound up alone in a strange room talking to my wedding dress.

"My watch says it's only ten o'clock, Poppet. Open the

door."

Two hours until the day of our wedding. That should be just enough time. It also would prevent me from staying up all night staring at the ceiling.

"Hold on." Scrambling over to the wardrobe, I tucked the bag inside and closed it.

When I opened the door, Alexander filled the doorframe. His arms hung overhead, clutching the wood. The biting scent of bourbon hit my nostrils and I stared at him. "Have you been drinking?"

"I had a drink with Edward. Unofficial stag night." He stalked forward. "Nothing wild, Poppet."

I relaxed a little knowing Edward had the good sense to cut his brother off the night before his wedding.

"My king bed is missing its queen." He moved closer and his scent reminded me of the day we'd met, spicy and sharp. I'd wanted to kiss him then—to know what he tasted like. But one taste wasn't enough. It never would be.

"I have something for you," I said coyly.

"Poppet, I thought you'd never offer."

"Keep it in your pants, X." I darted to the dresser before he could grab me and picked up a small red box. "I found this when we were moving. I'd bought it months ago and never gave it to you."

"Can I open it?" he asked, holding out his hand.

"It's silly," I warned as I handed it over to him. "I thought I'd give it to you tomorrow, but then I realized I'll hardly get you alone."

"Oh, you'll get me alone." He smirked as he lifted the box lid. He drew out the small wax stamp and studied it, a grin tugging at his lips when he saw what it said.

X

"For when you write me letters," I whispered. "There's sealing wax as well. I know you have your own, but—"

"It's perfect," he stopped me as he dropped it back in the box and took out the wax. "Do you like my letters?"

I nodded, my eyes closing temporarily as his wicked words drifted to mind, accompanied by flames of all the times he turned them into reality.

"Yes," I breathed as he circled around me, tapping the thick bar of sealing wax against his palm. "Write me one now."

He pressed against my back, his lips dropping to the curve of my neck. "Poppet."

"Hmmm," I murmured dreamily.

"I've been picturing you all night with white silk shoved up to your waist." One hand snaked around my waist, capturing my breast. Alexander's fingers kneaded through the fabric of my dress until my nipple stiffened sharply. My breasts grew heavier as he massaged them until they were swollen and hot. "Tomorrow I'm going to take your luscious tits into my mouth, claim them right through your wedding gown, and suck them until you come."

My hips moved against his and he continued to compose his sinful promises. "I'm going to take you to church and then I'm going to find the first dark corridor and worship you."

I moaned, needing his devotion now, longing for his hands to continue to tease and torment.

"Thinking of claiming you as my bride is making me so fucking hard. All I can think about is watching my wife sink onto my cock." He abandoned my breasts and pressed a hand to the mound between my thighs. "Do you want to be claimed?"

"Yes," I murmured, my hips writhing against his hand.

He nipped my earlobe. "I'm writing a letter, Poppet, but if you insist."

Drawing my zipper down my back, he peeled my dress off my shoulders as he unhooked my bra until my swollen breasts were free. Then he slowly pushed it over my hips until it puddled at my feet, leaving me in my garter belt and stockings. His fingers traced the straps before he plucked them free one by one and jerked down my panties.

"Crawl up on the bed and inspire me," he ordered, stroking his cock through his trousers.

I climbed onto the bed slowly and spread my knees, giving him his first glimpse of the surprise I'd planned for our wedding night. Belle had escorted me to the salon the day before and I'd braved the wax room. I'd never gone completely bare before but the low hiss of his exhale told me he approved.

"That is very inspiring." He drew his hand down my slick sex, murmuring his approval. A moment later I tensed as I heard the metallic click of his belt unbuckling. Silence fell between us. "There's nothing to be afraid of. I'll never strike you like that again."

"I know," I said in a small voice.

"Turn over onto your back," he instructed.

Rolling over, his gaze smoldered into me as he carefully removed the belt and laid it on the bed. "This will never hurt you again."

"I know," I repeated, wishing I could control the reaction I had to it.

"I'm going to show you that," he said, picking it up and moving to the side of the bed. "Put your hands over your head."

Taking a deep breath, I lifted my arms and crossed them.

"What's your safe word?"

"Brimstone," I whispered.

"If it's too much or you want me to stop, use it." He slid the leather strap under my wrists and wrapped it around them, gently binding my hands. My breathing sped up with each coil until finally he pulled the belt tightly through its buckle. "I love when you obey me, Poppet. When you show me you trust me with your pleasure."

Alexander returned to the foot of the bed, running a hand through his black hair as his eyes raked over me. Leaning down, he urged me to bend my knees, opening myself to him.

"Spread your legs. Show me how wet your cunt is for me."

I widened my thighs until my hips ached. The pulse in my clit throbbed as the sensitive nub met with air.

"Pain and pleasure," he murmured as he stripped off his clothes. I was captive to his gaze, held in place by more than the belt he'd used to restrain me. Tiny emissaries of pleasure rippled along my skin as he stood over me, stroking the wide shaft of his cock. "If I was writing a letter to you, I'd sign my name." His finger wrote an X across my inner thigh before it descended to my drenched folds and thrust inside me.

"Then I would slide it into the envelope," he continued as he pumped his finger leisurely. "Do you know what I would do next?"

My head twisted against my bindings, and I bit the

tender flesh of my upper arm, trying to contain the orgasm clawing its way free.

"You can't come yet. I haven't finished with my letter."

His finger withdrew, leaving my hole pulsating against the sudden emptiness.

"Look at me," Alexander said a moment later, but I shook my head. "Look at me now or I'll go back to my room until I'm sure you've learned your lessons."

I forced my eyes to open and meet his.

"Very good." His fingers flicked and a moment later a match blazed to life. The flame traveled along its thin path until it died at his fingertips. "It's very important to me that my letter remains private. It belongs to me just like your beautiful cunt. Tell me who it belongs to, Clara."

"You," I panted, my hands wiggling against the leather strap. I needed to get free—needed to pull him into me.

"You'll want to hold still for this," he warned as he lit another match and held the flame to the wick of the sealing wax. "Otherwise this could get messy."

My teeth sank into my lip, my body going rigid with the expectation of pain as I watched the fire claim the base of the wax. Alexander held it over my breasts patiently. A thick bead of paraffin formed at the tip, drooping lower as it bloated until it seared across my stiff nipples. Its heat faded quickly, but it fed the slow burn growing inside me. Another scorching drop spilled across my left breast, and I cried out as the tension at my core mounted.

"You look so fucking gorgeous right now. I love watching you squirm until it hits and then you melt along with it." He dripped a path down the valley of my breasts to my navel. "Lift your ass in the air."

I arched up, balancing precariously as my heels sank into the mattress.

"That's right," he hissed. "I love when you spread your legs in those fuck-me high heels. But you have to stay very, very still for me. Can you do that, Poppet?"

I nodded, a whimper escaping my lips as I tried to keep myself from swaying. Wax splattered down my sex, the swelling of my folds preventing its heat from hitting my engorged clit. I bucked against the hot liquid, feeling it harden as another drop streamed across my tender flesh.

"Signed, sealed and delivered," he murmured, puffing out the wick. Alexander abandoned the wax on the bedside table and knelt between my spread thighs. A hand slid under my ass, supporting my shaky legs and his cock nestled against my aching seam. My back arched up, seeking the contact I so desperately craved. He'd drawn and quartered me, stretched me beyond the limits of my restraint and I couldn't wait any longer. His free hand hooked around my thigh, bringing my left leg around his waist. "Wrap them around me. I want to feel those heels digging into my tailbone as I fuck you."

My legs circled his hips and he sank into me, with a low groan.

"You've been such a good girl, so patient while I played with you. Now I'm going to make you feel so good." He glided inside me, burying himself deeper with each precise stroke. His hand moved to my lower belly, and he pushed the rough pad of his thumb against my clit as his cock pummeled me. Lights exploded across my vision and I cried out, my thighs clamping against his waist. I dug my heels in for leverage as I rocked hard against his groin.

"Fuck yes," he hissed as he released into me, impaling me

while I unraveled on him. "I love you, Clara. I love you so
fucking much."

My legs fell open as I collapsed against the bed. A
moment later, he pulled my wrists free of the belt, massaging
them tenderly. My arms stayed over my head, my face
pressed against them as I quaked with the remnants of my
climax. His weight shifted off the bed and I heard water turn
on in the ensuite bathroom. I sensed his return, but I couldn't
move. I couldn't look at this man who had pushed me to the
breaking point and held on as I fell over it.

Alexander scooped me into his arms and carried me into
the shower. The hot water washed over me, melting the
remaining tension from my limbs.

"Can you stand?" he whispered, nuzzling my ear.

"I think so." I wasn't entirely positive I was right about
that, but as he lowered me to my feet, he kept his hands on
my hips until I'd regained control of my legs. Carefully he
pulled away the wax and then washed away the oil. I leaned
into him, luxuriating in the sense of completion I felt when
he cared for me. This is what our marriage would be—push
and pull, give and take.

A half an hour later, I kissed him goodnight at the door,
already longing to be in his arms again. He tugged the sash of
my robe tightly around my waist.

"See you in the morning," he said meaningfully.

"I'll be the one in white," I teased.

Closing the door behind him, I pressed a hand to my
chest as my heart raced. In the morning, we'd be joined in the
most intimate way possible. We had a lifetime of nights like
this ahead of us, and I was ready for each and every one of
them.

CHAPTER EIGHTEEN

Pulling down the wrinkled covers, I decided it was time to go to bed. Otherwise I was going to fall asleep at the altar. But before I could untie my robe, someone knocked at the door.

Apparently X wasn't going to take my demand that he couldn't see me after midnight seriously.

"Am I going to have to call Norris to drag you away?" I asked as I swung the door open, knowing that saying no to Alexander was already a lost cause.

But it wasn't him at the door; it was his father. The King raised a questioning eyebrow at my appearance, and I adjusted my robe quickly.

"Were you sleeping?"

That was one excuse for how I imagined I looked like right now. I smoothed my tangled hair back and shook my head.

"I was trying to sleep." It wasn't exactly a lie. I had considered going to bed.

"I didn't think women slept the night before their weddings."

"Perhaps not." I shifted on my heels, wondering how long we were going to make small talk. I couldn't imagine why he'd come all the way to Clarence House to speak to me unless it was to threaten me or lecture me. As I was getting married in the morning, I wasn't in the mood for either.

"May I speak to you about an important matter?" he asked.

I hesitated. It was past eleven, but I was never going to sleep. I stepped into the hallway and shut my bedroom door behind me. There was no way I was going to be alone with him.

I followed as he led me through a corridor into a sitting room swathed in masculine colors and decor. Traditional leather chairs sat next to an unlit fireplace and floor-to-ceiling bookshelves lined the walls. The dead eyes of animals bored into me as I entered. It was another room I hadn't discovered yet, but considering the collection of hunting trophies on the wall I wasn't certain I'd be back.

Albert paused at a serving cart and pulled the stopper on a decanter. He poured himself a bourbon, but I hung back, staying closer to the door. What was I doing here? The sooner I got this over with, the better.

"Alexander has not been entirely honest with you, Clara." The King swirled his bourbon and watched thoughtfully as the amber liquid spun, coating the sides of the glass. "Nor have I."

"Imagine that," I said coldly. How was it possible that in a house staffed by hundreds of people, no one was around to save me from this conversation? I crossed my arms over my chest and stared him down. If he thought he could sway my decision to marry Alexander by producing some unsavory tidbit about his past, he was mistaken.

"Tomorrow you will wed my son, but it will not be a *legal* marriage."

My bravado faltered, and I took a step back. My fingers instinctively found the edge of a bookshelf and gripped it for strength and also to stop myself, because every fiber of my being wanted to slap him. "I'm sure the hundreds of guests planning to attend will be surprised to hear that."

"I have no plans to make it public knowledge," he assured me. "But you should be aware. Alexander, as my heir, requires my permission to marry. My *written* permission, and as you know, he's made it quite clear he has no intention of asking me for it."

"Alexander told me—"

"What he wanted you to think. He didn't tell you the truth. I'm afraid that's a trait he picked up from me." His smile was tight-lipped, and it deepened the lines on his face. He looked tired—worn down from the years he'd spent maintaining his fierce grip on the country as well as his sons. "If you marry tomorrow, you can continue living with my son. Perhaps even bear him a child. But for all intents and purposes, there will have been no marriage. As far as the palace is concerned, you will have no claim to the benefits or protections afforded the monarchy nor will your children. They will be illegitimate, and you will be his mistress."

"Why are you telling me this now?" There was no purpose to it. He could have informed me of this months ago if he wanted to put a stop to our marriage. Maybe he was even more cruel than I'd suspected. I couldn't think of

anything more vile than waiting until hours before the ceremony to deliver this news.

"Because unlike my son, I believe you deserve to know."

"There's more to it than that. You're hoping I'll cancel the
wedding." If I walked away tonight, it would save the
monarchy and Alexander the embarrassment of having to
admit to an invalid marriage.

"I know you think me the villain." He paused as though
to give me time to challenge him on this fact.

I didn't. I thought him much worse than the villain. I had
for some time, and he'd done nothing to convince me otherwise. He could claim to have my best interests at heart but it
was a lie. "You basically just told me I would be your son's
whore, so you're right. I don't think very highly of you."

"A crude choice of words, but I suppose if you prefer that
to mistress." He took a long draft, his Adam's apple sliding
violently as he swallowed. Running the back of his hand over
his mouth, he regarded me with narrowed eyes. "He was
intended for Priscilla. I believe you've met her."

"I've had the *pleasure*," I admitted, not bothering to hide
my distaste. She'd been like the rest of the Royal Brat Pack:
privileged and self-involved. "I believe she made a joke about
my weight. Such class. What a loss for you that Alexander
went against your wishes. I had thought you wanted him to
marry Pepper."

"There was a time when Alexander wouldn't have cared,
you know? He would have married who I wished to avoid
having to deal with me. That disillusionment would have
helped me with the Pepper situation." He smirked and
shifted in his seat until his arms rested on his knees. "I heard
you paid her a visit."

"I'm certain she tells you everything."

"Not anymore," he said with emphasis. "Pepper is no longer a friend of the family."

"Whatever will we do at parties?" This was, perhaps, the first piece of good news I'd heard all day, but it didn't come close to soothing the rawness creeping into my throat.

Albert motioned for me to take a seat. I tugged my robe together tightly and settled onto the leather cigar chair, shifting to be certain that my thighs remained covered. The King had repeatedly proven himself to be a twisted man, not only having an affair with a girl who could have been his own child, but also directly stating he wished his son had died in Afghanistan. I never quite knew what to expect from him, even after months of being in his presence.

"I make you uncomfortable," he noted as I squirmed under his gaze.

My eyes flashed nervously to him. It was as if he knew exactly what I was thinking. Yet another characteristic of his that unnerved me.

"I make many people uncomfortable," he continued, smiling wolfishly. "Most can't see past that I'm King. Others get the wrong impression of me when we first meet."

"What impression was I supposed to get?" I asked flatly. "Or are we rewriting history? You were horrible to me on our first meeting and our second and practically every meeting since then. You were tolerable at Christmas, which was a surprise."

"Balmoral is the closest to a normal home that this family has, so it tends to make me sentimental," he said, speaking of the Scottish castle where the Royal family gathered for the

Christmas holidays. "Generally, I regard sentimentality as a weakness."

"I got that *impression* when you told your son you wished he had died at war," I bit out. Whatever he was playing at, I wanted no part of it. Even if it meant there would be no wedding in the morning. Only a truly sick individual would get in bed with King Albert, and I was happy where I slept.

"Alexander's lack of respect angers me," he explained, "and on more than one occasion, we have both said things we regretted."

"You sent him to the warfront," I said pointedly.

"I sent him to become a man!" Albert roared, spilling his drink on the Oriental rug. "Before he became lost to guilt and grief. He wanted to be treated like a man, so he sought out perversion—and dangerous company. He had no idea what he was getting into. I gave him what he truly needed by sending him away. I forced him to grow up!"

Hot anger coursed through me. Alexander had needed his father's love as well as his punishment. A fact that still escaped Albert. I stood and dipped into a curtsy. "I'm afraid I must take my leave of you. Thank you for being honest with me. I'm certain Alexander only wished to protect me from further insult by not telling me that you'd refused to consent to our marriage. Regardless, tomorrow *is* the most important day of my life—whether or not you sanction it. Tomorrow will be about Alexander and me. Not the hundreds of guests or the fancy luncheon or the balcony kiss. Tomorrow I *will* commit my life to his. I will become Alexander's wife in all the ways that matter and fuck you for suggesting otherwise."

Turning on my heels, I padded toward the door.

"You remind me of her," he called.

I stopped in my tracks and spun to face him, silently cursing my curiosity. "Who?"

"Elisabeta," he admitted. He placed his empty glass on an antique side table. Pushing to his feet, he swayed a little as he crossed toward me.

"I might be a British citizen. You might be the King, but to me you're just a man—and I don't obey you, unlike your wife."

To my surprise, he chuckled under his breath. "My wife was obedient in the public eye, but she had a fire about her. Greek woman usually do."

His eyes were far away as he recalled his late wife. Albert stepped closer and the harsh scent of bourbon prickled my nostrils. His eyes drooped a little as he straightened up to lord over me. "She questioned every decision I made. Elisabeta was my equal. When I see you and Alexander together, I know he's met his own match."

I sucked in a breath, genuinely shocked to hear him say that.

"Then why oppose our marriage?" I asked him in a soft voice, struggling to wrap my mind around the insane and abrupt turns this conversation kept taking. "Do you hate your son so much?"

"Hate?" he echoed. "You think I hate my son?"

"I'm not sure," I admitted, "but he thinks you do."

"Someday, God willing, Alexander will sit on this throne and perhaps then he'll understand. Emotional distance is the only way to be an effective monarch."

"But it's not the way to be an effective father." My chastisement was gentle but firm. Choosing not to pander to him anymore meant calling him out on his bullshit.

Because we were no longer rewriting history. We were being honest.

Still, I was gambling by even continuing this discussion. I'd avoided contact with the King for months to protect myself from his painfully blunt disapproval of my lack of pedigree. But I'd also avoided him to prevent exactly this. Alexander didn't want a relationship with his father. He'd made that clear. "Let's not pretend that you've had your sons' best interests at heart."

"My wife was the one who helped me become a father. When I lost her, I lost that ability. Perhaps that seems like an excuse." He shrugged and nearly lost his balance.

My hand shot out to steady him. "Maybe it is. Maybe it shouldn't be anymore."

Maybe it's just the bourbon, I thought.

"You're so like her." His words slurred slightly as he repeated himself. "That's why I refused his request. That's why I've tried to tear you apart."

"That's not a reason," I whispered. Tears smarted my eyes and I blinked them away. I'd be damned if he was going to see me cry again.

"It's not just your fire, Clara," he explained, shaking his head sadly. "You're beautiful like she was, but just as fragile." His hand snaked around my wrist and squeezed. "I could snap your arm in half. You're so breakable."

"Stop." I tried to tug free but his grip only tightened.

"Too lovely for this world. Alexander knows that." Albert jerked me forward, causing me to stumble and fall into him. "He knows he'll lose you just as I know—and that will be what finally destroys him. It's what destroyed the part of me that cared."

His breath was hot and I closed my eyes, straining my face away from his. He was somewhere else, caught in a web of memories, and I had no idea what to expect. The fact that he saw Elisabeta when he looked at me wasn't comforting. Between his intoxicated state and his broad upper body, I couldn't fight him if I tried. And then as suddenly as he'd drawn me close to him, he released me. I darted away from him, stopping only when I reached the door.

"He'll never lose me," I promised. I had no idea why I felt the need to reassure him, except maybe that I also needed to reassure myself.

"I hope that's true. Sincerely. I only want to protect the family that I have left."

"They don't need you to protect them." Why couldn't he understand that? How had his perspective grown so warped? "They need you to care about their happiness."

Silence fell over us. I had nothing left to say, and he could no longer deny that I was right. We both sensed it, just as we both sensed something shift between us. I would never love Albert as a father, but for the first time I felt that I understood him a little.

"Good night." This time I didn't follow rules of etiquette to take the proper leave of him. We'd spoken to each other as equals. It didn't seem necessary to point out our differences now.

He said nothing more.

Back in my temporary bedroom, I locked the door and stood in the oppressive silence. Finally, I opened the door to the wardrobe and stared at the only thing inside. With trembling fingers, I unzipped the overstuffed garment bag and drew my wedding dress out. I traced the delicate lace that covered the silk bodice. I'd sent Alexander to another bed tonight to avoid bad luck. It had found me anyway. There would be a wedding, but it wouldn't be long before the press discovered our marriage was a sham. There would be a scandal that I might have avoided if I'd chosen deference to the King rather than confrontation.

Still it didn't seem to matter. I'd meant it when I told his father that I would marry Alexander in the ways that truly mattered in the morning. I would give him my body, my heart, and my soul. And no act of King or country could stop me.

CHAPTER NINETEEN

ALEXANDER

I stood before the mirror, tugging my sleeve to my wrist and fastening my cufflink. Edward passed me my jacket when I'd fastened the other, and I shrugged it on, swiftly fastening each of the seven gold buttons. I adjusted my shirt under the banded uniform collar and stepped back.

"Well?" I held open my arms.

"Dashing," he assured me. "Clara won't be able to keep her eyes off of you."

"I'd prefer that she couldn't keep her hands off of me." Sitting on the small bench at the foot of my bed, I laced up my patent leather boots.

It had been some time since I'd worn my Royal Air Force uniform, even longer since I'd worn a ceremonial one. This one had been tailored on Saville Row, created specifically for the wedding using the finest Venetian cloth and gold embroidery thread. It was strange to put it on. It symbolised both my past and my future—the old and the new commingling in a way that wasn't comforting. I dismissed the thought, reaching for my hat. For a moment I imagined Clara wearing it—and nothing else. The vision made my cock twitch, which was unfortunate given Clara's request that I not see her before the ceremony.

At least I knew how I'd be spending my wedding night.

The door to my bedroom opened and my father strode, uninvited, into the room, already clad in his own Naval uniform.

"The Irish Guard?" he said to Edward, studying him for a moment.

Edward tugged at the hem of his crimson jacket, a tight smile stealing over his face. "My highest rank."

"Your only rank," our father corrected him.

"Not all men need go to war," I said in a lowered voice, drawing his attention to me. My brother had endured years of his attacks while I was serving in Afghanistan. It was time for me to bear the brunt of our father's abuse, particularly since I was to blame for his foul mood.

"How are you liking the house?" he asked me.

My eyes narrowed as I tried to read him. Everything with my father was a trap. The only way to avoid becoming snared was not to move.

That was not an option.

"We're settling in. Clara is a little overwhelmed, of course." I kept my answer light, but I chose not to thank him. It was my birthright to claim residence at Clarence House. There was no need to flatter him with false gratitude.

His lips turned under as he rested one hand on the scabbard of his ceremonial sword. "I'm certain that she is."

"With time, it will be easier for her," I assured him.

"That brings me to the point of my visit." He turned to Edward and smiled wanly. "Can you give us a moment?"

Edward glanced to me, no doubt wondering if either of us would be left standing when he returned. Bowing his head, he exited the room, pulling the door closed behind him.

"This is unnecessary," I warned my father. He'd come to levy impotent threats about the legitimacy of my marriage to Clara. Over recent weeks, he'd been increasingly resistant to discussion about my security concerns. It seemed he'd chosen my wedding day to remind me that today's ceremony was a ruse.

"As you know, without my sanction of this marriage, it will be considered invalid in the eyes of the state. Any children Clara bears to you will be illegitimate and not awarded the Royal status."

I gritted my teeth, an angry swell burning through my blood. I'd expected his resistance to my marriage, but that did nothing to alleviate my fury. "I plan to have no children, so that should not be an issue."

Shock flitted over his face. It was the first time he had looked genuinely surprised for as long as I could remember.

"You see," I continued, "you've taught me quite well. Children are a duty, a cross to be borne for the sake of the monarchy. Regardless of legitimacy, I see no need to taint the Royal blood any further with my perversion, as you call it."

"I assume your bride is aware of your preference for this?"

I nodded. We had discussed it. Undoubtedly there would come a time when she questioned that decision, but I was certain by then she would understand the full responsibilities that came with the crown.

"I suppose issues of legitimacy are of no importance to

you then." He rubbed his palms together, his chest expanding on a deep breath.

"None at all." My response was firm, calculated. He'd expected to sway me, but I couldn't be positive what his end truly was.

"You've been quite clear on your decision to marry Miss Bishop," he mused, "but despite my refusal, you've not exercised the one option you truly have to ensure your marriage is legal."

"You've made it clear that I've had no options," I said through gritted teeth.

"Rescind the throne." His words hung in the air between us. They were neither a suggestion nor a demand. It was a statement of fact.

I did have an option, but it was one I was unwilling to exploit. Not while Clara's life was in danger.

"I'd expected you to," he continued. "You've made your distaste for your birthright obvious enough, constantly eschewing tradition and decorum in favour of more secular proclivities."

There was a note of disgust in his voice, but he waved a dismissive hand.

"You have been made aware of the situation involving Clara," I said. "You've refused to help." Regardless of his intentions to prevent Clara's protection as a Royal, he couldn't stop me from protecting her. Unfortunately remaining under his thumb with access to our family's wealth was the only way to afford such security.

We stared at each other for a moment. Two men in uniform unwilling to affect the slightest compromise. My father broke eye contact first, strolling across the bedroom and picking up a framed picture of Clara and myself.

"I was thinking of your mother last night." His hard features softened as he spoke of her. His rapt devotion to her had proven time and again that he had a heart.

"I imagine she would have liked Clara," I challenged him. My mother had been a dutiful wife, but as I grew older I understood that her true duty rested with her children.

"Do you know that the doctors informed her that carrying Edward to term could jeopardise her health?" he asked me.

I froze, unable to move. He rarely spoke of my mother save to paint her as a saint. She had died when I was six, far too young to truly know her. My father had given us glimpses of her through offhand remarks, but they were sketches of who she was. He'd never completed her portrait.

"It was a risky pregnancy from the beginning, but when the first doctor suggested she abort, she fired him." A smile curved over his lips at the memory. "Your mother took her responsibilities as Queen very seriously. She was careful to stay at my side without ever raising controversy. But no man could tell her what to do. Not her doctor. Certainly not me. It's perhaps why I have such a difficult time looking at your brother. People assume I disapprove of his lifestyle, but truly, it's the pain of knowing she chose him."

"She was his mother," I said coldly, my hands balled into fists at my sides. "But you are his father—a *duty* you've never seemed to comprehend."

"I don't flatter myself that she would approve of my parenting." He placed the picture on the nightstand and regarded me with distant eyes.

"You shouldn't."

"Such strong words from a man who places no value on children."

He was baiting me, dangling an irresistible morsel over me—and I couldn't stop myself from biting. "I place no value on servitude—on this life."

"The crown continues with or without you, Alexander. I assume your brother won't produce an heir either." He shrugged at my wary expression. "I am kept abreast of his relationship with David, even if *he chooses* not to flaunt it."

"I guess he assumes you won't condone it."

"There's no point," he said. "His progeny will never claim the throne."

"So your line dies," I pointed out, drawing satisfaction just from saying it.

"I told you I was thinking of your mother, but I failed to tell you that it occurred to me yesterday evening how she might feel about today."

The fact that he'd considered anyone's feelings was new. It was convenient that the person was dead.

"I think she'd like Clara," he said slowly. "Actually, I think she'd be quite happy if she were here today."

"If only that was a position you shared with her." I was growing tired of the trip down memory lane. Neither of us would yield—it wasn't in our blood.

"I spent a lot time considering that and I came to a realisation. Your wife is your choice. May God have mercy on her pitiful soul. Only I can choose the direction the monarchy takes after today though." He cleared his throat, tugging at the collar of his uniform. "No man should want this duty.

You've operated for years under the mistaken impression that I enjoy being King."

"Mistaken?" I repeated. No one who took such pleasure in ordering people about could not enjoy the position.

"Blood has been shed throughout time by cruel men who want the throne. The best of us have taken it despite ourselves. That's why you will ascend following my death."

"And if I don't want it?"

"You will take it," he said with certainty. "Good men do not shirk responsibility."

"No, they do not." I didn't trust myself to say more. Our pieces were in position but neither of us could move to check the other. It was a draw.

"I thought about taking this to your fiancée, but I don't want to spoil her day by showing up at her door." He retrieved a folded envelope from his pocket and passed it to me.

"How uncharacteristically thoughtful," I muttered as I broke the wax seal. Sliding out the enclosed papers, I scanned them before lifting my gaze to him.

"If you're thinking of refusing, you should know I've already filed official duplicates. The mandate is in order."

I gripped the documents tightly, knowing they changed everything. One granted Clara the title of Duchess. The other was the decree sanctioning our marriage.

"Why?"

"Perhaps because she would have wanted..." He trailed away, not offering the other motivations he might have.

I hardly cared. Two simple pieces of paper. That was all it took to confer the highest level of security for her.

I swallowed, my jaw tensing, and nodded my thanks.

"No doubt you have things to attend to before the ceremony." With that he took his leave.

I was down the hall and in front of her door, papers in hand, before I realised that Clara had no idea that she'd been about to wed me illegally. I paused, catching the laughter that floated from inside the room. I pictured her for a moment, breathless. Her cheeks pink with excitement. She'd fought for this day—for me.

Now somehow we'd both won. Turning away from her room, I went back to the bedroom and collected my gloves and hat. In a few hours we would be man and wife. The rest could wait.

Her happiness was all that mattered, knowing this would only jeopardise that. Later, I would tell her she was a Duchess. Later, I would take her to our marital bed and make love to her as my wife. For now, I unbuttoned my jacket and slid the papers into my breast pocket, over my heart.

The space she already occupied.

CHAPTER TWENTY

He arrived with the crowds, set up camp, and waited. Waited until the excitement reached fever pitch along the route to Westminster Abbey.

There were so many people—swarms of them. They descended on London like vultures, hoping for a taste of a life they could never have. It disgusted him to walk among them, but the plan had to be followed precisely.

The plan.

He couldn't have done better himself, though he now acted alone.

Police swept the streets, checking lamp posts and sewage drains. Officers walked amongst the crowd, confiscating bottles and fireworks. Routine, perfunctory tasks to ensure there would be no disturbances to the blessed fucking event. But the security plan he'd been given kept him a step ahead.

At dawn the officers would rotate shifts, stopping to chat with their colleagues just as the people behind the barricades did the same. Their awareness would be compromised by the air of revelry on the streets.

He navigated through them easily. One man was easy enough to let by and people were always so fucking polite. He followed the security perimeter, staying far enough from the actual barrier as to not draw attention to his movements until he finally saw it: a horse tied near a barricade.

Its rider was out of sight. Approaching it, a little girl looked up to him, stroking the bit of muzzle the animal had managed to push through the bars. Her mother stood next to her, busily gossiping with a friend.

"Isn't she beautiful?" she asked.

He smiled and held a finger to his lips. "Can you keep a secret?"

The child's eyes widened and she bobbed her head.

Slowly he reached through the bars, caught the reins and freed the animal.

"She should be able to walk around."

The girl nodded again and turned her attention back to the creature.

He stepped a few meters away, out of the girl's sight, and drew the slingshot from his pocket. The irony made him smile. All of what would come—started with a child's toy. Drawing it back, he shot a small pebble squarely into the horse's hindquarters. The animal reared, its hooves crashing back down on the pavement before it bolted down the street, finally catching the attention of the crowd—and the officers.

He saw the girl tug at her mother's coat, but the mother shooed her child's hand away, caught up in the unexpected excitement. Police officers scattered, some moving to avoid the stampeding beast, others attempting to stop it.

He faded into the crowd, moving quickly to the row of nearby shops near where the horse had fled. Ducking into an *alley, he waited, staying still as they had trained him, until an officer darted close by.*

Alone.

An easy target.

The officer never saw him. He never heard the rock fly through the air. By the time it hit his neck it was too late. Now that he was stunned, the stranger struck.

One twist and the officer's neck popped. His body went limp. It was so much easier to kill a man than he'd expected. Dragging his body into the alley was more difficult, though not impossible.

He stepped onto the street a few minutes later, abandoning the stripped body, along with the slingshot, in a trash bin. The toy had been useful, but it was only a child's plaything— nothing like the metal wedged cold and heavy in his waistband.

Smoothing his stolen uniform down, he marched back toward the cathedral to do a man's work.

CHAPTER TWENTY-ONE

ALEXANDER

Eight minutes had never taken so long. My arm ached from acknowledging the crowds as the borrowed Bentley drove leisurely along the official procession route toward Westminster Abbey where I would see my wife for the first time.

Next to me my brother was at ease, a charismatic smile gracing his face as he waved.

"You're much better at being Royal than I am," I informed him as the car turned toward Whitehall.

He glanced at me and shook his head. "I'll remind you of that when the whole of England is up in arms about my engagement."

"Your engagement?" I repeated, turning to stare at him. "Were you planning on telling me?"

"You've had quite enough on your mind, which is why I made Clara swear not to tell you until after the wedding."

Another bombshell. "Clara knew?"

"Of course, she helped me pick out the ring."

"I can't believe you two kept this from me." But no part of

me could be angry. Not when my brother had a chance at the happiness I had found.

"Obviously I couldn't keep it from you," he pointed out. "Which is why I stole your thunder."

"You only made this day more perfect," I said, clapping him on the shoulder as the car pulled to the entrance of the gothic cathedral. "Although it is strange to think of my little brother getting married."

"Says the notorious womaniser," Edward shot back as the passenger door opened.

An officer saluted us when we reached the red carpet leading into the abbey. Just past the gates Edward and I paused to wave to the crowd. It was expected. Mostly another photo opportunity for the press. But I felt an odd sense of pride surge through me as I regarded the crowd. All my life I'd resented how the press laid claim to my personal life. I'd expected to feel the same today. Instead, as the onlookers cheered and waved Union Jacks, I felt grateful. These people had embraced Clara. I had no misconception they were here to see me.

She was as much their princess now as she was mine.

Edward leaned in beside me. "Pausing for a photo op? The tables have turned. Unless, of course, you're flipping them the bird."

"I'll flip it to you if you're not careful," I warned him.

He sighed and strode forward. "Get inside before you upend the monarchy. Clara deserves one drama-free day."

Invited guests had already arrived, but we stopped in salute as two familiar faces appeared in our path.

"At ease," Brexton ordered with a chuckle.

I ignored him and regarded my former commanding officer, Squadron Leader Kelly. "Sir."

"Your Highness," he bowed.

My hand reached out and caught his forearm in a firm, friendly shake. "Now that formalities are out of the way, how are you?"

Kelly cocked his greying head toward Brexton and grimaced, drawing out his considerable wrinkles. "I've had to babysit this one all morning. How do you think?"

"In my defence," Brexton interrupted, "I have a bet going with some of the guys about how many hats we can collect."

"Hats?" Edward asked. He looked to me for answers, but I shrugged.

"There are a number of lovely ladies wearing hats here today. It makes it easier to keep track of which ones we can get into dark corners at the reception." He paused, winking at me. "There are bonus points for feathers and unique colours, of course."

"Brex, it's good to know some things never change." I shook my head, unable to hold back a laugh.

"We're doing it for you, poor boy. It's the end of an era."

I nodded solemnly, though I wondered if they knew I was content to see that old life draw to a close. Taking our leave, we continued through the crowd, stopping to make polite conversation on our way to the Chapter House. When we were finally alone in the octagonal chamber, I turned to Edward. "I suggest you elope."

"As if Father would sanction my marriage." He rolled his eyes, but I didn't miss the edge of pain in his tone. I knew the ache of rejection when I heard it.

The papers in my pocket, officially condoning my

marriage, grew heavy, reminding me that anything was possible. Yesterday I would have said the same thing. "We'll have to work on him. Look on the bright side."

"Which is?" Edward asked.

When Clara and I had returned from our honeymoon, I would appeal to our father, choosing to believe I could sway his apathy towards his youngest son.

"At least, David is British." I grinned at my younger brother, bumping my elbow against his. The weight I'd carried for the last few months had lifted. Things were finally falling into place, and I wanted Edward to feel as light as I did.

"He does have that on his side." He paused, regarding me with studious eyes.

"What?" I prompted.

"I'll admit I didn't expect to see you this happy."

I inclined my head. "Neither did I."

Trumpets sounding my father's fanfare echoed through the chamber.

"The guest of honour," Edward muttered. "It will be nearly time then."

"In a moment," I stalled, wondering where my personal security advisor was.

Norris entered. My pulse sped up, returning to normal when he smiled.

"Your uniforms have always suited you," he said as he approached us.

Despite his long years serving the King, Norris wore a tailored morning suit. It was a calculated move. I'd arranged for him to be seated with Clara's family. To most he would appear as another guest, but it reassured me to know he was on her other side.

"The guard reports no suspicious activity," he informed me.

The police and guard had run continual sweeps of the streets, dismantling light posts and checking sewer drains for bombs. But I was more concerned with the guests and the crowd gathered along the procession route. "Anyone of interest among the crowd?"

There was only one person of interest to me. I didn't have to tell Norris that. Daniel had vanished from the grid again after he'd managed to breach our engagement gala.

"A few kooks," he said, "and there was an incident with a horse."

I raised an eyebrow just as Edward repeated, "An incident with a horse?"

"Something spooked it and took off near Whitehall, made it all the way to Parliament Square before a chap caught him." He clapped a hand over my uniform's epaulette. "We're in prime shape if the worst we have to contend with is wild horses."

We laughed. Norris's hand stayed planted on my shoulder. My father's fanfare ended, and I couldn't help but think that my true father stood with me here under the vaulted ceiling of the chamber. Albert may have granted me permission to marry Clara, but Norris had protected her. He'd guided me as I continued to cock things up during our courtship. I was only standing here today because of him.

"Thank you." My words were thick, coated in emotions I never knew how to express.

"It is not my duty, but my privilege."

I embraced him in a warm hug. He pulled away, placing his hand to his nearly invisible earpiece. "Clara has arrived at the West entrance. It's time."

I inhaled deeply and squared my shoulders.

"Last chance to run," Edward whispered as we exited toward the East Cloister.

"Not a chance in hell."

We emerged into the sanctuary. I barely processed the presence of the guests. I nodded as they smiled and wished me well as I passed. Over three thousand people were in attendance and all I could think of was the one climbing the front steps. I met my father's eye as I approached the altar. Next to him my grandmother was absorbed in reading her programme.

As we ascended, I counted each step. They were the final ones I would take before claiming Clara as mine forever. Edward stood next to me, our backs turned as the congregation began to sing the processional hymn, signalling Clara's march had begun. Every instinct in my body compelled me to turn. I wanted to watch her approach, to see her choosing me as I had chosen her, but I held to decorum. Next to me, Edward glanced over his shoulder, a wide smile splitting his face.

"She's on her way," he told me. I glanced to him and his face said it all.

A deep peace settled over me. The moment had come and there was no doubt. No trepidation. In that moment, my life made total sense. Each moment brought her closer to me until finally I heard the rustle of silk and footsteps on the stairs.

And then she was at my side. She paused, allowing her

father to lift the veil from her face. She placed her delicate hand in mine and I drunk in the sight of her. An unexpected lump settled in my throat. She was here. She was mine.

"You are perfect," I whispered, and a slight flush stole over her porcelain features. Someday I wouldn't be able to recall what her dress looked like or that she had chosen pearls instead of diamonds. But I would recall the blush on her cheeks. The blood-red roses she carried. And this feeling. Oh God, I would remember this amazement.

The Dean of Westminster approached us. He spoke, but I didn't hear what he said. His words didn't matter. Only mine did.

"I will."

Our eyes stayed locked as he repeated himself until she uttered a soft, "I will."

He began the vows, pausing to allow me to repeat after him, but as I opened my mouth, a murmur rose from the guests. My hand tightened over Clara's as I glanced out to the crowd.

Impossible.

It was the only thought that filtered into my conscious thoughts before he raised his gun and fired the first shot. I heard the crowd erupt in panic as my father stepped into the aisle to confront the rogue police officer.

His name was on my lips but I couldn't bring myself to call it out, even as my arm lashed out to draw Clara behind me.

"Stop!" My father's command boomed and echoed over the clamour of the crowd.

"She belongs to me!" Daniel screamed. He swung the

gun in wild arcs, sending guests scattering. "She will never be your whore!"

I lunged forward and agony rolled through me. My knees buckled but I locked them in place as the next shot rang out. Norris flashed before me as I stumbled forward.

"Clara." I managed the order before I fell. No other words were necessary.

Two more cracks split the air, followed by one last ominous pop. I crumpled to the floor of the cathedral, my eyes trained on the vast, arching ceiling. And then she was there. I wanted to soothe her, to erase the fear marring her beautiful face. Her arms scooped under me, cradling me. The warmth of her drowned out the panicked crowd even as a coldness seeped through my blood.

"Alexander!"

I could hear the plea in her voice, and I watched in horror as crimson soaked across white silk. My fingers fumbled for her, needing to draw her close, needing to know she was safe. Her hand caught mine. She didn't let go until they pulled her away. Without the balm of her touch, I faded into night on a Friday morning.

CHAPTER TWENTY-TWO

B arricaded in a waiting room, I paced the floor, train thrown over my arm, as I tried to ignore the muddy red stains covering my wedding dress. No one was telling me anything. No one was allowed in. I was certain if I stopped circling the room, I would go crazy. I couldn't process the events of the last few hours. If I allowed myself to stop and focus on even the smallest detail, it tore through me. Daniel hadn't injured me, but I was bleeding internally, my own mind slowly killing me, as Alexander bled on a surgical table somewhere down the hall.

My stomach roiled at the thought and I caught myself against the wall.

"Wake up," I whispered, my small voice carrying over the empty space. This was a nightmare. None of it was real.

But I'd felt the slippery heat of his blood on my hands in the cathedral. I'd felt his hand slip from mine as medics lifted him onto a stretcher. I'd heard the wail of sirens.

If this was a dream, it had been hewn from the darkest fears I kept locked inside me.

The door clicked open and Belle peeked in. I broke down at the sight of her in a t-shirt and jeans, no longer in her bridesmaid's dress. The helpless look on her face assured me that this was real. Alexander was dying somewhere in this hospital, and I was dying with him. All of my manic energy deserted me as I sank into a crumpled mess of silk and tulle on the tile floor. I wanted to cry and scream. I wanted to rip off the silk and lace that reminded me of everything I'd lost today.

Of what I still had to lose.

Belle dropped to her knees, abandoning her bag to wrap her arms around me. I didn't resist her as she pulled me closer. But her presence didn't make it okay. It didn't take away the stabbing agony in my chest. It didn't fill the pit at my core. It opened me to the pain. The tears frozen in my throat thawed, clawing free in wrenching sobs. We didn't speak for a long time. I let her hold me until the sobs wracking my body calmed into ragged breathing punctuated with gasps.

"I brought you a change of clothes," she whispered, stroking my hair soothingly.

"I feel like I'm being held prisoner. No one's telling me anything. No one will let me see him. I'm going crazy," I rambled on. It was the smallest of comforts to no longer be talking to myself. "Where is everyone? Where's my family?"

"Being interrogated." Her voice was quiet as if she anticipated my reaction. Her hand found mine and grasped it tightly. "Edward is in emergency meetings. He managed to send me a text message, but I haven't heard anything since."

"My family is being questioned?" I asked in disbelief.

"Everyone is being questioned."

"This is ridiculous! It was Daniel. Everyone saw him!" I pulled away from her.

"Daniel is dead. I know that much."

Relief swelled, cresting for a brief moment, before crashing away again. He was dead. I thought I hadn't wanted it. After today—after he tried to take Alexander away—I no longer granted him sanctuary in my thoughts. I could only hope he'd been dragged to hell.

"Clara." Belle's voice dropped again. I shook myself from the haze of my thoughts and looked to her. Bad news was written across her face, telling me what she couldn't bear to say.

The world grew black at the edges as my vision swam. I pressed a hand to my forehead, trying to ward off the dizziness. "No!" I shouted, stopping her as she opened her mouth to continue. "No! I don't...I can't..."

Belle's hand shot out and caught mine. "Clara, you need to hear—"

"No!" The scream exploded from deep within me, liberating all the fear I'd kept carefully compartmentalized since my arrival at St. Thomas's hospital. I wrenched away from her and tried to stand but the blood pounding through me grew louder and louder until darkness overtook me.

MY ARM THROBBED. The hum of fluorescent lights grew louder. I blinked, my eyes meeting unfamiliar walls. Reaching over, I fumbled with plastic tubing as I tried to figure out where I was. Unwanted memories flashed in my head. Blurry. Jagged. A nurse swam into view as bile rose in my throat. She rushed forward as I covered my mouth with my hand, producing a small, plastic bucket with the ease of someone with years of experience. She held it in place as I wretched, emptying my stomach of the little food I'd eaten earlier this morning.

This morning. It felt like a lifetime ago. In so many ways, it was.

She hovered near me until I waved her away. Falling back against the hospital bed, I managed one word. "Water."

"Slowly," she advised as she helped me take a sip. "Give your stomach a moment to settle."

"It was just..." I struggled to find a way to explain that I wasn't ill. Not really. "I'd forgotten and when I woke up, it all came flooding back."

"That's common with traumatic experiences." She patted my hand with one hand as she adjusted a monitor with the other. "Of course, it could also be..."

She trailed away, giving me a knowing look as she wrapped a blood pressure cuff around my arm. A hint of a smile played on her lips. Any warm feeling I had toward her vanished. My whole life had been destroyed. Every plan I'd had for the future gone in one violent minute. Another memory flashed through my mind: Belle's face right before I blacked out. I grabbed for the bucket again, my body rejecting the water. But when that was out, I continued to heave, convulsions wracking my body. Any moment now I'd be forced to hear what she's tried to tell me.

"Shhhh, everything's going to be okay. The doctor will be here in a moment to answer your questions," the nurse said in a kind voice, which made me hate her even more.

I didn't have any questions, and she was wrong. Nothing

was going to be fine. Not anymore. I had nothing. Nothing to ask. Nothing to know. Nothing to live for.

I laid back and stared at the white ceiling overhead. Did they paint hospital rooms in such sterile colors so patients would have one less thing to process? White walls and sleek silver instruments—a blank palette. It seemed like the wrong choice. My world had already been stripped of color. Of meaning. Being here only reminded me of that.

Heavy footsteps informed me we'd been joined by someone. The doctor. Someone else. I didn't care.

"Miss Bishop," a deep voice greeted me absently.

Hearing my own name stole my breath. I wasn't supposed to be Miss Bishop. Everything had changed, but that hadn't.

He continued when I didn't respond. "I want to assure you that your privacy during this time is of the utmost importance to us. Our entire staff has been reminded of our confidentiality policies."

"Can I see him?" I spoke in a voice so small that I didn't recognize it. Could I really handle seeing Alexander's body? My eyes shut involuntarily as I wished I hadn't been so adamant about him not seeing me on the day of our wedding. Now I'd never feel his hands on my body again, never feel his skin warm on mine. He'd given his life to save me, but without him I had no desire to live.

"Nurse Taylor will remove your IV in a moment."

"Why do I have an IV at all?" I asked. I was alive. My heart was beating—even if I wished it wasn't.

"Given the events of the day and your condition—"

"My condition isn't an issue," I cut him off. "I don't know

who you spoke to, but my eating disorder is under control. The fluids aren't necessary."

A concerned look came over Dr. Andrews' face, and his eyes flickered to meet the nurse's. Gesturing for the chart, he scanned through its contents without another word. Meanwhile panic snowballed in my chest. I needed to see Alexander. I needed to have a final moment alone with him.

"Please," I whispered. "Just let me see his body. Please let me say goodbye."

The doctor froze, mid-page flip. "I'm sorry that won't be possible. The body was removed by the King's Guard hours ago."

I had no energy left to scream. None left to cry. A hollow chill seeped through my veins, numbing me entirely. I'd taken the ultimate risk by allowing myself to love a man like Alexander. He burned too bright, soared too high, ran too deeply for this world.

I was always going to lose him.

I just never imagined it would end like this. And it hurt. It hurt worse than any pain I'd ever felt. The agony carved through me and took up residence in my bones. My blood was cold fire in my veins, a stinging reminder that I was here and he wasn't.

But grief was the price of love, and if I had my choice now, I would pay it again.

"You can see Alexander, of course," Doctor Andrews continued. "He isn't awake from surgery, but the operation went well. He's in stable condition. Not completely out of the woods, but his prognosis is quite strong."

My mouth fell open and I shook my head, fresh tears

pricking at my eyes. Warmth flooded through me. Life flooded through me. "W...w...wait. Alexander is alive?"

"Yes." Doctor Andrews looked as confused as I felt. "I assumed you had been told."

"You said his body had been removed." My finger shook as I pointed it at him.

Doctor Andrews sat on the edge of my bed and took a deep breath. "Not everyone made it. The King is dead."

Guilt mixed with my relief. Tears fell freely down my cheeks as I realized that Albert had given his life for his son's. A final sacrifice that muddied everything I thought I knew about him—everything Alexander believed to be true. When Alexander finally woke up, he'd have to confront that, and I needed to be by his side.

"I need to see him." I tore at the tape holding the IV in my arm, and Nurse Taylor rushed to stop me.

"We'll arrange for someone to take you there." A vein tensed in Dr. Andrews' jaw. "But before that I have to ask. Miss Bishop, are you aware that you're pregnant?"

CHAPTER TWENTY-THREE

P*regnant.*

THE WORLD STOPPED, and I stared at him.

The need for confidentiality. Their seemingly unjustified caution. Suddenly it all made sense.

"That's not possible." But even as I spoke, I felt the truth. I'd known. I'd known for weeks that something was different. But that didn't explain how it was possible. "I'm on the pill."

"The pill is not one hundred percent effective in preventing pregnancy. There's always a possibility a woman can become pregnant." Dr. Andrews' eyebrows knitted together as he consulted my chart. "We won't know until we perform an ultrasound, but according to your hormone levels, it appears you're quite far along."

"How far along am I?" This couldn't be happening. I'd woken up this morning expecting the happiest day of my life and instead I'd experienced the ultimate roller coaster—and the ride wasn't over. Pregnant. I couldn't be pregnant. We weren't even married yet. This couldn't be happening.

"Months, I would guess. Based on your blood work at least three months, possibly more."

"But I haven't had any symptoms." My hand pressed instinctively to my stomach, trying to anchor what I was being told to something tangible. I cycled through the last few weeks looking for clues that I'd somehow missed. They were there. The stomachaches and mood swings. Feeling possessive of Alexander to the point of obsession. Crying. I'd mistaken them for anxiety and sentimentalism.

"It's not unusual for a woman to not realize she's pregnant, particularly if she's been distracted by other life events."

Like a wedding, I thought. I'd had plenty to distract me, but how could I have not noticed that I was pregnant?

"I've had my period," I told him. None of it fit together, because I wouldn't let it. "How could I have been pregnant for months with a period?"

"An ultrasound will determine if there might be an underlying cause for your bleeding," he continued. "It could be the placement of the placenta or minor breakthrough bleeding that you misinterpreted. We can perform the ultrasound now if you'd like."

Alexander should be here. The thought was almost out of my mouth before I swallowed it back. A baby was the last thing that he needed to worry about. I pushed away the painful realization that this wasn't good news. Not only was it the last thing he needed to worry about, but it was also the last thing that he wanted.

"Would you like to wait for your fiancé?" he asked as if he could read my thoughts.

I shook my head. "No, I don't want to cause him more stress."

And I couldn't wait. I needed answers. I needed something concrete to prove to me that this wasn't all a dream. Because at the moment I couldn't be certain I wasn't trapped in a nightmare.

"I'll send for a machine," the nurse said.

"I can go to the machine," I offered. The thought of sitting here, plugged in to tubes and monitors while waiting for answers was too much to bear.

"Given today's events, it would be better if we brought it to you," the doctor suggested gently. "I can only imagine that you'd like to keep this quiet until you've had a chance to speak with your family."

My family. I'd have to tell them. I'd have to face them and explain that all of today's terrible events had happened because of me. I'd have to tell them why Daniel had attacked the wedding. I'd have to explain that I'd known about the threat. Then I'd have to tell them I was pregnant.

I'd have to tell Alexander.

And then I'd have to face the fallout.

I'd lose all of them. Maybe that was for the best. Being close to me was dangerous. The hand on my stomach wrapped protectively around my hip as if I could cage my unborn child and protect him.

But the person he needed to be protected from was me.

The doctor stood to leave and I caught his arm. "My friend, Belle Stuart. She must be here still."

He looked to the nurse, who nodded.

"She's in the waiting room, miss," Nurse Taylor informed me. "Would you like me to deliver a message?"

"No"—I shook my head—"I'd like her to be here. Could you get her for me?"

"Of course."

Time stood still while I waited for her to return with Belle. The only movement in the room was the blinking line on the heart rate monitor, but my eyes were glued to the hand over my stomach. It was impossible. Even as my memory provided more and more evidence to the contrary, I couldn't believe it.

Belle flew into the room, stopping short of my bed and pointing shakily at me. "Thank God you're alright, because I plan to kill you. I cannot handle any more of this craziness, Clara Bishop."

"Then you better sit down," I said softly, patting the side of my hospital bed.

She did so reluctantly, her eyes trained on me as if any moment I might faint again.

"The doctor said you were okay." There was a note of accusation in her tone, resentment at being lied to.

"I'm pregnant." I forced the words out, desperately needing to say it and wanting to hold it inside at the same time.

"Did...what? Huh?" Belle fumbled for words, her eyes darting from me to the nurse and back again. "Did you know?"

"Of course I didn't know!" My voice pitched up, growing loud enough that Nurse Taylor stepped forward anxiously.

"Well, you haven't been drinking for weeks," Belle said, crossing her arms and staring me down.

"I haven't wanted to drink. The stress has been making me queasy."

Belle narrowed her eyes and waited for me to realize what I was saying.

"Oh." I couldn't think of anything else to add.

"Are you one of those women from the telly? You know, the ones where they go to the bathroom and a baby comes out?" Her disbelief softened into a teasing tone. "I guess this means Alexander doesn't know."

"Believe me, I would have told you if I knew." Saying the words was a practice run for the more difficult confession I'd have to make later. Dread crept under my skin at the thought.

"I know," she said softly. "How far?"

"I don't know." I had to push the words past the lump forming in my throat. "He said maybe three months. They're going to give me an ultrasound."

Belle did her best not to look shocked by this revelation, but it was in her eyes. She reached forward and squeezed my hand. "Can I stay with you? I'd like to see the baby."

The dam burst and grateful tears rained down my cheeks. I could only nod.

"I'm going to be right here with you," she promised as the doctor wheeled a cart into the room. He swiftly closed the door behind him. "Let's see if we can get a peek."

Nurse Taylor bustled forward and pulled down the hospital sheet to my hips. "Pull your gown up, love, and I'll hold this."

I wiggled the thin gown up to reveal my abdomen. Out of the corner of my eye I saw them exchange a look. Glancing down I saw what had attracted their attention. In the light of recent information, it was obvious that the few extra pounds I'd put on were a little more than that.

"This will be cold," Doctor Andrews warned as he

squeezed a glob of jelly over my stomach. "Don't panic if we can't see anything. It might be too early for an abdominal ultrasound."

"And if it is...?" I trailed away as fear circled my heart and constricted. I wasn't certain if I was more afraid that he would find something or that he might not.

"We'll have to do an internal scan," he explained as he smeared the jelly around with the probe, his free hand flicking a switch. Next to me the machine's screen came to life, filling the room with a gentle whooshing sound followed by a racing heartbeat.

And there he was.

I knew him as soon as I saw him.

I knew he was a boy. I knew he was mine and Alexander's. Our flesh and blood. Our love combined to create the most beautiful sight I'd ever seen.

"Meet your baby," he said, turning the screen so I could have a better view.

There were a million questions on my tongue and none of them mattered. There was only him. My little majesty. My fingers stretched into the air as if I could reach out and touch him.

"Is he a *he*?"

"The baby is being a bit shy. I can't tell you if it's a boy," he said. "In a few more weeks your doctor can perform another scan to tell you, but the baby looks healthy."

I stared at the screen in rapt devotion as he measured and made notes.

"As I suspected, you're currently measuring about four months along."

"Four months?" I repeated in shock. "How could I be four months pregnant and not know it?"

"Most first-time mothers don't feel the baby until four or five months, even then most describe initial movement as feeling like tiny bubbles. It would be hard to overlook at this stage. And there's the issue of the placenta, which is anterior and quite close to the cervix. That could account for your bleeding. We'll want to monitor that, but all of this is very normal in early pregnancy. You shouldn't worry." He hit a few buttons and a moment later a long sheet printed from the ultrasound machine. "First picture."

I cradled the sheet to my chest. I'd spent the last several hours wishing I was dreaming, but I wanted this moment to be real. I slid my finger across the edge of the paper until I felt the sharp, familiar sting of a paper cut. Tears of joy—the tears I never expected after today—streamed down my face. Belle's hand tightened around mine, drawing me back to the present. I turned to find her crying, too.

"He's beautiful," I whispered to her.

"So it's a boy, huh?" she teased, swiping at her eyes with her free hand.

"I know he is." I couldn't explain it. No more than I could explain how an hour ago a baby was the furthest thing from my mind and now it was the center of my world. The thought of carrying Alexander's child captivated me. Maybe it was a sign a light in the darkness that had consumed us.

I'd been wrong. The worst day of my life—a day filled with unimaginable pain and fear, a day filled with disappointment and grief—had still managed to be the happiest day of my life.

CHAPTER TWENTY-FOUR

Dressing slowly, I considered how foreign my body felt to me. I was nourishing another life—I had been for months. I'd been betrayed by my womanhood. Despite the love that had taken up residence inside me, I couldn't ignore that fact. I had to push it aside though and focus on the other realities I needed to face. When I was finally allowed to see Alexander, I couldn't be wearing a hospital gown. Seeing me like that would add undue stress to him, which wouldn't help his condition.

The yoga pants and the soft over-the-shoulder sweater Belle had brought me were a soothing replacement after spending hours in the gown. I needed to be comfortable in my own skin, especially as I processed everything that I'd just learned. In the bathroom, I stared into the mirror. My reflection was out of place in this setting: hair still waving over my shoulders, my make-up precisely applied for cameras. I twisted on the hot water and splashed it over my face. But I wanted it all off. Pumping the soap dispenser, I lathered it over my face and rinsed with scalding water. I grabbed a towel and scrubbed until no remnant of today remained on my skin, leaving it tight and red. I yanked out the pins that held my hair out of my face and pulled my hair back, securing it loosely at the nape of my neck. I wanted to look ordinary.

Because I needed to feel ordinary.

I was Clara Bishop. Nothing more and nothing less. I hadn't married the Prince of England today. I was still a nobody. Somehow that made me feel safer.

As I sat on the bed, slipping on a pair of flats, Nurse Taylor knocked on the door. "I can take you to your fiancé now. If you're ready."

I wasn't ready, not by a long shot. But I knew I would never be prepared. My imagination seized my thoughts, inflicting horrible images upon me. I'd seen him fall in the sanctuary. The powerful, brutal man I loved brought to his knees by one cowardly act of violence. My place was at his side, though.

And I had to tell him.

Every impulse in me wanted to crawl back into the hospital bed and hide. Instead I pushed to my feet and followed her toward the critical care unit.

"We've locked down this wing of the unit," she explained as she led me down a quiet corridor. Security guards lined the walls, motionless as statues as we passed. With each step I took closer to Alexander, my anxiety grew.

"How is he?" I asked her softly.

"I'm not privy to that information," she told me. "But I assumed you'd want to speak with him immediately."

That was a reasonable assumption, so why was I suddenly so afraid to face him? How could I feel this compulsion to be with him and run at the same time?

"He's going to be angry." I'd spoken out loud without meaning to.

"Surprise is not anger," she said carefully. "He might need time to adjust to the idea of being a father, but don't assume he won't want the baby."

But he wouldn't want the baby. I knew that, because he'd been very clear about not having children. This wasn't in his plans. Of course none of today's events had been in his plans.

She paused at the door to his room. "This is as far as I go."

"Come with me," I blurted out, suddenly wondering why I'd sent Belle to check in with my family.

"I'm not cleared to enter that room, miss." She gave my shoulder a squeeze. "You'll do just fine."

Taking a deep breath, I touched my belly, hoping to gain strength from the love I'd recently discovered. My hand dropped away as a guard opened the door for me.

The lights were dim in the room, turned low so he could sleep. Everything was motionless—still—so I didn't move. I merely soaked in the sight of him, watching his chest rise and fall in shallow heaves. I closed my eyes and concentrated until I heard the rasp of his breath under the oxygen mask. In and out. In and out.

No sound had ever been so precious to me.

And I knew then, that no matter what, we could get through this. Love like this—love that consumed and ravaged, it was a living, breathing thing. It demanded more because it returned more. This love was for the brave, and that's what I had to be right now.

Movement stirred out of the corner of my eye and I whirled around, one hand clutching my chest and the other landing protectively over my belly. Norris said nothing, just regarded me in silence as his eyes traveled over me, stopping briefly when he spotted the hand on my stomach. I let it fall away, shifting self-consciously, and when I dared to meet his eyes, it was clear that he knew.

Neither of us spoke for a long moment until, at last, he pushed to his feet and walked toward Alexander—our common ground. He looked to me and nodded, a signal to say it was okay. Sucking in a shaky breath, I joined him on the other side. Alexander filled the bed, his broad shoulders dwarfing it, and I couldn't make sense out of it. I couldn't wrap my head around his silence. It was as if a fire had been extinguished inside him, and I'd burnt out along with it.

"He's going to pull through, Clara," Norris told me gently.

"How bad is it?" I asked, unable to tear my eyes from him even though I couldn't bring myself to reach out and touch him.

"The first shot avoided any major organs, but the second one nicked his subclavian artery. That's why he was in surgery for such a long time." He paused and turned his tired eyes toward me. "I apologize for leaving you alone. I felt my place was here."

I swallowed and offered him the small smile I could muster. "It's okay. I didn't need you."

"He would have wanted me to stay with you."

I couldn't deny that he was probably right about that. "I won't tell if you won't."

"Tell me what?" a dry voice asked.

I dropped to the bed beside him, my fingers finding his and fumbling to twine our hands together. One eye opened and then another.

"Thank god," he breathed, trying to lift my hand up to bring me closer. He winced and let it fall back to the cot.

"Not so fast, X." I leaned forward and brushed my lips over his knuckles, still clinging to him.

Alexander couldn't move his head, but his eyes raked across me, and the chill that had descended over me slowly evaporated under the heat of his gaze. "You weren't hurt?"

I shook my head as the tears brimming in my eyes spilled over.

His eyes darted to Norris, narrowing as he took in his old friend's haggard appearance. "You look like hell."

"You put me through it." But the joke was hollow. There was no mistaking the emptiness in Norris's voice. I felt it, too. The sorrow and the confusion this day had wrought upon us all.

We both knew there were hard conversations to come. There was no way to hide that from Alexander.

"Who?" Alexander asked.

"You need to rest," Norris said, but there was no bypassing the question, just as there was no way to save Alexander from the fate that had been suddenly thrust upon him.

"Who?" he repeated firmly.

"I'm sorry," Norris said. "Your father is dead."

I braced myself, tightening my grip on his hand, but Alexander remained silent. A muscle in his jaw twitched, but his face was placid.

"There were papers in my coat," he told Norris.

"I have them," Norris assured him. The bodyguard placed a hand on Alexander's uninjured shoulder. "Your brother has been handling the situation."

"By situation, you mean he's deciding what to do next?" Alexander clarified gruffly. "That is not his responsibility."

"X, I think—"

He cut me off, his tone brisk, "Edward will not bear that burden."

"He's more than capable of making arrangements and handling the inquiry."

"I'm not questioning his competence. I am questioning my own," he said, "as will the people the longer he's forced to assume my role." Alexander turned his attention to me, leveling his gaze until it held my own. "Clara, I need you by my side."

"I'm right here," I promised him. "Always."

Alexander looked to Norris. "Find the chaplain. I want to be married immediately."

"Not like this," I said quickly. "It can wait."

It had to wait. I'd never seen Alexander vulnerable before and I couldn't take advantage of that. Alexander deserved to know what he was walking into. I couldn't marry him without telling him about the baby. I refused to. But there were more pressing matters at hand.

"It cannot wait."

I looked to Norris as I fought to contain the anxiety curling through me. If he was going to demand to be married, I couldn't put off the truth.

"Can we have a minute?" I asked Norris in a small voice.

His head bobbed, but the look he gave me was one of pride.

I was doing the right thing. I focused on that as he disappeared into the hallway to wait.

"I understand this is not how you pictured your wedding," Alexander said before I could speak.

"I don't care about the wedding," I cried out. Choking back an anxious sob, I clapped my free hand over my mouth and shook my head. Everything was wrong. It was all happening too fast—much too fast. Refusing his wish now would hurt him, but it was for the best. He'd understand why later. "You're in no position to make this decision."

"I'm the King of England," he said, a strange edge coloring his words as if he was trying them out. His lips turned down, but he recovered immediately. "It's not what we planned."

He spoke each word in a measured tone, absorbing what he was saying. But I knew it was too much.

"I can't marry you," I whispered, my head dropping to stare at our clasped hands. "Please don't ask why."

"Clara, look at me," he commanded. "None of this is your fault. However, if you've changed your mind..."

His last words were strangled and I couldn't bear it. "I want you, X. That hasn't changed."

"Then what has?" he asked in a low voice.

"I know that your father refused his consent," I fumbled, looking for any way to avoid this a while longer. "The marriage will be invalid."

"The papers I asked Norris for grant that consent. My father delivered them this morning. They also grant your first title, which will hardly matter soon. If you have no further objection..."

The sharp, double-edge of grief swept through me. This morning I'd been willing to marry him without permission, believing it to be my choice. The fact that his father had changed his mind, coupled with the sacrifice he'd given only confused me now. It mixed with shame and sorrow, stealing my breath. Albert had removed the final obstacle to Alexander's happiness, and now I had to erect a new one.

"I do," I said, "but I don't know where to start."

"At the beginning," he suggested. "Judging from the looks of it, I've got nowhere to go."

Four months ago. That's where it began. I shook my head, my thoughts filtering through the day's events and landing on the blood-stained floor of Westminster Abbey. I knew then that it began in darkness, in the void of grief that had swallowed me and returned me to this world completely changed.

"Belle came to me," I started, gaining strength as he nodded encouragingly. "No one was telling me anything and when she came, I thought she was there to tell me you were gone." The words fell softly from my lips.

"I'm here."

It was a simple reassurance, but my stomach bottomed out. *For how long?*

"I couldn't handle it. The whole day had been so overwhelming, I fainted." Embarrassment flushed my cheeks.

"You're alright though?" he confirmed. "The doctors checked you out."

I swallowed over the rawness in my throat, nodding slowly. "They did, but they found something."

Alexander grew very still, his silence spurring me forward.

My words rushed out. "I didn't know. You have to believe that. I didn't plan it. I have no idea how it happened."

"Clara," he interrupted in a strained voice, "what did they find?"

"A baby," I whispered.

The soft confession settled heavy over us. I dared to look up only to discover his expression blank, as unreadable as if he'd drawn a mask over his face. Silence stretched between us, the tension between us drawing taut. One wrong word and it would snap.

"How far along are you?" The question was direct, purposeful, without a hint of softness. He'd grown hard before my eyes, steeling himself against a future he didn't want.

"Four months," I admitted.

"You were taking your pills?"

Another question of clarification, but the hidden accusation in it stung.

"I was."

He didn't release my hand but his went limp as if he no longer wanted to hold it. I rocked a little, trying to soothe the savage ache building inside me.

"I suppose it's not surprising, given our sex life." The words were cold. Clinical. They were as detached from this reality as I felt.

"That's why I can't marry you." My voice cracked, splintering on my tears. I blinked against them, hating the evidence of weakness when I needed to be strong.

"Had events occurred differently, you would have married me this morning. Am I correct?"

"Yes." I forced the word out.

"Would you have been scared to tell me if I was already your husband?" he asked.

"I don't know," I admitted. I'd lost the ability to contemplate alternatives. There was already too much to process. There would be no solace in what-ifs.

Minutes ticked by, neither of speaking. "I don't see how this changes things. Norris will send for the chaplain."

"This changes everything," I whispered. It already had. I could feel the shift between us.

"I still choose you." His voice softened just enough to draw my eyes to his. For one brief moment the curtain he'd drawn lifted and I knew it was true, and then it descended again.

"Get the chaplain," he said with a note of finality I didn't question. "We're getting married."

For months, people had discussed the wedding of the century down to the tiniest detail. In the darkest hour before dawn on the eleventh of April, it took place without fanfare or cameras. Six people were present. Alexander agreed to wait long enough that we could call those closest to us to our sides as witness.

His hand stayed closed over mine as he spoke his vows clearly. "I, Alexander, take you, Clara, to be my wife, to have and to hold from this day forward; for better, for worse, for richer, for poorer, in sickness and in health, to love and to cherish, till death us do part; according to God's holy law. In the presence of God I make this vow."

I repeated his vows, pausing after each to absorb the words. It was such a simple thing to recite the familiar promise. It was entirely different to mean them.

When he pronounced us husband and wife, I bent to kiss Alexander as our small audience cheered.

"For always," Alexander added quietly as we broke apart.

Always would never be long enough.

CHAPTER TWENTY-FIVE

Buckingham Palace was empty save for the dead. Despite the frantic funeral preparations occurring behind closed doors, there wasn't a soul in sight. I'd found myself in the throne room, staring absently at the empty seat I was expected to fill. I didn't belong here. I never would. Regardless of the splendor and wealth that dripped from the private rooms of the grandiose estate, I was grateful that we would continue our residence at Clarence House for the fore-seeable future.

Or so I had been told via one of Alexander's new private secretaries. I'd have to learn to ignore the frustration that seethed inside me at every turn, even if it meant accepting personal messages about my life from total strangers.

Instead I told myself I should be grateful for the opportu-nity to leave Clarence House, which didn't yet feel like my home, after being mandated to remain inside for the last two days. I hadn't even been allowed to leave to visit Alexander, but the crushing thing was that I suspected this mandate had come directly from him. Norris had driven me here this morning, informing me that Alexander planned to come here directly following his release from St. Thomas's.

"Excuse me." I stopped a maid. "Can you point me..." I trailed off. I wasn't certain where I needed to be.

She curtsied, keeping her head low. "Your Majesty may follow me."

There was definitely no getting used to this.

"She's not Queen yet," a caustic voice interrupted.

I spun around, finding myself face-to-face with Alexander's grandmother. Her age showed in the fine lines surrounding her narrowed eyes and pursed lips, but it had no effect on her presence. She was a Queen, and she was letting me know it.

I supposed it hadn't been coincidental that I'd not seen her in the hospital following the shooting.

"I was informed you married my grandson in the hospital. I'm not entirely certain it's legal to marry someone under the influence of opiates, but you've landed your prize"—she shooed away the young girl with a dismissive wave—"*despite* everything. And soon you'll have a throne, but you aren't the Queen yet."

"I assure you I haven't been running around with a scepter and the family jewels," I said, my anger getting the better of me. The suggestion that I was happy about any of this didn't merely irk me, it infuriated me.

I'd been prepared to assume my role as Alexander's wife prior to the wedding, but I hadn't learned yet what would happen when the throne fell to him. The possibility had been so remote it hadn't even occurred to me to ask.

"You will learn your place in this family," she hissed, spittle flying from her lips.

I bit my lower lip, trying to contain my rage. I might not know all of the etiquette and protocol for the situation I was in, but I did know that I now outranked her in this family.

She knew it as well.

I'd had enough contact with Mary to be quite certain this wasn't completely a result of grief. Still, I couldn't divorce myself from the fact that she had just lost her son. Possibly because I had an actual beating heart in my chest and possibly because the mere idea sent my unpredictable hormones into a tizzy.

"I am very sorry for your loss, Your Highness."

"What do you know of loss?" Her lips drew into a grimace. "You know nothing."

She left me there and retreated down the hall. A moment later her voice carried through the empty passage followed by another familiar one.

I chose to look on the bright side. At least I knew where Alexander was.

I peeked into the private chapel through the doorway, relieved to see Edward and Alexander standing a few paces away, but remained out of sight when I saw Mary was still there. Alexander and Edward had enough to worry about without me stirring the pot.

"It's a poor show," she said condescendingly to Alexander. I'd missed how he had disappointed her this time, but I could guess she'd once again blown something out of proportion. "The Prince's Vigil is a time-honored tradition."

"Alexander is still recovering. I will be taking vigil around the coffin as well as the Duke of Sandringham, Elliott, and William." Edward stepped closer and took his grandmother's arm. "Alexander should have a moment alone with our father."

"He never wanted one before," she accused as Edward led her toward the door. I stepped back and pressed myself against the wall, wishing I could become invisible.

But she caught sight of me as soon as they exited.

"I forgot to tell him his whore was here."

Edward halted in his tracks and rounded on her. "That is Alexander's wife and my sister. You will show her the respect she is due."

She shot another withering look in my direction but didn't apologize. "I'd like to leave now. I must continue packing."

I supposed that regardless of Alexander's decision not to move into Buckingham, she didn't want to stay here. Her husband had died years ago and now her son was gone as well. Part of me almost felt sorry for her.

Stepping toward the chapel entrance, I paused. Alexander stood before his father's body with his back to me. His broad shoulders slumped as if carrying a heavy burden. He spoke to him in a low voice that carried through the otherwise quiet room.

I was torn between leaving and staying. In any other circumstance I might have some clue what to do, but this was way out of my comfort zone. His actions this week had suggested he didn't want me around, but it didn't change the fact that he needed me. I was certain of that.

The vows I made to him echoed in my mind. This was clearly a for better or for worse scenario. We were in this together, and if he'd lost sight of that, it was up to me to show him.

"Grand gestures are useless when you fucking die during them. If you loved me that much all along, you should have just said, you bastard," Alexander said. The pain and isolation I'd felt for the last two days also colored *his* voice, sending a pang of regret tightening in my chest.

He stormed from the room so quickly he walked right past me. I moved out from the shadows, but he continued on. If he realized I was here, he was ignoring me.

Alexander pulled his phone from his pocket and dialed. "News?" he demanded without greeting the receiver. "Unacceptable. This situation needs to be contained and sorted. I'll accept nothing less."

He paused, obviously listening to a response I couldn't hear.

My heart was in my throat and I swallowed against it. Whatever was going on, I needed to trust that he would be up front with me. The past few days had been extreme circumstances. Nothing more.

"Then deal with her," he snapped before pocketing the phone.

Deal with her? Me? Another woman? Given that roughly half the earth's population was women, the options seemed endless. Coldness flooded through my limbs, and I shook it off. I was being paranoid, a symptom of being kept alone without information. If I wanted to know what was going on, I only needed to ask.

"X," I called before he could get any farther away.

He turned, momentarily startled, but his face was unreadable when he saw me standing behind him. His handsome face was drawn with exhaustion and his usually messy black hair even wilder than normal. I longed to go to him, take him in my arms, and give him whatever small reassurances I could.

"How long were you there?" he demanded.

"I wanted to give you some privacy." My voice was so small that it nearly got lost in the cavernous passage.

"You have no business being here."

I took a step back, my resolve to stand by him faltering for a split second. Squaring my shoulders, I decided to remind him exactly why I was here. "Your wife and son's place is at your side."

"Son?" he repeated, a surprised look darting over the beautiful face I hoped our child would share. "Then you've had another ultrasound."

A brittle edge crept into his voice as he spoke. Pain? Regret? Disappointment? I couldn't be certain. Perhaps it was all three.

I shook my head, my hand folding over the small proof of my pregnancy. "No. It's just an instinct."

"I had no idea you had medical training," he said coolly. The mask slipped back into place, preventing me from reading his thoughts and emotions.

But his jibe had hit its intended mark. I forced myself to ignore the sting it had caused. I couldn't expect him to be himself after the dramatic change in our circumstances.

"No one has informed me of the funeral arrangements," I said, trying to change the subject. "Can I help?"

"It's being handled." He dismissed my question as if I'd had no business to inquire regarding the services and continued down the hall. "Funeral plans are always in place for sovereigns. Remind me, we'll need to discuss our own funerals at the earliest possible convenience."

The life growing inside of me fluttered in protest, mirroring how I felt about the morbid suggestion. He was distracting me from the issue at hand.

"But I will be walking with the family behind your father's coffin for the funeral procession." I had to speed up to keep pace with his long strides.

Alexander stopped once more and faced me. "I'd prefer if you didn't."

He could have slapped me and I would have been no less hurt.

"I am a member of this family. I am your wife," I reminded him, lowering my voice as a few staff members scooted quickly by us.

"I'm only thinking of your condition." But his eyes stared past me as he spoke, his fingers flexing with pent up energy.

"What about your condition? You were shot!" Apparently Alexander was going to take on all of his late father's responsibilities—including driving me crazy.

"I'm fine, Clara."

My name sounded cold on his lips. It was the way one spoke to a stranger—the way one condescended to a stranger. This week had tested my resolve, diminishing my strength, and I needed him to hold me. We needed each other.

"Don't be this way," I whispered. "Don't shut me out."

His hand shot out and grabbed my wrist. He twisted it behind my back in a fluid motion that awakened the hunger I'd chosen to ignore the last few days. Taking my chin in his free hand, he leveled his gaze to mine. "I never shut you out, Clara. Sometimes I wish I could. But you are always in here."

"Prove it," I dared him.

He drew my hand over my head, shifting his weight in

the same moment to pin me to the wall behind us. My free fingers brushed against velvet and I grabbed on to the drapery as his mouth collided with mine. A leg slipped between my thighs and the toe of his shoe kicked my heel, spreading my legs wider to grant him access. He ground his hips against mine, pistoning his groin so that I could feel the heat of his cock.

He drew back, his lips a breath away from mine.

"Does this prove it?" he challenged me, panting heavy and hot on my face. "This is what you do to me, Clara. You make me so fucking hard that I'm going to have to fuck you right here when it is neither the time nor place for such an act."

He released my wrist and reached down to unbuckle his trousers. I pressed my hand to the wall, bracing myself as he wrenched my skirt around my hips. Pushing aside my panties, he drove inside me.

I bit my lip to restrain from crying out. I wanted to wrap my arms around him, to hold him as he fucked me relentlessly. But that wasn't what he needed. He was lost, fueled by a primal urge I recognized from our past. He'd taken me like this before—when he wanted to claim me while remaining detached.

He was punishing himself.

Tears leaked down my face, overwhelmed by the euphoria and confusion forming a volatile cocktail within me as he pushed me to the edge. It was more than I could take, and still not enough.

"Your cunt is squeezing me," he rasped. The hand clutching my jaw slid lower to cover my neck. My breath caught as he held me gently by the throat. "It's going to take everything I have—just like you."

I cracked open, pleasure spilling from me and mingling with shame. Alexander groaned, unleashing a guttural cry that filled the hallway, as hot jets of cum filled me. He held me like that for a moment, his tip still twitching inside me, and then he withdrew without a word. He buckled his trousers, and with one brief glance in my direction, he walked away, leaving me trembling and breathless. Sated—and completely alone.

THAT NIGHT, I lay in our new bed, watching shadows play across the wall and trying to ignore the empty space next to me. After this afternoon's display in the hallway, I shouldn't have expected anything less. But telling myself that did nothing to relieve the hollowness that had taken up residence in my chest.

My imagination drifted to where I was supposed to be: a private beach in the Maldives. But it only reminded me of how utterly alone I was. A tiny, unmistakable flutter stole my breath away. I stayed motionless, waiting to feel it again—to feel him again. Love poured through me, filling the cold emptiness that had occupied my chest only moments before.

I was wrong. I wasn't alone.

My hand skimmed my stomach, wondering if it was normal to feel so much love and fear for the fragile life growing inside me at the same time.

The door handle turned and a slant of light broke across

the room, falling over the bed. A moment later a shadow loomed on the wall, but it stayed still.

I wanted to turn over and reach out to him. I wanted to call him to my arms. I wanted to, but I didn't.

The door closed, shutting out the light and leaving the space beside me empty.

CHAPTER TWENTY-SIX

I nervously adjusted the hat my mother had sent over the evening before so that the netting covered my eyes. Turning in the mirror, I caught sight of the soft curve under my black dress. Maybe I'd been blind to it before, but it seemed more pronounced each morning. Searching my closet, I discovered a long, black jacket. I slipped it on, grateful for the additional camouflage.

I hadn't been in the public eye since the day of my wedding—the day that had brought me to this one. There'd been little to prepare me for what was expected, but I knew I needed to be here, regardless of what Alexander wanted. He wasn't the only person close to me hurting today.

A small part of the official funeral procession had gathered in the foyer. If Alexander saw me enter the room, he ignored me. He was breathtaking in his fitted black suit. More than anything I wanted to go to him. I wanted to be by his side. Instead I stole across the room to Edward's. He caught my hand and looked me over, his brows knitting together as he not-so-surreptitiously eyed my waistline.

"How did we not see that?" he asked.

Well, that confirmed that. I swallowed, shaking my head to let him know to drop it.

He tilted his head in understanding, then bent close to whisper in my ear. "Are you feeling okay?"

I managed a slight nod, a lump forming in my throat. Between Alexander avoiding me and generally pretending the baby didn't exist, no one had asked me that.

"You look stunning," he added softly. "Pregnancy agrees with you."

I wanted to appreciate his words. The trouble was, I wanted Alexander to be the one saying them.

Norris appeared beside me and gestured to a vintage Bentley parked near the curb. "Ma'am."

"Are you riding with me?" I asked Edward hopefully.

He opened his mouth to answer just as Alexander slid into the back of the Bentley. "No."

"Never mind." I tugged at my jacket to make sure it was completely closed.

Edward gave me a quick hug.

"His mind is elsewhere," he reassured me, but his eyes tightened as he spoke.

A lie was easier than the truth.

Norris held open the door for me, nodding as I slipped into the backseat. I squirmed into place. I wanted to move closer to Alexander, but I couldn't bring myself to pull him from his thoughts. He stared out the window, not bothering to acknowledge that I had joined him.

Heat prickled at the corner of my eyes, and I turned from my husband to my own window. A hand closed over mine and I glanced over to find him still gazing stonily into the distance. I shifted my attention back outside.

No words passed between us, but our hands remained clasped tenuously, even as we arrived at Westminster Hall. There was a moment of hesitation when Norris opened the door, neither of us quite ready to let go of the other. And then Alexander's head swiveled in my direction, offering one brief smile before he released my hand.

The funeral procession itself would travel from the hall to Paddington Station, according to what I'd read online. I waited in the car for a moment, taking in the crowd of sailors who would pull the carriage conveying the King's coffin. The carriage itself was draped in the vivid colors of the King's Standard. It was hard to imagine him in there. Despite the brief glimpse I'd had of him while his body laid in rest at Buckingham, I hadn't visited his body. He'd righted some of the wrongs he'd committed, but, in the end, it didn't feel like enough.

The back passenger door swung open, and Alexander's hand extended to help me out of the car. But as soon as I was on my feet, he turned to discuss something quietly with Norris.

The April air was muggier than I expected. Heat bloomed up my neck and cheeks, and I crossed my arms over my chest protectively as I realized I shouldn't have worn a coat. Then immediately uncrossed them. I was in the midst of an official state funeral. My wounded pride, and more than moderate discomfort at being here, had to be pushed aside. Keeping my head down, not quite ready to acknowledge the large crowd gathered to pay witness to the King's final march, I moved to stand behind Alexander.

"Ma'am?" Norris cast a concerned look at me.

I forced a smile onto my lips. My fingers clutched at my collar. I just needed a little more air.

Norris cleared his throat, capturing Alexander's attention. My husband turned to study me.

"I'm fine," I said, sensing I was being tattled on. Making a decision, I unknotted the belt of my jacket to slip it off. But before I could, a brief dizzying wave washed over me. I stumbled forward as Alexander's arm shot out to catch me.

He took a step closer to me, lowering his voice so that we couldn't be heard over the crowd. "The processional takes two hours. Norris will take you home."

I shook my head as my thoughts continued to swim. My place was here with him. I needed to show him that.

"This isn't up for discussion." Alexander motioned for Norris, and the trusty bodyguard gently gripped my elbow, leading me back to the car.

Between the sudden vertigo and the shame coursing through me, I didn't have the energy to fight him as he guided me back into the car. But as the door slammed shut, I couldn't help but think it wasn't the only one that had just closed.

BACK INSIDE MY BEDROOM, the weight of the day caught up with me. I was here instead of carrying out my own responsibility. This afternoon Alexander would leave for Windsor, where his father's body would be interred. He would do all of that without me.

Ripping free the pin holding my hat, I threw it across the

room and collapsed against the wall. I pulled my knees into my chest, obliterating my stockings in the process. Rocking back and forth, I liberated everything I'd tried to suppress for the last week.

Week. My life had been shattered in a moment a week ago. How could time seem to move so quickly and slowly at the same time? I was still reeling from the assassination, unable to process that it had actually happened, as though it had been a fleeting nightmare—and yet, it had been the longest week of my life, made worse by Alexander's constant absence.

A soft knock startled me, but I stayed silent. Alexander could send anyone he wanted to check on me, but it wouldn't alter the memory of his rejection. If he needed reassurance that I was okay, he'd have to come himself.

The knock grew more insistent, and finally the door flew open.

"I'm coming in and don't try to stop me!" Belle yelled right before her concerned face appeared around the door.

"Hey," I managed to squeak past my tears. "You should be at the funeral."

"No one will miss me," she said dryly, sinking down to sit next to me. I dropped my head to her shoulder and she hooked an arm around me.

"I miss you," I whispered.

"I'm right here. Chicks before dicks, right?" Belle squeezed me closer. "Now tell me what's going on."

"I don't even know where to begin." But her invitation opened the floodgates and I poured out every confusing moment from the last week.

"I understood most of that," she said, "but, darling, I'm

going to need you to take a deep breath. I'm not an expert but I'm pretty sure this stress isn't good for the baby."

"Easier said than done," I sobbed.

Belle hugged me tightly and let me cry until there were no tears left.

"Stupid hormones," I muttered finally, my chin still trembling. "I should warn you that I'm being a tad dramatic these days."

"Your crazy ex-boyfriend almost killed you on your wedding day. I don't think you can be dramatic enough," she pointed out. "And I feel like a total arse because I don't know what to do. Normally I'd advise that we should drink copiously to drown our pain, but..."

She reached down and patted my stomach, but my attention hitched on one word. *Our*. Belle was in pain, too, and I'd been too distracted to reach out to her.

"Oh my god." My voice broke as fresh tears welled in my eyes. "I forgot about Philip. I am a terrible best friend."

"You get a pass on this one." She rubbed my back soothingly. "According to the best friend triage system, attempted murder and unplanned pregnancies trump getting cheated on. Everyone knows that, and if it makes you feel better, the whole thing has distracted me from the wanker, so...thanks."

A giggle broke past the rawness bottlenecking in my throat. I'd forgotten how good it was to laugh.

"Also I'm moving in with Aunt Jane and she's going to teach me how to have lots of torrid love affairs," Belle informed me.

"Of course she will." I smiled, recalling Aunt Jane's view on taking lovers. Belle would have her hands full keeping up with her. "Is there space for me? Plus one."

"Always," she promised, but her brow wrinkled thoughtfully. "He loves you, Clara. Anyone can see that."

"I can't," I whispered. I *wanted* to but the haze of lies and distance had made it impossible. "He doesn't want the baby."

"He doesn't know he wants the baby," Belle corrected me. "Wasn't this the guy who said he couldn't love? He loves more fiercely than anyone I've ever met—except maybe you. You two are going to get through this."

I wished I could believe her. I wished a lot of things. But wishes—like happy endings—were for fairy tales.

CHAPTER TWENTY-SEVEN

Belle stayed with me until the next morning while I waited for Alexander to return from the funeral. We fell into an easy rhythm, watching movies and eating junk food. It was the perfect distraction from all the things happening outside my control. For a little while I even believed it could last.

"Your mobile is ringing," Belle said as I came out of the bathroom. "It's your mum."

I sat on the edge of my bed and held out my hand.

"Are you sure?" Belle asked. We both knew exactly why she was calling.

"Where were you?" she demanded before I even had a chance to say hello.

"Good morning to you, too." I flopped back onto the bed, clenching my eyes in preparation for the attack.

"Alexander barely said a word yesterday evening," she continued.

"You saw him?" I asked, stunned.

"Of course, we went with the funeral party to Windsor. I

assumed you would be there." She heaved a sigh that I could feel through the phone line. "Especially after I bought you that hat. That was Jane Taylor."

"Perspective, Mother," I snapped.

"Do you know what the tabloids are saying?" her voice lowered. "That you're pregnant. They have pictures of you nearly fainting at the start of the procession—and thank god for that, because I don't know when you'll get to wear that hat again—and then you disappeared entirely! *Entertainment Today* has started an entire blog devoted to the Royal baby bump watch."

I'd fallen silent as she prattled on, a sour taste flooding my mouth.

"Clara," my mother said, but I didn't respond. "Clara?"

"I don't feel well," I said softly. "I should go."

"Oh my God, you are pregnant," she breathed.

Acid rose in my throat and I dropped the phone, rushing for the bathroom with Belle on my heels. I clutched the porcelain as Belle hovered over me, holding back my hair.

When the heaving had calmed, I sat back and clutched my stomach. "I just left my mother on the phone."

"I have no doubt she'll call back." Belle began riffling through the vanity drawers until she found my toothbrush and toothpaste.

She pulled me to my feet and I took it half-heartedly. "I can't do this."

"Yes, you can," she murmured, watching me over my shoulder in the mirror.

"How do you know that?"

She wrapped her arms around me, dropping her chin on my shoulder. "Because you have to."

An ANGRY VOICE wafted down the hallway and I paused, momentarily torn. Alexander had come home hours ago and shut himself in his private office. My stomach churned as I considered that he might be dealing with publicity fall-out from my little spell yesterday.

"You can't keep avoiding each other," I said as though saying the words out loud might help me believe them.

I waited at the door for silence, trying hard not to eavesdrop. That proved simple since Alexander only seemed interested in barking vague orders at the other party. When he hadn't spoken in several minutes, I knocked briskly on the door and sauntered in.

There was no way I was giving him a chance to shut me out. Not this time.

"I heard about the tabloids," I admitted. I knew he had no love for the gossip rags that had spewed lies about his family for years, but I also suspected he might be more sensitive to their intrusion at the moment based on how tightly he'd clung to privacy for the last week.

"Speculation was inevitable the moment we were married." He leaned back in his chair, affording me a better view of him.

It was entirely unfair that he could look so drained and so hot at the same time. The slight circles under his eyes only highlighted the strong curves of his face. Stubble peppered his jawline and drew attention to his sinful mouth.

I lost track of why we were at odds as my body carried me closer to him. I wasn't thinking. I was acting on pure, primal instinct—the same instinct that had pushed me into his arms in the first place.

"I arranged for a new personal car for your use. A Range Rover," he continued, shifting papers across the desk. It smacked of someone trying to look busy.

Suddenly, I remembered why I was upset with him.

"I don't need a new car." I twisted my wedding ring around my finger, my eyes darting to check if he was still wearing his. He was. "The Rolls-Royce is fine." I didn't add that a new car was even more pointless considering how rarely I went anywhere these days.

"I will be attending more meetings, and you have your own appointments. There are other...considerations to keep in mind."

My mouth gaped. Not only was he going to ignore me, but he was going to ignore the baby as well. "Considerations? Christ, X. He has a heartbeat."

"Speaking of," he said without missing a beat, "your prenatal care has been arranged with our private family physician. You should speak directly to him if you have questions or concerns."

I crossed my arms over my chest, the simmering anger I'd felt earlier blazing into fury. "I should, huh? Where do you fit into this? Should I send you a birth announcement or am I allowed to tell anyone?"

"I've been advised that, given the current situation, we should wait a few more weeks before we announce—"

"Advised by whom?" I demanded, smashing my fist on the desk. My hand smarted from the impact and I jerked it back, rubbing out the pain. Alexander stiffened, his posture going rigid as I challenged him.

"You and me, remember?" I started to lean forward so I could force him to meet my eyes, but then I drew back and recrossed my arms as I peered down at him. "*Nothing changes between us.* That's what you said, so why are all these people suddenly advising us on how to handle our lives? I can't hide this pregnancy forever, and I don't want to."

His head tilted back, shifting his attention to the ceiling. "You're being unreasonable. The doctor told me to expect hormonal fluctuations—"

A glass paperweight flew past his ear and cracked against the plaster. Alexander's head fell forward and he stared at me. I shrugged. "Hormonal fluctuation."

I didn't wait to see how he responded. Instead I walked as calmly as my rage would allow back to our bedroom. I was certain he'd have plenty to say about that one, but for now the look of total shock plastered across his face was good enough.

Grabbing a pair of tan riding boots from the closet, I dropped onto the bed.

Alexander's muscular frame filled the doorway, a dangerous glint sparkling from his eyes. He ran a finger over his lower lip as he watched me pull a boot over my leggings.

"Going somewhere?"

"Apparently I have a new car," I snapped. "I thought I'd get out for a bit."

"It's dark out and the weather is bad." Alexander shifted, moving a few feet closer before stopping again.

"The last time I checked, I was an adult, or are you giving me an order, Your Majesty?"

"Practice good judgment, especially when speaking to me," he advised.

"Practice good judgment?" I repeated. The time for good

judgment was long past, and we both knew it. Pushing onto my feet, I started for the door. "Fine. *I'll* do that when you do the same. Tell me what's going on. You aren't attending state meetings at midnight."

He yanked on his tie, letting it drop loosely around his neck as he undid his top collar button. "My business doesn't concern you."

"Like hell it doesn't," I exploded. "You don't get to decide to cut me out of your life. That's not how love works. We're bound to each other even if you walk away."

"That's what you think this is about?" Alexander moved so quickly that his hand was around my waist before I'd processed his question. The other caught my chin and directed my eyes to meet his. Inside me a low spark lit, beginning to simmer, as he held me captive. "You think I'm walking away?"

"Late meetings? Private phone calls? What am I supposed to think?" I wasn't asking, I was pleading—pleading for him to tell me my fear was misplaced. My anxiety took over, spilling every paranoid thought I'd had for the last two months at once. "I know this isn't what you wanted. You didn't want to be King. You didn't want to be tied to this life. You didn't really want to get married, and you certainly didn't want—"

"Shut up. Just shut up." His lips crushed against mine, his hands sliding under my ass to lift me into his arms. We were in motion, colliding recklessly, too caught up in reaching each other to consider the consequences.

There were things that needed to be said. Realities that needed to be dealt with. But in that moment, all that mattered was the hands seeking me out as we struggled to find each other in the darkness that had consumed our lives.

Alexander laid me across the bed, but I knew this was where his gentility ended. The need to possess—to claim—radiated from him, but that didn't mean he was in a rush. Far from it. He moved to the bedside table, dropping his cufflinks casually on the mirrored tray. Then he turned his attention to his buttons. *One. Two. Three.* The tension in my core doubled as the final button popped open and he shrugged off the linen shirt with the sleek grace of a predator readying himself to kill.

I had missed his body. He'd withheld it except for the quick fuck in the hallway. I couldn't be sure if his distance was meant to punish me or to punish himself. All I could think of was feeling the smooth hardness of his chest against my breasts. I longed for the warmth of his skin on mine. I needed nothing between us—no clothes and no lies.

My fingers found the edge of my blouse, but before I could shrug it free, he pounced. Two strong arms bracketed my body, locking me in place and preventing any movement.

"I'm not walking away. That's not what I do," he growled, sending a ripple of anticipation coursing through me. "That's not what *we* do. We fight and we fuck and we love each other. We never walk away."

I gasped, my head falling back onto the mattress as he pressed between my legs. Even through the layers of clothing still separating us, his erection stabbed against my swollen sex, awakening the hunger I'd held in check through the pain and suffering of the recent past.

"I chose you, Clara. Do you still choose me?"

"Yes." It was a whisper. It was a prayer. It was a vow as solemn as the one I'd made by his hospital bed.

His mouth dropped to trace kisses along my jaw. "All the things that happened to us—they haven't defeated us. They haven't destroyed us. They've strengthened us. I couldn't do any of this without you—" he pulled back and fixed his gaze on me "—so don't ever fucking suggest I want to walk away again."

My eyes closed in answer to him, lost under his spell, intoxicated by the rush of emotions provoked by his unflinching confession.

I had needed to hear it, but it had also needed to be said—and that was a fact I couldn't ignore. Too many things had gone unsaid between us lately. We'd been tiptoeing around the truth, trying to ignore how drastically our lives had been altered.

And how much more they would change in the next few months.

I shifted the hand still clasping the edge of my shirt and spread my fingers over my belly and the space where our child grew inside me. "I can't do *this* without you either."

Alexander jerked back, settling in a crouch as a horrified look passed over his beautiful face. I wanted to touch him, to reassure him, but I knew it would only cause us both more pain.

"The lies and the secrets you're keeping from me," I continued, pushing up on to my elbows to level a glare at him, "they have to stop. I've never been more frightened. Not the night Daniel attacked and not at Westminster. I feel like I'm losing you, and I need you. *We* need you."

The horror on his face faded to a calculated distance, and

the fire that usually burned in his blue eyes hardened to cold sapphire as he stared at me in stony silence.

A sob choked from me, momentarily closing my throat. How could I explain to him how I felt? How much I needed his reassurance now? Especially when he looked at me like that?

"Those days were short-lived panic. I feel this in my bones. It aches like a cancer slowly spreading and eating me alive. I can't live like this." My voice caught again as my heart tried to silence me. I was afraid of facing the future alone, but even more afraid to say what I knew had to be said. Inside me a soft thump tapped against my splayed fingers. Normally it would have barely registered with my conscious mind, but right now it was the only sign I needed.

All the fear over the pain I might face couldn't compare to the love that I felt for this child.

"If you choose me, then you choose this, too. I chose you, and I want to choose you every day for the rest of my life, but I can't choose you over our child. I *won't* choose you, because this is our baby. This is our love given flesh and bone."

I waited for him to speak, my heart breaking a little more with each second that ticked by. When I lost count, humiliation washed over me.

So much for fighting.

I scooted to the edge of the bed and stood. Alexander watched without a word, still squatting. We were inches apart, but he made no move to stop me. No move to touch me.

I opened my mouth, unsure what to say, and only one thing came to my mind. But before I could speak, his phone vibrated in his pocket.

Our eyes locked and deep within me I knew this was the moment where everything would become clear—where my future would be laid bare. He drew it from his pocket and held it to his ear. "Give me a moment."

With a flick of his thumb, he muted the call but I was already halfway out the door.

"Take all the time you need." I shook my head, wondering why my tears had stopped falling.

He inhaled sharply, shaking his head. "My secrets protect you, Clara."

"Your secrets have broken us."

I didn't wait for him to try to stop me. I knew he wouldn't. He'd made his choice.

CHAPTER TWENTY-EIGHT

The guard didn't question me when I pulled out in the new Range Rover, even though it was well past midnight. I'd grabbed my purse and nothing more, but no one had stopped me. There had been a time when I wouldn't have left our home alone. A time when Alexander would have insisted on an escort. A time when he would have sent Norris to intercept me.

Times had changed.

It didn't hurt as much as I might've expected to have him stop caring. I'd fought him on the guards and the security constantly. In a way I was finally getting what I wanted. No, it wasn't the lack of concern that hurt. It was the denial.

Alexander could claim to love me. He could fight for me and, for that matter, fight *with* me. But he'd denied the one pure element of our love: our child.

There wasn't room for more pain. My heart couldn't shatter any further without turning to dust and blowing away with my very breath.

I adjusted the seatbelt and pulled past the Clarence

House gate. A group of intrepid reporters leapt to attention, splashing through the rain to get their shots. I pressed the gas pedal to the floor, screeching forward, wheels spinning, as I took off down the street.

They'd gotten a few shots. I blinked against the spots of light persisting in my vision. There would be speculation, and I couldn't care less. I finally understood that there would always be speculation. But now I also knew that my job wasn't to avoid it. That was impossible. My job was to protect our baby from it.

I didn't want him to grow up without Alexander, but I refused to stay and play pretend. I'd seen how resentment could poison the relationship between father and son. I couldn't allow that to happen. The greatest gift I could give to Alexander was a normal life for our child, even if that meant a life without him.

He couldn't see that now. I could only hope someday he would, and that someday he would understand when he was no longer blinded by guilt and grief.

I merged onto the M1, which was relatively empty at this hour. *Normal* people were at home in bed, sleeping before work. *That* was what I wanted. Normalcy. But I'd have to find it first. A few taxis sped past on the way to one of the nearby suburbs. Rain battered against their service lights as they ferried people to chosen destinations.

I had no idea where I was headed. My chest was as taut as an overstretched rubber band, and I gasped for air against the tears lodged in my throat. I wanted to cry. I willed myself to, needing to free the ache trapped inside me. I was desperate for the baptism of grief that would wash away my mistakes.

But this wasn't an ordinary relationship ending. This was the relationship that defined every moment of my life, both my past and my future. Alexander was as inextricable from me as the blood and veins and the beat of my broken heart. So what did it matter what direction I chose? Every path forward was colored by the absence of him.

My headlights flashed across a mile marker: *Scotland*. I would go to Balmoral while I considered my options. There were people to call, a doctor's appointment to cancel, a whole life in need of maintenance in the city I'd left behind. But for now, I wanted to be alone, and the highlands seemed the perfect place to retreat from the crown.

THE RUMBLE of my stomach half an hour later, followed by an impatient flutter from his little majesty, reminded me that I'd skipped dinner. Rubbing my belly, I exited the motorway to find a petrol station.

"Momma's sorry," I cooed, wondering if the baby could hear me yet. It felt good to talk to him—to have a palpable connection with someone I loved, even though I'd never met him. "I'm going to start taking better care of both of us."

Ten minutes later when I made my way out of the shop with a bag of crisps and a juice, I promised myself that I would do better tomorrow. I popped open the bag as I input the destination into the Range Rover's navigation system. With the storm, it was getting harder and harder to see directional signs. Balmoral was just over eight hours away. I was pretty sure I could make it on sheer determination alone. I needed as much distance between Alexander and me as possible. An entire country was a good place to start.

I pulled back on to the M1 and flipped my wipers to full blast. The rain had picked up, building from a late spring drizzle to a downpour. Lightning split the darkness ahead, and the crack of thunder that accompanied the flash vibrated through the Range Rover. But what made me nearly jump out of my skin was the piercing ring of a phone a few seconds later.

Crap on a cracker. I'd turned off the sound on my phone, but it must have connected to the stereo's bluetooth automatically.

"Alexander calling," a pleasant female voice informed me.

I hit the voice command button on the steering column. "Reject call."

It was too dark and too wet to risk searching for my phone in my purse to turn it off. Maybe it was my newly minted maternal instincts kicking in, but there was no way I was taking a hand off the wheel. When the phone rang for the tenth time in the space of twenty minutes, I pulled to the side of the road, grateful that no one else was out at this hour, and dug my phone free. Edward's face smiled on my screen with this incoming call though. Apparently Alexander was calling in favors. I considered for a moment before I hit accept. I wasn't running away, so there was no reason not to be honest about my plans. I just wanted to be alone, and I knew that was something Edward could understand. "Hello?"

"Clara!" Edward's voice filled the cabin. "Are you okay? Where are you?"

"I'm fine," I assured him, scanning the road for a sign or

mile marker, but between the pounding rain and pitch black-ness, I couldn't see anything but a few feet in front of me. "And I have no clue."

"Say put," he ordered. "There's a tracker on the car. I'll send someone to find you."

"Of course there is," I muttered. "I'm not lost. I'm on my way out of town on the M1. It's too dark to say where exactly, but there's no need to send anyone. I have a navigation system."

"I'd feel better if I did."

"Edward," I said, lowering my voice secretively, "it's over. I left him. I can't come back."

There was a pause before he finally spoke again. "Just tell me where you're headed. I'll come."

His offer dislodged a fresh batch of tears that had started brewing the moment I'd heard his voice. I swiped at them, frustrated to have added heartbreak to hormones. "Balmoral."

"Balmoral?" he repeated in shock. "Christ, that's near half a day's drive. Pull over to the nearest village and I'll meet you. We can go anywhere you want, but it's late now. You should sleep."

"Edward..." I trailed away when I heard his muffled voice. He was talking to someone else. Someone in the room with him.

I didn't have to ask who it was.

"Clara." Alexander said my name with such power that my body responded as if he was next to me. My nipples stiff-ened as goose bumps rippled across my skin. My tears fell faster now, matching the incessant beat of the rain, and the impatient kick in my belly made me cry harder. I guess little majesty could hear us, and he knew his daddy's voice.

"Please stay where you are," he spoke smoothly, but there was a frantic edge to his words.

"I had no idea *please* was in your vocabulary." I couldn't remember hearing him say it before.

"When you tell me that you're going to listen, I'll say thank you." His voice took on the charming huskiness that had first lured me into his grasp.

I shook my head before I realized he couldn't see me, but I couldn't bring myself to say no. Silence stretched between us, emphasizing how far apart we truly were, until the boom of thunder broke through the void.

"You've already walked out," he said. "I can't handle it if you say goodbye tonight, too. Let me bring you home."

"I can't," I finally managed. "I can't come back. We both know how this ends, X. You warned me from the beginning. *You* told me to run."

"That was when the most I knew about you was your name."

"You warned me and you came for me anyway." My words were caught between accusation and memory.

"I couldn't stop myself," he admitted. "You sighed so perfectly when I touched you."

I closed my eyes, soaking in his confession. Even if I could forgive, it didn't change anything.

"Have I ever told you that?" he continued. "Have I told you that this perfect flutter of breath escapes your lips when I take your hand or wrap my arms around you? I live for that sound. I crave it. It took me a long time to understand why such a simple thing could have such an effect on me, but now I know. It's the sound of utter contentment—the sound of total love and trust. And you made that sound the day I met you. I'd been waiting my whole life to hear it, and I didn't even know it."

"X, don't," I broke in, swallowing hard. My fingers reached toward the dash and the sound of his voice.

He isn't here, I reminded myself, slamming my fist onto the steering wheel.

"You know so much more about me now, but you're still keeping secrets," I whispered. "I've watched too many people I love turn a blind eye to lies. I don't want to live like that."

"It's not a secret." His tone shifted from soft recollection to fierce dominance instantly. "I'm—"

"Let me guess?" I interrupted with an angry sob. "You're protecting me? From what? Pain? I don't need you to lie to me. That doesn't protect me; that hurts me."

"Goddammit, Clara," he roared, his words booming through the confined space. "Someone killed my father. They—"

"Daniel," I interjected. "Daniel killed your father, and Daniel is dead."

"It's not that simple. Someone provided him with information, with a weapon—I have a duty to find out who."

I drooped in my seat, bracing my forehead against the steering wheel as exhaustion suddenly overcame me. "Why would you keep that from me?"

"Because you've been busy with more important things," he snapped. "Things that don't remind you of that day or of him."

"No." I said it so softly I doubted that he heard me. "I've been busy being lonely, because you shut me out."

"We can get through this." His voice softened again.

"Alexander—" A knife twisted in my chest, but I knew what I had to do. I knew what I had to say. "—there is no *we*."

"Never say that again," he commanded. "You and me, we're..."

I lifted my head, struggling for the right way to explain and knowing there was no magic word that could sever the bond we shared. "X, I—"

The sickening crunch of metal stole my words from my lips and drove the air from my lungs as my body was thrown hard against the steering wheel. The world spun. Glass cracked and showered over me as I became weightless, soaring without wings. My only anchor was his voice, screaming my name—until even that was gone.

CHAPTER TWENTY-NINE

ALEXANDER

E verything stopped. The world stood still and the only thing stirring was the sound echoing through the phone.

The scrape of metal.

The smash of glass.

Then silence.

"Clara!" But I already knew she wouldn't respond. My stomach twisted and I lurched to my knees, heaving stomach acid onto the floor.

Flames blazed to life, surrounding me. I fell back *and stared at my hands, but there was no blood even though I'd felt the glass in my palms.*

"Alex!"

My gaze searched the fire, looking for the voice, but I was alone in the devastation.

A million questions raced through my mind, seeking answers. This wasn't right. This wasn't where I was meant to be. Something under my hand vibrated. I lifted it to discover a phone. The screen flashed.

Call disconnected.

Why would I have a phone? My eyes darted back to the accident, only to discover I was in my father's office at Buckingham.

No, *my* office.

It was a fucking dream.

No, a memory.

No!

It was happening again.

It was happening *to her.*

"Alex!" Shaking accompanied the voice and I looked up to find Edward peering over me.

He snatched the phone out of my hand and called her name.

I shook loose some of the fog. I had to tell him she wasn't there.

Disconnected.

We'd been disconnected.

It was my fault.

Metal shrieked in my ears and my fists pounded against them. I had to make it stop.

Edward spoke. He was on the phone. I had to tell him. "Norris is on his way there now, but call the local police and hospital."

Norris. Police. Hospital. It wouldn't matter, she was already gone.

No, she isn't, a small voice told me. *It's time to fight.*

I pushed to my feet. I had to fight. There was time.

Clara.

Clara needed me. This wasn't a dream. It wasn't a flashback.

My stomach threatened to heave again, but I held it down. "Where is she?"

"Norris was already on his way, and we've contacted the local police. She's about fifty miles outside of London, near Salford."

"I need to get to her." I was out the door without another word. Edward followed on my heels.

"Alexander, medical professionals are on their way."

"Do they have a medivac?"

"I'm on that," he promised. "You need to go now. Norris is too far away, but I'll find a driver."

"Get me a helicopter," I snapped.

"Emergency responders are on their way," he repeated, ignoring my request.

I spun and shoved him against the wall. Right now I didn't care if he was my brother or if he was trying to help me. I only cared that he listened. "Get me a goddamn helicopter."

"You can't fly in this weather." He pushed me away, shaking his head.

"Six years flying over war zones says I can," I hissed.

"Killing yourself won't save her," he said softly, reaching for my shoulder, but I shook him away.

"Not saving her will kill me." I strode through the hall toward the stairs that led to the helicopter pad, calling behind me, "Get me a helicopter."

"I'm on it," he said without further argument. His eyes met mine across the hall. "You aren't going to lose her."

No, I wasn't.

. . .

"WE REPEAT: flying in this storm is not advised."

"Air control, this is an emergency," I shouted into my headset as I buckled in and started the engine.

"What's your pilot ID?" a frustrated, disembodied voice demanded through my earpiece.

"Alexander Cambridge, King of fucking England," I snapped back.

"Sir," the man's frustration immediately shifted to panic, "you can't go up in this storm. We can't allow—"

"Then arrest me," I shot back, "but first give me my goddamn flight clearance."

The blades sliced through the air, sending rain ricocheting across the windscreen as I opened the throttle and pulled on the collective, pressing my foot to the left rudder petal. I'd flown in worse conditions, but I'd had a much cooler head. Partly due to my training with the Royal Air Force and partially because I hadn't cared if I returned from any of the missions I flew. I tried to find that place of detachment now.

Focus on the mission objectives.

Work from your list.

Don't think too far ahead.

In weather like this I needed to stay in the moment or I was fucked. The thought of Clara, bloodied and soaked on the pavement, swam to my mind and I shoved it deep inside me.

"Focus." Fear couldn't control me. Fear couldn't save Clara. Only I could do that. Her life was all that mattered, even if she walked away from me after.

The helicopter shuddered when I shifted from ascent to forward motion, but I adjusted smoothly despite the rain. I knew that only good pilots could land in the dark. Only great pilots could land in a storm in the dark. For the first time in my life I thanked God that I'd been sent to Afghanistan. Had every moment of my life been leading me to her? Had my mistakes actually served a purpose?

Edward's voice filled my ear, relaying information about the status of the rescue team with air traffic interrupting every few minutes to remind me that touching down was going to prove difficult—and that getting back up in the wind might be impossible.

I beat on against the rain, slicing a path through the storm. Of course she had to be in the middle of fucking nowhere with no true trauma center nearby. Not one that I trusted to treat her. I wanted to hold her and shake her and kiss her at the same time. I sucked in a deep breath, mentally preparing myself for the reality that I'd be unable to do any of those things immediately.

A burst of wind swiped at the side of the chopper, rattling the entire vessel. If my calculations were correct, I would arrive any moment, but there were no flares on the ground yet.

"I hope one of you bastards has the sense to put down some flares," I muttered, forgetting my headset was on.

"Norris has been in contact with the local police," Edward reassured me over my headset. "He's given them strict instructions for handling the scene. He was about half an hour out from the scene and should arrive shortly after you."

It hardly made me feel better. I should have sent him after her immediately. Then this would never have happened. But I hadn't expected her to leave London, because I hadn't realized until it was too late that she was really leaving.

"Hey, get everyone off this line," I told him. "I want to talk to you."

A few moments later, my brother spoke again. "Just me, Alex."

"If I don't make it out of this. Marry David. Two Kings aren't going to destroy the monarchy."

"I don't think it works that way," Edward said wryly.

"Who the fuck cares. You'll get to make the rules."

"Sorry, I'm not interested in the position," he informed me. "You're coming back after you take care of my sister. Get her and that baby back here in one piece."

"Will do," I said in a clipped tone, unwilling to allow the emotions brewing inside me to boil over. I shut off my headset and shut down my brain. No one could help me land this now. It was up to me. Wind caught the rudder and I clutched the cyclic, white-knuckled, fighting to maintain control as the helicopter threatened to spin.

A vision of Clara, her porcelain skin glowing, flashed through my mind. Sunshine fell in sheets over the room, brightening the tranquil space and lighting upon her. She smiled shyly and glanced down at the bundle sleeping peacefully in her arms.

I jerked back on the cyclic, regaining control but losing the image. A moment later I armed the brake for descent and began to lower the aircraft. "I'm coming, Poppet. Just hold on."

The helicopter touched down roughly and my head whipped forward. I might be a little out of practice, but I would take it. On the ground the storm had abated, lifting the cloud cover enough for me to get a handle on my position as soon as my feet hit the soggy ground.

Asphalt glistened in the moonlight and I slogged toward it, battling the wet, overgrown grass of the countryside. I couldn't risk blocking the road for incoming emergency crews, but I was within a mile of the accident if all the information fed to me in the air was accurate. I was close to her, but the thought did nothing to soothe the savage fear flooding through me. Emergency lights blinked just over the hill.

Focus.

Don't think too far ahead.

I locked my panic into the darkest recesses of my mind and forced myself forward.

When I reached the road I saw it. The 4x4 rested on its roof, completely flipped onto the shoulder, a pool of shattered glass surrounding it. It wasn't tall enough. The frame had bent in the crash. Before, it had comforted me that she'd taken the Range Rover—but seeing it now I knew it didn't matter. Bracing myself, I raced forward but the closer I got to the violent scene the harder I fought to focus as old memories seeped into the moment.

The other car burst into flames and I ran to it, pushing past a fireman, but when I reached it there was nothing but the crushed remains of an older four door. The entire driver-side had been peeled back like tin can. Sarah's dead eyes bored into me from the driver's seat. I stumbled back with a gasp but when I forced myself to look again, a stranger stared blankly at me. He was dead. There was nothing I could do for him.

Clara. Focus.

"Sir!" A police officer hauled me away from the car, but it only made the rift between reality and the past worse.

The scene bombarded me, overwhelming my senses with latent memories of the crash that killed my sister. The cloying smell of spilled petrol hung in the air and I fought a wave of revulsion. This wasn't six years ago. This was now.

But the weight of the moment collapsed onto my shoulders—the acrid scent of blood and burnt rubber nearly proving too much.

There were going to be questions. How would I explain this to my father?

Jonathan tugged at me, but I held her tightly as if I could breathe life back into her. Why hadn't I driven? They shouldn't have been at the club.

A strong arm jerked me onto my feet, and I snapped out of the flashback to find Norris pulling me out of the street.

"Get yourself together!" But I didn't wait for him to continue. I wrenched free and sprinted the last few meters to the 4x4.

"Hey." A medic caught my arm, trying to hold me back, but I shoved him out of the way. It was surrounded by first responders, one of which was rushing forward with a hydraulic cutter.

Norris caught up to me as I reached the 4x4. "Don't let the past come between you. Not now that you have promised 'til death do us part."

His words tore through me. I had promised her. And all I'd done was make her question the sanctity of my vow.

I fell to my knees at the side of the crushed vehicle, barely aware of the glass and metal I landed on. Behind me, Norris intervened on my behalf with the first responders as I crawled through the battered window.

Clara's head hung like a rag doll. Blood ran jagged across her face. She wasn't moving, but she was wearing her seatbelt

Good girl.

I squeezed inside and reached for the hand that rested protectively on her belly.

It wouldn't look like this if she was... It would be limp.

But all the logic in the world didn't make it any easier to press my thumb to her wrist. Clara uttered a soft cry when my fingers closed over her skin and the tiny shred of hope I'd tucked away inflated.

"Poppet," I said softly. "Wake up."

But she didn't stir again.

"Don't move her," an impatient, unfamiliar voice admonished me from outside the car. I'd ruffled someone's feathers. "We're going to cut away the door."

"How long?" I barked, knitting my fingers through hers.

"Not long. Please come out."

"I'll come out when she's out."

"Your Highness..."

"Exactly." That put an end to it.

When they were ready for the saw, I reluctantly shimmied free and a rough hand closed over mine, helping me to my feet.

"They say they won't know until she's out," Norris said in a low voice.

"Did you inform them about the baby?"

He jerked his head in the affirmative. "You won't be able to keep the pregnancy a secret after tonight."

"I don't care," I murmured, my eyes glued to the extrication in front of me. "As long as she makes it, we'll handle the fallout."

Norris paused and regarded me for a moment with wise, sad eyes. "Pray, for her sake, they both make it."

A flurry of activities startled us apart, and we rushed forward as the last of the car gave way to the saw.

"Gently," a medic yelled as they freed her from the seatbelt. She sagged against them when they cut the buckle.

I pushed my way forward as they tethered her to a stretcher. "What now?"

"We'll take her back to city and hope –"

"No hope. No try. She makes it tonight. Got that?"

"Unfortunately she's lost a lot of blood and there's the possibility of internal bleeding. I need you to prepare yourself. I can't guarantee your wife or your child will survive this."

My hands were around his shirt collar before I processed what I was doing. "Unacceptable!"

Norris shoved me back.

"How can we help?" he asked.

"Just follow the ambulance." The medic glared at me as he adjusted his shirt.

"How far is it?"

He hesitated. "An hour."

"Does she have an hour?"

"We don't have a choice, sir."

"I can get her there. If you can keep her stable."

"Civilians generally don't—"

"Do I look like a civilian?" I stopped him. I whipped around to Norris. "Make sure she's secure and stable. The helicopter is half a kilometer due north."

"I have to protest," the medic interjected. "Despite your experience, flying a patient takes—"

"I learned to fly when I was fighting for something I didn't believe in—and I never lost a soldier." I stared him directly in the eye, for once grateful to be born King. "She's safe with me."

CHAPTER THIRTY

ALEXANDER

"Your Majesty," the doctor bowed his head in formal greeting.

I waved my hand, losing patience with everyone's formality. "Alexander. How is my wife?"

"She suffered a fairly traumatic brain injury that's caused her to slip into a coma."

I sank into a chair and nodded for him to continue. "This isn't uncommon following severe trauma. The good news is that we've got her oxygen levels stabilized."

"When will she wake up?"

"That's difficult to say. Some patients come out of comas in hours or days..." He trailed away but I knew what he was leaving out.

Others never came out.

"The hospital has been placed on lockdown to ensure..."

He prattled on but I didn't care. It was too much to wrap my head around. Hours ago I thought I'd lost her and it nearly killed me when she walked out. Now...

"And the baby?" I forced myself to ask. I'd seen the car, so I expected his answer.

"It's too early to say. We focused on your wife's condition, because, frankly, the baby can't survive without the mother at this stage." He placed a hand on my shoulder, but it was anything but comforting. "Call your family. Don't be alone."

Alone. The concept echoed through me.

There were people to call. People who would help and those who needed to know. But without her, I would always be alone. I tugged my phone out of my pocket and stared at it. Norris was addressing any possible hospital security issues. I should call Belle and her parents. But maybe it was because of the hopelessness yawning inside me, draining every bit of fight I had left, I couldn't bring myself to dial. It seemed impossible that the whole world didn't already know on some subconscious level.

The door to the waiting room opened and I sucked in a deep breath. More news already couldn't be good. But when I saw my brother I began to cry.

Edward took the chair beside me and just waited. No questions. No status updates. Having him here made me feel better and worse at the same time. His presence comforted me but it also meant this was real.

It meant I was losing her, too.

I was losing everything.

I RESISTED Edward's suggestions that I rest, choosing instead to split my time between pacing the halls and staring blankly at the waiting room door. We'd been informed that they were running a blood panel and I could see Clara soon. The minutes stretched interminably, each ticking past in a vacuum of emotion, as we waited for news that never seemed to come. Edward excused himself to take calls and handle the matters that I'd normally oversee. He ghosted to and from the waiting room without a word, and I was only barely aware of his presence.

When Dr. Sullivan finally reappeared, dark circles rimmed his eyes, but he smiled reassuringly. "Your wife is doing well. All of her vital signs are strong. We'd like your permission to run an ultrasound to check on the baby."

"Of course," I agreed, quickly adding, "on the condition that I can be present."

He hesitated and a fresh surge of fear tightened my chest. "If that's your wish, you certainly may be present. However, you need to prepare yourself. The baby's heart rate is strong on our external monitors, but the baby's situation is unstable."

I nodded my understanding, even though the warning was a moot point. No amount of preparation could ready me in the event that something happened to either of them. But I owed it to her to be there, and more than that, I wanted to be there. Clara was the source of my strength. Now I needed to be strong for her.

Edward stood and clasped me in a tight hug as Dr. Sullivan waited for me by the door. No words passed between us, but when he pulled back our eyes met and he jerked his head tersely in a sign of silent solidarity. I didn't ask him to come with; I needed to face this alone.

The hospital room was spacious, but the bulk of it was occupied by the bed and a number of machines quietly analysing and recording Clara's condition. It was eerily quiet, but the sight of her slammed into me with brute force. I'd braced myself before entering but I hadn't truly been prepared for the sight of her, small and pale, surrounded by tubes and IVs. My stomach flipped as I drank in the sight of her, at once relieved to see the slight movement of her chest as she breathed and also horrified by how utterly still the rest of her body was. The left side of her face was swollen purple from the head trauma, providing a garish contrast to her waxen skin. Every impulse in my body compelled me to go to her, rip out the needles, and scoop her into my arms. I fought the urge to carry her away. This was what she needed, no matter how difficult it was to ignore my instinct.

Dr. Sullivan gestured to a chair next to the bed, and I walked to it slowly, taking my place at her side.

"Can I touch her?" I asked in a soft voice, unable to take my eyes off the woman I loved.

"Yes," he assured me before turning his attention to the nurse as she wheeled in the ultrasound machine.

The others faded into the background as I laced my fingers through hers. Her hand was soft and fragile in mine. It was alarmingly cold, devoid of the comforting warmth that I usually found in the simple gesture. A machine by her bed chirped frantically and my gaze flew to the doctor, who was studying her heart rate.

"That was...interesting."

I swallowed hard, my mouth and throat dry, and waited for him to continue.

"Comatose patients sometimes show increased vitals in the presence of a loved one." He smiled encouragingly. "I'd say she knows you're here."

I squeezed her hand, hoping for another sign but her

pulse remained steady. It was selfish to hope that I could somehow draw her out of this, but it didn't stop me from trying.

The doctor continued to speak, explaining what we would see and what he was doing with each step as he prepared for the test. A nurse squeezed in next to me, drawing back the bedclothes and rearranging Clara's gown, but I didn't budge.

My eyes stayed on her, watching for the flicker of her lashes, willing her lips to part.

Say something.

But there was no further sign that she felt me. I was adrift. Unmoored. I clung to her hand—the brittle thread that connected me to this world.

A hum filled the air followed by a gentle whooshing, but I didn't turn away. I lifted her hand to my lips and pressed it there, desperate to fill the void that stretched between us.

"Alexander," the doctor called my attention back to him, "there is someone I'd like you to meet."

It took every ounce of determination I had to turn away from her, but when my eyes landed on the screen, the heavy weight on my heart suddenly lifted.

"She looks perfect," Dr. Sullivan said, relief coloring his voice.

"She?"

"She," he confirmed.

"You were wrong," I said to Clara, my vision still locked on the tiny creature dancing on the ultrasound monitor.

She.

She.

She.

Warmth flooded through the emptiness I'd been carrying. It burst through my chest, coiling around my heart and anchoring me to this world—to my family. I'd found the meaning I'd searched for in a place I'd feared to tread. The darkness that had shadowed my life lifted and there was only her. And I finally knew, beyond a doubt that, of all the things I'd done wrong, of all the mistakes I had made, I must have done something right.

Dr. Sullivan hit a button and the screen went blank. I blinked, immediately missing our child. He reached down and drew a sheet from the attached printer and handed it to me. I held the picture of my daughter in one hand and my wife's hand in the other. How was it possible in the face of such traumatic circumstances to feel joy?

"Can I stay with them?" I asked as the nurse wiped the remnants of ultrasound jelly from her and readjusted the sheets.

The doctor thought for a moment before agreeing. "I'll have the nurse bring in another cot."

"That won't be necessary," I told him. The chance that I would let go of her hand was minuscule—that I would take my eyes off of her: impossible.

"Eventually, you'll have to sleep. They're going to need you to take care of them." But he didn't fight me on it further.

"Doctor?" I stopped him before he could exit the room. "You said she can hear me, but can she understand what I'm saying?"

"Accounts vary from survivors. Some can recall everything from their time in the coma with vivid detail. That seems to be rare though. It's typically almost as though the body redirects normal function to healing. Many describe it as dream-like. They recall voices and light but they can't remember more than you or I might upon waking from a dream. But research, and my own experience, has shown that patients' vitals change in the presence of loved ones, like we saw earlier." His hand gripped the handle of the door. "There's only one thing that every patient I've had come out of a coma state has shared. They all felt trapped—lost, if you will—until something called them back. If Clara is caught in darkness, she needs you to lead her to the light."

He left me alone, but I no longer felt the crippling isolation that had consumed me in the waiting room. They were with me. I knew that.

"Clara." Her name fell from my lips—an intonement rather than a command. "I wish I could demand you'd wake up, but we both know you can be stubborn."

I paused, drawing a breath for strength. "I love that about you, Poppet. It drives me wild when you challenge me. Maybe that's why I can't keep my hands off of you."

"I hope she's like you," I continued. "Headstrong and brave. I know she will be, because she already takes after you. I didn't believe I could want anyone—need anyone—until you told me off that day for smoking at the Oxford and Cambridge Club. I couldn't even tell you that I didn't actually smoke, because I enjoyed how sexy you were when you were irritated. Before you, I never understood want. And I never could have believed I'd want to bring a child into this world."

"The doctor told me to lead you out of the darkness, but how am I supposed to do that? You are my soul, Clara. You healed me, and I shut you out to punish myself, to seek retribution. I am darkness. How can I be your light?"

Leaning forward, I covered the soft swell of her belly with my other hand, holding our child—protecting her. "I want this life. I choose this life. I want you. I want *her*."

"I don't know if I can bring you home. But I'm not leaving you—*either of you*. I'm never letting go again," I vowed.

I lowered my head to our clasped hands and repeated my promises until my mouth was too dry to speak—until my quiet words became silent prayers.

CHAPTER THIRTY-ONE

ALEXANDER

"**G**et. Some. Rest." Belle managed to make a simple statement into an order. She kicked her flats off and folded her legs under her. "Have you been out of this room today?"

"He hasn't been out of this room this week," Edward tattled, drawing a chair next to Clara's best friend.

Both turned and stared me down.

"Did you choreograph that?" I asked. The truth was that having them here made this ordeal easier to bear. After a week of remaining in stable condition, but with no further signs of progress, I was losing hope. Their presence provided a distraction from my inability to do anything for my wife and daughter.

"Don't you have a country to run?" Belle asked pointedly.

"Thankfully," I nodded in Edward's direction, "I have him for that. It's a largely ceremonial job anyway."

In fact, it wasn't. Edward provided a buffer to the barrage of inquiries and requests stacking up in my absence, but soon a decision would have to be made.

And I knew where my rightful place was.

I gripped Clara's hand tighter.

"Just be thankful I got him to start showering," Edward told her.

I'd finally convinced him to stop bringing me button-downs and trousers. I drew less attention from other patients in a t-shirt and jeans. My free hand ran across the scruff on my jawline. The five minutes a day he'd convinced me to leave her side hadn't allotted time for a shave.

"You're just going to have to deal with a beard," I whispered to her.

Belle and Edward did an excellent job of pretending not to notice when I spoke quietly to her.

"It's two," Belle said ominously.

"Batten the hatches," Edward added.

I'd abused my power by insisting the two of them had twenty-four hour access to Clara's room, and they'd taken shifts, slowly perfecting the art of being here enough to be supportive while still knowing when I needed a moment alone with my wife. The same couldn't be said for the Bishops. I'd tried not to take it personally that Clara's vitals only shifted in the presence of her mother, especially after the doctor quietly informed me that it appeared to be a sign of duress. Madeline had arrived with luggage, and I'd promptly had Norris arrange for nearby accommodations—and for them to be subject to regular visitation hours.

Clara's mother arrived in the room, fluttering around with the chaotic presence of a ruffled hen. She snatched up the chart clipped to the foot of the bed and pored over the notes, unleashing a barrage of questions.

"Has she shown signs of awareness? How is the baby's heart rate? Have you asked about another ultrasound?"

"Mother," Lola interceded, trying valiantly to rein her in. It was a lost cause, but I appreciated it nonetheless. Clara's sister could be a touch abrasive, but after a week of keeping Madeline in check, we'd begun to bond.

Madeline took up residence on the other side of the bed and stroked Clara's forehead softly. "Wake up, baby girl."

Despite the frenzy she brought with her each day, I couldn't fault her commitment to her daughter. The overly-coiffed woman I'd been introduced was absent, replaced by a mother in trainers with a ponytail.

"I'm going to speak with the doctor," she announced. "We've been asking for that ultrasound for days."

She had her daughter's best interests at heart, but she also wanted to control the situation. I'd allowed small requests to be met. However, things were quickly coming to a head between us.

"There's no need," I stopped her before she could reach the door. "I've spoken with him, and we've decided it was medically unnecessary."

I had decided that. Dr. Sullivan had been more than willing to perform the procedure.

"This is ridiculous," she fumed. "Is it too much to ask for an assurance that my grandbaby is healthy?"

"They're monitoring the baby's heart rate. Everything is fine," I assured her, noting that Clara's blood pressure was elevated.

"I'm sure the doctor has a reason," Lola said, crossing to her mother and leading her back into the room.

"It's not unreasonable," she rattled on, and Clara's pulse

jumped. "I have a right to know that my daughter is healthy. She would never keep me from seeing an ultrasound."

"She hadn't even told you about the baby," Lola finally snapped. She planted her hands on her hips. "She's five months pregnant and you just found out, so stop assuming you know what she wants!"

"Don't speak to your mother in that tone of voice," Harold admonished her to the shock of everyone in the room. Most of the time I forgot he was even there.

Lola attempted a response, but he cut her off.

"That's exactly the point. This family can't continue to lie to one another." But instead of sounding angry, he sounded hurt. He ran a hand over his thinning patch of hair.

"That's rich coming from you," Lola said coldly.

The heart rate monitor beeped frantically, and my eyes flickered up.

"We all make mistakes—" Harold began.

"Except Clara," Lola interrupted.

"Enough!" I roared, standing so quickly that my chair flipped over. "*Everyone* out."

"Alexander! She might hear you." Madeline clutched her chest.

I advanced toward them, finger pointed at the door. "Out!"

"I hardly—"

"Out!"

Edward and Belle took the cue and started herding them all to the door. I caught my brother by the arm and whispered, "Get Norris."

Norris appeared moments later, stepping in and shutting the door swiftly behind him.

"One Bishop at a time," I ordered.

He chuckled appreciatively. "Understood. How is she?"

"Holding on." I'd been giving him the same information all week. I didn't have any more information to give him, and it shredded me to know it.

"She's strong," he reminded as he took his leave, "and so are you."

Normally the silence that echoed in the room chipped away at the last remnants of my faith, but right now I welcomed it. Glancing back, I discovered Clara's heart rate had returned to a steady rhythm.

"You still like it when I take control, Poppet?" I said to her.

Her lips twitched, and I froze. It had been my imagination, just a symptom of too little sleep and too much desperation.

Still...

Sitting at the edge of the bed, I took her hand again. "Was that a smile? You do like it when I get bossy."

This time I knew I didn't imagine it. I swallowed hard, still resisting the possibility that this actually meant something.

I moved closer and tucked a strand of hair behind her ear. She sighed.

"Do you remember the story of Sleeping Beauty?" I whispered. "Wake up, Poppet."

I brushed a kiss over her lips, but she remained still. Being a gentleman was getting me nowhere. Of course, it never had with her. Clara's body responded to touch—to dominance—but given her current condition, I'd have to rely on suggestion.

"I'm not Prince Charming and I'm not asking."

Her lashes fluttered.

"Maybe I need to find other ways to wake you up," I suggested, dipping my lips to kiss her neck. I nudged the hospital gown down with my chin, and continued my descent down her bare shoulder. "I've got something better than true love's kiss I could try."

"I'm pretty sure a prick got me into this trouble in the first place," she croaked past dry lips.

My arms were around her before I could think better of it, pulling her close to me until she winced and batted me away. But I wouldn't release her entirely.

"Water?" she asked hoarsely.

I dove into action, spilling water all over the tray table next to her bed, before finally bringing it to her lips.

"Whatever else you want, Poppet."

She groaned and dropped her head to her shoulder, staring at me shyly. "Eggs and toast and butter and jam. I'm starving."

I hit the call button and she grabbed my hand.

"And then I'd like you to tell me the rest of that story, but only if they live happily ever after," she whispered. Her eyes were wide and hopeful.

"They did," I promised. "King, Queen, and Princess."

"Princess?" her voice piqued with surprise.

"Princess," I confirmed, finding her lips again. "A beautiful, perfect, princess. Clara, I—"

But I was interrupted as the nurse bustled into the room and cried out in shock at the scene in front of her. Clara laughed tiredly and I tucked myself beside her for the few

precious moments I had before they'd be poking and prod-
ding her.

She twisted toward me, love shining brightly in her eyes.
I had so much to tell her, but it could wait. We had all the
time in the world.

CHAPTER THIRTY-TWO

I stretched my legs out, pressing them against the floorboard, and savored the exquisite soreness in my limbs. After being stuck in a hospital bed for a week and a half, I relished even the smallest movements. Few things in this world felt better, I realized, than a hot shower, shaved legs, and brushed teeth. Well, I could actually think of a few, but considering the swarm of security accompanying me back to London I decided not to think about that.

"Hungry?" Alexander asked, taking my hand. His other stayed firmly planted on the steering wheel of a brand new Land Rover Discovery. He was dressed down for the drive home in a tight, black shirt that hugged his athletic form and showed off his coiled biceps. He flashed me a quick smile that made my stomach flip.

"Have something in mind, X?" I said suggestively, leaning across the center console.

"Uh-uh, Your Majesty. You are on bed rest," he informed me.

"I'm not Queen yet."

"You're my Queen."

I melted a little, but I couldn't be sure if that was from what he'd said or how sexually frustrated I was. The last few days before my release had been full of teasing kisses and double entendres, but he'd held back, never allowing things to get past innocent flirtations. "The doctor said rest," I corrected him.

"Poppet, do not tempt me, or you won't be getting any rest at all." His eyes darted to check his blind spots as he took an exit.

I suspected that he was being more protective than he let on. "The doctor said sex was fine."

"I'm sure sex usually is *fine* for most people." He winked at me, flashing a wicked smile. "But that's not how I do it. That's not how we do it. Don't tell me you've already forgotten?"

Forgotten? Definitely not. I was trying not to remember. After a few more days stuck in that hospital bed, I was restless and hormonal. Between visitors and doctors, we'd barely had a moment alone. I was ready to be home with my husband.

"What do you think of the car?" he asked.

"Don't think I don't realize you're changing the topic," I accused. I gave the inside a cursory glance. "It's okay."

The truth was that it was sexy as hell. Tan leather seating and polished woodgrain trim. Not to mention that the passenger seat actually had a massage function. It was incredible, but it still couldn't compare to the sinful man driving it.

I'd never actually been in a car with him behind the wheel before, and I hadn't pressed the issue when he slid into the driver's seat.

"*Okay?*" he repeated. "First of all, you better like it, because its safety features are unmatched and there's plenty of room for the baby."

I turned to stare at the five seats behind us and looked back at him. "There's room for a small army."

"I thought we might need the space in the future."

I didn't miss the suggestive tone of his voice. The hand resting on my belly rubbed my small bump, hoping our daughter felt as safe and loved as I did in this moment.

"You're quiet," he pointed out.

"I'm happy," I murmured. My gaze turned dreamily to the scenery outside the window. "Take me home."

He raised my hand to his lips. "Your wish is my command."

Alexander's hands stayed clamped over my eyes as he led me down the hall of Clarence House toward our bedroom. My anticipation mounted with each step, but despite my pleas he wouldn't give me a clue as to what he had planned.

"Almost there," he promised as he turned me gently to the left instead of the right.

"We aren't going to our bedroom?" I asked, confused.

"You really have a one-track mind, Poppet," he whispered in my ear. "Constantly trying to get me naked and in bed."

"You're evil," I told him.

He laughed. "You're impatient."

I was impatient. After an hour stuck in traffic next to him, my body ached for his. I was fairly certain I could convince him to see my side regarding the bed rest issue. I just had to get him alone first.

"Here we are." He released me and rested his palm on the small of my back as I blinked.

"Oh." Tears prickled in my eyes as I absorbed my surroundings. The walls had been covered in a champagne wallpaper that glistened elegantly in the afternoon sun streaming in to the expansive space. Pale pink silk swathed the large windows that overlooked the gardens of Clarence House. Alexander led me to a large tufted chair that had been positioned next to a fireplace with a carved mantle. When I sat down, it tilted slightly, and I realized it was actually a rocker. I swallowed against the emotions welling in my throat. An ornate dollhouse sat in the corner surrounded by stuffed animals and baby dolls. A rocking horse rested parallel to my own seat. And on the far wall, under a canopy of lace, a gilded crib waited for our baby.

It was more than I could have imagined. More than I would have allowed myself to imagine a short while ago.

"Do you like it?" he asked.

I looked up to him, struck once more by his brutal and powerful bearing. He was a force of nature that had swept me away long before I'd realized I was in danger of falling for him. But he was so much more than that, and I knew now that time would continue to reveal more of the beautiful soul that lay hidden under his commanding presence. He had conquered me, claiming my body and stealing my heart, and now I knew he would cherish me as I did him for the rest of our lives.

"How?" I asked. "You never left my side."

"That is the power of a smartphone and a brother with good taste," he admitted. "Although I did okay everything."

"You told me you weren't romantic," I accused, swiping at the happy tears streaming down my cheeks.

"I suppose that means you like it?"

"I love it." I sprung to my feet, briefly wondering how much longer I'd be able to do that as I patted my growing belly. Wandering around the room, I discovered an abundance of small touches that doubled the ache of joy in my heart. A vase engraved with the crest of the Oxford and Cambridge Club held a bunch of petite pink roses. A tiny but exquisite replica of the London Eye perched on a shelf next to her crib. Next to it rested a candid shot of Alexander and me kissing on the night he asked me to marry him.

"I thought," I said slowly, searching for the right words through the mist of emotions clouding my thoughts, "that I would never feel at home here, and although it does still feel like a dream, I can see it now. I can see us here. All three of us."

Alexander caught me from behind and wrapped his arms around my waist, crossing his hands protectively around my belly. "I understand. I spent my whole life in places like this, and I never felt as though I belonged either. But now I know. Home isn't a place, Poppet. Not for me. You are my home."

He released me, but before I could reach out and pull him back, he dropped to his knees before my feet and pressed his head softly against my midsection. My fingers wove into his hair and held him there. We clung to one another—man and wife, vine and branch, heart and soul.

Alexander buried his face into me as he pressed his lips lightly to the swell of new life I carried. His mouth moved, brushing a whisper through my shirt's thin material, but I heard it.

"I love you, princess."

He'd once believed those words a curse. He'd withheld them to punish himself for the past. Hearing him say them now to our child stole my breath.

Tears swam through my eyes as he tilted his head to gaze at me. This was the for always he had promised me that night on the London Eye. We'd had to fight to get here, and I had no doubt that a life together wouldn't always be easy. But Alexander was worth all of it.

"I didn't know how to handle it when I found out you were pregnant. After he tried to take you from me, the thought that you were carrying our child made the weight of that day too much.

"I always wanted you both," he said softly. "But I knew I didn't deserve you—how could I deserve her?" He kissed my belly once more. "I went back to the dark places. I sought revenge so that I might."

I caressed the side of his face, running my fingers over the stubble, and took his chin. "I'm with you, even in darkness."

"And there, you are my light," he murmured in a rough whisper.

"Always," I promised.

For a moment, neither of us spoke, we simply drank in each other's presence, soaking in the peace we'd finally found. Then Alexander's hand slipped under the hem of my shirt and kneaded the flesh of my hip. "I have a confession." His lips curved into a wicked smirk that set off an alert between my legs.

"Your body is so incredibly sexy, Poppet. I've barely been able to concentrate for weeks watching it change."

I raised a skeptical eyebrow, but he shook his head, catching my shirt in his hands as he stood and lifted it over my head. "You look so fucking luscious. I just want to taste every last inch of you."

Yes, please.

Without a word, he swept me into his arms, cradling me close to his chest where I could hear the beat of his heart, and carried me across the hall to our bedroom.

"Are you forgetting the staff?" I asked him wryly, but I didn't try to cover myself.

"Sooner or later, all three hundred of them are going to learn that I can't keep my hands off of you." His mouth twisted into a cocky smile as if imagining each future encounter with a shocked household member.

He lowered me to my feet but kept an arm hooked around my waist. His hold on me tightened as his other hand cupped the nape of my neck possessively.

A moan spilled from me as he slanted his head and began the agonizingly slow journey down my neck to my collarbone. His tongue followed the curve of my breast as his hand freed it from my bra.

"I didn't think these could be any more perfect," he murmured, "but I'm a man who can admit when he's wrong. So full and soft—they're absolutely delicious."

My laughter at that statement gave way to a gasp as he flicked the tip of my nipple with his tongue. He circled it leisurely, and I sighed with approval, even as desire inflamed me. My blood heated, pounded with uncontrollable hunger, as it traveled in rivers of want that pooled into the swollen mouth of my need.

"Oh god...please, X..."

"Tell me what you want," he commanded. "My mouth on your lush cunt?"

"Yes."

My breathing was coming as fast and hard as I wish I was.

His lips abandoned my breasts and sought the sensitive spot behind my ear. "Do you want my cock?"

"Please...please."

"You're going to have to be clearer with your instructions." His hot breath sent shivers cascading down the back of my neck. "I've taken the day off to worship you, so tell me how you want to be fucked."

"Hard," I cried.

His tongue clicked disapprovingly. "You're supposed to be resting."

"Fuck resting!"

"That's precisely the idea." His fingers hooked over the waistband of my jeans and shoved them roughly to the floor. Alexander wasted no time sliding his hand under my panties. His thumb dove deftly past my folds and planted itself over my throbbing clit.

"I'm going to make you come again and again," he said silkily, "*my way*. Soft and slow, Poppet."

"Oh, please," I whimpered, bucking against him. "I need to play. I need more."

"And you'll have it...in four months," he added. His teeth sank gently into the bow of my neck. "Think of it as months of foreplay. Although, satisfaction *is guaranteed*."

"Just make love to me," I pled.

He didn't need further coaxing. He gripped the collar of his shirt and jerked it smoothly over his head as my fingers unbuckled and unzipped. He stepped out of his pants and lunged forward, catching the elastic of my panties and snapping it. Our mouths collided as he lifted me against him. I wrapped my legs around his waist, circling against his cock, my desire turning liquid at the contact.

Alexander carried me to the ornate bench at the foot of our bed, holding my ass firmly over the crest of his shaft as he took a seat.

"Carefully," he warned as my hips strained to lower myself over him.

My eyes sought his and locked on. I knew what he needed to hear. "You aren't going to hurt me."

"What if you're wrong?" he asked. "I'm not a perfect man."

My fingers twined through his hair and held him in place, refusing to allow him to turn away. "Love isn't perfection. Love is when two imperfect people choose not to give up on each other."

"I'll always choose you above everything."

I clenched my eyes shut and pressed my forehead to his as his powerful grip relaxed, allowing me to sink down until I was sheathed to the root. Alexander's hands rocked my hips as he thrust inside me. My hands sought him, closing over his jaw and sculpted cheekbones for leverage as I surged against him. We moved in a sensual rhythm, taking our time.

"This is my home," he groaned, his pace increasing only slightly.

My yes was lost in a sudden blissful cry as he shifted,

piercing me deeper, and I fractured against him, falling into a million pieces that only he could join together. Our love was ecstasy and pain, birth and destruction, light and dark. It existed outside of time and distance, stretching infinitely into the unknown. I clung to him, to the answers I'd found in his arms, no longer afraid of what the future held for us, knowing we would face it together.

CHAPTER THIRTY-THREE

January

Dawn stole across the floor as I waited, listening to my wife's soft breathing. On cue, a low keening trembled from across the room. Clara stirred, sighing sleepily as she began to push down the covers.

"I've got her, Poppet," I whispered. I drew the blanket over her and kissed her neck swiftly before I slipped from the bed.

The cry ratcheted in demand as I padded toward the bassinet.

"Have you been forgotten, princess?" I murmured.

Elizabeth calmed at the sound of my voice, and I scooped her into my arms. Her head wobbled slightly, a clear look of disapproval on her face, before she finally buried it against my shoulder. I brushed my lips over the dark wisps that curled over her crown.

"Your mum needs sleep," I informed her, cradling her to

my chest. I heard Clara rise and start toward the loo. "Daddy kept her up all night trying to make you a playmate."

"Is that what you were doing?" Clara called softly from inside the ensuite.

I swayed to unplayed music, earning a contented gurgle from my audience. Love swelled in my chest as a tiny hand fumbled for my chin. It was my favourite part of the day: waking up to my wife and daughter.

Clara's body pressed against mine, her hands curving over my shoulders as she matched our gentle rhythm.

We danced in the subdued light of early morning until Elizabeth realised her mum had joined the party.

"Someone is hungry." I passed her to Clara, one hand hovering near her neck. "When you're finished I'll change her."

Clara kissed me on the cheek before she swept over to the chair by the hearth. I watched as they settled down to nurse before I took my turn in the loo.

When I emerged, Clara was rocking Elizabeth. Sunlight streamed through the gaps in the drapes, casting a faint glow on her porcelain skin. I froze, my gaze fixed on the sight as the edge of a memory skirted through my mind. Elizabeth's finger wrapped around her mother's as Clara hummed her back to sleep. Our daughter smiled dreamily before resuming her suction.

"She's laughing," Clara whispered with delight and my chest tightened. Every day brought some new small moment to amaze us.

I ruled a country, but these two women were my world.

Elizabeth's mouth dropped away from her mother as she

fell deeper into her dreams, and I lifted her from her mother's arms. Clara released her reluctantly.

"Go back to bed," I ordered her.

"A little bossy today, X." She feigned annoyance as she crawled back under the covers. "Someone should crown you King of England. Oh wait…"

"Tease all you like, because you're coming with me," I warned as I carried Elizabeth back to her bassinet, deciding not to wake her for a nappy change. I laid her down and turned on my wife.

Drawing the sheets down, I crept over her. She popped open one languid eyelid as I pushed her satin nightgown up and ran my lips from the hollow of her neck down.

"I heard what you were plotting," she said, not quite able to stifle a gasp of pleasure as I brushed my mouth over her nipples. They'd been off-limits for the past few months as she acclimated to motherhood, but this morning I couldn't resist. Tracing the swell of her breast from peak to valley, I moved down, circling around her navel with the tip of my tongue before I paused to place a soft kiss over the scar on her lower belly. The number one reason I'd been unable to convince her it was time to fill another room in the palace.

"I can't help it. You've gone and gotten even sexier. It makes me want to do crazy things to you." I meant it. Clara's body had softened with motherhood into a voluptuous wet dream. I'd nearly lost my mind during the first six weeks post-partum and I'd been making up for lost time ever since.

"Crazy like have another baby before Elizabeth's even two?" she asked.

I placed a palm on her thigh and her legs flowered open in invitation.

I continued my descent, kissing along the inner curve of her leg. "I think we should at least practice."

"Practice sounds good," she said breathily as my tongue split her seam and danced over her engorged clit.

"I thought it might." I hooked an arm around her leg and drew it roughly up, bracketing my shoulder against it for leverage as I continued my assault.

Clara's hands clawed at the sheets, grasping for a pillow to stifle her cries, as I relentlessly tongued her, reminding her exactly how great practicing could be. Her muscles tensed and then she burst, her body shaking as she came.

She laid there, quivering in silence while I kissed along her thigh. When I pulled away, she tossed the pillow to the other side of the bed and scrambled to her knees. Her breasts spilled from her nightgown as she gripped the waistband of my boxer shorts. I leaned back soaking in the delicious sensation of her mouth on my cock. She sucked greedily until my balls tightened then pulled away.

My hand fisted over my shaft, moving slowly as she drew off her the satin slip, revealing herself completely to me. Her body was a marvel—all curves and temptation—and I watched in wonder as her hair spilled over her shoulder. She tossed the gown to the floor and crawled back to me, bringing her mouth to mine.

Her teeth nipped at my lower lip, giving the edge of pain to my pleasure. "I want to play." Lovemaking had become slow and rapturous since Elizabeth's arrival. I couldn't help wanting to spend every moment I had alone with Clara worshipping her.

"You won't break me," she said, giving voice to the concern I tried to hide.

Her eyes turned up to me, wide with invitation, and I felt the familiar, primitive stir of dominance.

If only she knew how helpless I was to resist her—that every ounce of control I exhibited was simply to prolong her pleasure. My hand lashed out, gripping her jaw and drawing her roughly to me. She moaned and I smashed my lips harder to hers. Whimpers slipped through as my tongue plunged inside her mouth sucking hers forcefully and drawing it deeper into mine.

I broke away, grabbing her hips and flipping her onto her stomach. My tongue trailed her spine as my fingers delved into her cunt.

"You're so wet for me, Poppet. So tight and so wet," I murmured before sinking my teeth into the soft flesh of her ass. "Kneel."

She pushed to her knees, dropping her bottom back on her heels.

"You've learned so much," I said approvingly, guiding the crown of my cock between her legs. I stroked it along her soaked sex, pushing it past her swollen folds. I rolled its tip over the bundle of nerves, drawing a raspy breath from her lips.

She shifted, dropping to open herself to me. It was the most erotic thing I'd ever seen—her hips circling wantonly over me. I drank in the sight until the temptation over-whelmed my restraint and I accepted her invitation.

I thrust into her with one smooth stroke and retreated. Angling my cock I took my time before I slid inside her again. My arms snaked around her torso, holding her in place as I hammered into her. I moved a hand to her throat, catching her jaw and stretching her. Clara's lips parted, sucking my thumb into her mouth.

Her cunt rippled over my cock, squeezing me as I forged ahead.

"I love when you ride me, Poppet," I whispered. "You look so fucking beautiful stretched over my cock."

I buried myself in her, releasing into her hard as she spilled over. I kept my hands wrapped tightly around her as she went limp. Gathering her in my arms, I guided us to the mattress and held her until she was still. Moving over her, I rocked inside her gently, locking my eyes with hers.

"Thank you," she whispered.

I couldn't help but smirk. "Anytime."

She blinked languidly, her tongue running over her lower lip as I rolled my hips. Her hand reached for mine. "I need your control. I crave it."

"I like to give you what you need," I told her, cruising along her jawline, "and I like to take what I need. Any and every way I can have you— I plan to. I love you."

"Promise?" she whispered.

My mouth closed over hers, sealing my vow as we found each other again.

CLARA's best friend swiped Elizabeth from my arms the moment she arrived, cooing and babbling to her. Belle had become our unofficial nanny since neither Clara nor I were comfortable with leaving her with a stranger yet. An inevitability we'd have to face soon. But with today's ceremony looming, we had both agreed it was best for Clara's anxiety if Elizabeth stayed with someone we knew.

"Are you certain you don't want to come?" Clara asked for the tenth time since Belle had arrived.

"You are taking my goddaughter away for two months while you go on your little trip," she accused, nuzzling Elizabeth's plump cheeks. The baby rewarded her with a throaty giggle.

"It's a goodwill tour," I corrected her. "Apparently this country's paternal leave policy doesn't apply to everyone."

"If only you had the power to change that," Clara teased as she stacked another set of nappies.

"We'd scheduled an American tour before…" I trailed off, not wanting to dredge up the past we'd worked so hard to put behind us.

"Before Elizabeth," Clara finished. Our eyes met and I knew we were thinking the same thing. Our world had begun with one another, but it hadn't started until her.

"Well, I don't mind missing it," Belle said, returning to the original topic. "How can being crowned Queen compete with this?"

She blew a raspberry on Elizabeth's tummy.

"Maybe we should just let them crown her now," Clara suggested, her lips twitching. "She's already ruling all of us."

"I think she needs more time." I took Clara by the arm and guided her away from the nursery, aware that we didn't have much time left before we were to exit for the coronation processional.

"What about you?" Clara asked softly. "Have you had enough time?"

I opened my mouth to say, of course—to reassure her. But

then I shook my head. "I don't think this is a job you can ever prepare for."

"You've been doing it for over eight months," she said as she disappeared into the closet. "This is merely ceremonial."

But it was also permanent, accepting the crown, being coronated was a commitment. My thoughts drifted across the hall to Elizabeth. There were a lot of reasons I didn't want to be King. But the two important ones outweighed everything else.

It wasn't just that I'd be able to offer them security and comfort but also because I would actually have the power to make the world a better place for my daughter to grow up in. I owed her that much.

I would give my life for either of them, but that meant giving it even without the threat of danger.

Clara stepped out of the closet in her coronation gown, her hand fumbling to pull on a satin glove.

I crossed to her and placed my hand over hers, calming her until she tugged it up.

"You've been doing this for eight months," I repeated her earlier words.

"It's easier to say that than to believe it," she admitted.

I stepped away, holding her hand up to inspect her. "You look so fucking beautiful, Poppet." Her ivory gown had been hand embroidered with hundreds of golden flowers.

"After today you're going to have to call me Queen," she joked, biting her lip nervously.

"Tonight I'll show you that I'm completely at your service, Your Majesty." My mouth slanted over hers, bringing her body into hard contact with mine. A moment later, she pushed me away, slightly winded.

"You'll never get through all these layers," she advised me.

"I do like a challenge."A rap at the door put an end to the discussion. "Tonight." My lips whispered the promise over hers.

LEAVING Clarence House was the easiest part of today's journey. After consideration, the coronation planning had suggested a different route than the one we had taken the previous April. Clara had refused, insisting that our lives couldn't be ruled by fear.

The hand clutching mine as we turned toward Westminster Abbey suggested this was more difficult for her than she let on.

Our nightmares of that ill-fated morning had subsided with time, but this was the first time we had been forced back to the cathedral. It wouldn't be the last as Elizabeth's christening would take place there upon our return from America. We'd jokingly referred to today as a practice run.

The security around the perimeter was tighter this morning. I'd personally appointed Norris to help oversee the operation, and he greeted us in full Blues and Royals uniform at the red carpet.

"Everything is in order," he said as we saluted one another. "And if you'll permit me saying it, you look beautiful, Your Majesty."

Clara glared affectionately at him. "That's worse than Miss Bishop." He accompanied us inside the entrance, bowing slightly as he took his leave.

"I couldn't do this without you by my side," I told her, drawing her eyes to mine as trumpets heralded our arrival.

Holding out my arm, she placed her hand over mine. We stayed like that for a moment, merely looking at one another before we moved hand in hand toward our shared destiny.

THE ROYALS SAGA CONTINUES WITH

Crave Me

Belle Stuart has given up on finding her own Prince Charming. That's a good thing, because Smith Price isn't charming. He's cunning, manipulative, and sexy-as-hell.

He's also her new boss.

She knows she should quit, but the opportunity is too good to pass up, which is why she shouldn't be surprised when she uncovers Smith's ties to the Royal family. Old, binding ties. Ones forged not out of friendship but something much more sinister.

Is he using her to get to her friends? Can she protect them even as she loses her heart to a man that might be a monster?

ABOUT THE AUTHOR

Geneva Lee is the *New York Times, USA Today,* and internationally bestselling author of twenty novels with varying amounts of kissing. Her bestselling Royals Saga has sold over three million copies worldwide. She is the co-owner of Away With Words, a destination bookstore in Poulsbo, Washington. When she isn't traveling, she can usually be found writing, reading, or buying another pair of shoes.

Connect with Geneva Lee at:
www.GenevaLee.com